THE
MANGOMAN

THE
MANGOMAN

RISHABH DUBEY

PARTRIDGE

To order additional copies of this book, contact
Partridge India
000 800 10062 62
orders.india@partridgepublishing.com

www.partridgepublishing.com/india

CONTENTS

PREFACE

The impossible of Yesterday is the Science of Today. The Digital Media has unified and enlightened the world to an unimaginable extent. Even Modern Politics is monopolized on the power of digitization. But the age old classical methodologies of 'Divide and Rule' remain intact. Polarization has been the key to the task and venture of winning the people. Take a bunch of people and make them realize their specific pitiable conditions in contrast to some other segments of society, they will empathize and succumb to your leadership. The world is now at a stage where there is a need for a true leader, who preaches unification over division, who holds the virtue of service high above the sin of domination. We need that one Ideal Hero possessing the virtues of the comic Super Hero.

You make a poker face when you see a cat being saved from a tree by a superhero, don't you? Let me ask you. What would you do if you were given the chance to gain the superpower of your choice for an hour? If I say that you can use it every day for an hour, then what? For how long would it drive an emergent stimulus to take a stand against the evil? For how long would it seem more predominant than meeting your partner, having a cup of coffee, eating a pizza, sleeping or hanging out with your friends. The adolescent mimic, the young braggart, the middle-aged avenger, the old anguished, which one would use it for some selfless good? Let's witness and watch these questions being passively imposed upon one Oday (pronounced Udai).

Oday is the silver-spoon fed son of a corrupt politician. All he has so far witnessed and known in life is the wrong. When an old blind lady wants to cross the road but is unable to, Oday would be the last one to help her. In fact, Oday would overlook her existence altogether. Moreover, Oday would never be out on the road to see her attempt to cross the road. He would rather be inside an air conditioned velvet-interior car. One day, God decides to grant him with the very power mentioned above (for specific reasons). The very first thing which comes to your mind is "I was a better choice than him". Apparently, anyone is a better choice than him. But is it so?

'The Mangoman' is a political satire, where the untoward and comical amalgamation of modern Indian politics with a superhero story, takes a critical turn. The hero with a common persona yet a special aura, only that hero can change the world. And the world is in a definite need of a prominent change. It needs a leader with only needs and no wants. Can Oday be the Leader? Can he become The Mangoman?

ACKNOWLEDGEMENTS

This novel owes its conception and existence to my dear friend Srijan Dwivedi, who introduced the concept of 'The Mangoman' or the 'Aam Aadmi' to me over a mid-examination and midnight telephonic conversation. The concept, originally introduced by my friend as a gesture to divert our minds off the seriousness of Chemistry, was soon realized to be a matter of discussion that turned quite serious. We ended pledging and promising each other that a day shall come whence we would be giving concrete shape to this concept. Thus I dedicate this work to us and our ideology of 'Think strange. Strange is New. New is Good.'

My inspiration towards writing has always been and will always be my father Mr. Triveni Prasad Dubey. Although it is rather impossible for me to even touch his level of excellence, for it can never witness a tantamount in all dimensions of space, yet I have always tried my best to live up to his expectations. He will always be the glacier of all the rivers and streams of thoughts that I know and perceive.

I am indebted to my mother Mrs. Rama Dubey for almost everything from my very existence to this very book. Her undying support is itself a testimony to the universality that it is, for because of her I am what I am and am going to be. Also, my ever innovative sister, Ms. Smriti Dubey, has always been the one who has actively and incessantly motivated me to write more.

I thank my real idol my elder brother Lt. Cdr. Saurabh Kumar Dubey who has been my noble guide, and intrinsic inspiration at every turn of my life and has always cared for me like a dedicated parent; and also my caring sister-in-law Mrs. Deergha Dubey who is the philanthropic guide I turn to whenever I am going through tough times.

Lastly, I am indebted to the intellectual minds whose innovative creations have been used to beautify the concept of the 'Mangoman'; And also, the ironical state of affairs of Indian Politics which moved me to compile it under one heading.

All in all, this book couldn't have been possible without any of you. So an explicit and candid whole-hearted thank you from me. I owe you all, something immensely greater than greatness. I owe you my salient thoughts and my profound dreams.

STATUTORY WARNING

The Chapters hence contain minor incidences of harsh
language being used. They are not meant to offend
the sentiments of the reader and have been placed
just to enhance the credibility of the natural dialect.
I do not seek to promote it in any way and am myself
a preacher of Clean Speech. The characters are mere
subjects of my imagination and not an object of my
opinion. Please tune in fine and enjoy. Thank you.

Rishabh Dubey

1

"Oday …. Oday…. ODAY… first the earthquake and now this…" came the dramatic whisper drenched in the symphony of a hopeful woe.

Oday (pronounced Udai) lay senseless on the leopard-tiled surface as Arjun tried to shake him up. Both of them were wearing yellow masks on their faces. There was absolutely no sign of movement on the part of Oday whose body harmonically oscillated in wiggles through Arjun's pushes and pulls. Nevertheless, ironically, the greatest problem right then was not that Oday lay apparently dead… although the problem was intensely affected by that mishap.

"Why is he not breathing?" asked Shalini who was also wearing a yellow mask.

Shalini was Arjun's girlfriend. Arjun was intimately associated with her. Only a female can reflect curiosity in a rhetoric. The usual interrogative sickened Arjun "Don't you say it…. Just don't."

"What else should I say then?" Shalini remarked.

"Okay… Darling… Neither your questions nor their answers are ANYHOW helping… Let's at least take him to the hospital," Arjun murmured loudly through his clutched teeth.

"Calm Down… They're still here" Shalini said "And also… what do you think we'd say once we reach the hospital? 'Look…. Our Fish Fainted'". Her ignorance seemingly added to the turbulence inside Arjun's head "Merman$_1$…. SHOW SOME RESPECT WOMAN". Probably some of the ignorance was adsorbed by Arjun who instantly slapped himself to sanity "Aqua… yes…. Water… How Can I? Arghhhh… Get useful… Get some water you haggard woman."

"Haggard…. Produce it yourself you bastard" Shalini said in an irritated tone.

"Girl… We have no time to discuss the righteousness of my posterity and conception… OR your beauty… And whom are you texting in this free time of yours? My friend is dying… or possibly even dead… get some water fast… my angel… my love… my Cleopatra," Arjun gratified.

"It is Ria. Her father passed away. It is the thirteenth day of mourning. Everybody was sending their sympathies on the whatsapp group so I thought I should join. Although I do not like the girl," Shalini said.

"Give me the bottle already," Arjun said in a desperate tone.

"Here's the last of it," came the gullible hand grasping the bottle.

Arjun splashed some on Oday's face but nothing happened. Then he gained a certain degree of enlightenment and turned Oday's head to show his neck. The neck, which might have surprised both the old as well as the new anthropologists. A large patch of nostril shaped grooves tightly held the skin. Something extra-terrestrial maybe. The holes opened up wide as soon as the water touched them. Oday regained his breath. His fin-shaped body structures protruded and retrieved back to toes and elbows and fingers.

"YEAH…. HELL'S HEAVEN… BULL'S FUCKING EYE… MERMAN MY MAN" Arjun's exuberance surfaced.

Oday shouted in a furious tone "Merman…. MERMAN…. NO MORE OF YOUR DEATH-MAGNET IDEAS. I would have punched you hard if I was not paralyzed."

Arjun got up and cleaned the dust off his pant.

"Who'd have thought this day would come, eh? A Luhar against a Luhar and a Teja against a Teja… A battle on equal grounds huh?" The rhetoric flowed sarcastically from Shalini's mouth.

"Yes… A Teja against two Tejas… Now who else would join the squad? My dad? Really… who'd have thought…? Never were there lies… There were just the wrong truths we ourselves chose… The reality was right there…" Oday said as a heavy sound of a helicopter rotor started reverberating through the building.

"That's our return ticket… Your Butler's here Shalini," Arjun shouted.

"I hope he brought my vanity," Shalini remarked.

"I hope he brought a sanitizer," Arjun followed.

Shalini's Butler got down from the helicopter and aided Arjun in carrying Oday to the chopper. Oday was made to sit in a wheelchair inside the helicopter. Arjun connected a small plug hanging out of the chair to a small socket in the rear of Oday's head. A man in a suit closely followed the copter staring down the eyes of Oday (who was wearing a mask revealing only his eyes). Oday stared back at him and remarked, "You shall not survive the next t…" "Bro… Want some?" Arjun interrupted waving an opened sack of McDonalds towards Oday. "Dude I am having my mome…. WAAAIITTT… IS THAT A McCHICKEN CHEESE?"

Oday said drooling for a bite of the burger. Arjun helped Oday have a taste of the meal.

Chewing down the crispy edges of the burger analogically and somewhat technically as a modern bureaucrat does to a nation's economic stronghold... he recalled how he did nothing better and worse still. His activated philanthropy, which was not so long ago dormant enough to be presumably negligible. The change was not so abrupt... Although it all sparked that very day. The day.... Oday recalled... Oday Luhar... the playboy spoiled brat of one of the most famous personalities in the state... the Chief Minister... Aditya Luhar.

"I'm not that Oday anymore...," Oday said assuming a tense façade after chewing down the burger.... "I'm just a nobody now... I am anybody.... I'm The Mangoman."

"Not with that name again please...Let's go already. Ananya must be waiting for us as such. Now let's get back to our country," Arjun said.

2

Oday Luhar was the eldest and only son and child of Aditya Luhar, the president of the ruling Ityadi Party and the Chief Minister of the greatest political centre of India, Uttar Pradesh. Aditya was known for his revered bloodline and political influence on other states as well. However, he was most famous for his generosity towards the younger generation. Not long ago had he started the student empowerment programme and had invested millions of rupees of the taxpayers to distribute laptops and smartphones to the students passing out of school. Never was there a first-hand witness... but reports were there that they had got laptops at the least. Although there was no guarantee that those laptops would get them into colleges and would pay their fees... but this was a good unpatented alternative to Aamir Khan's 'Aal Iz Well'. So good news for people who need laptops... you do not need money at all... You just need to have kids... Tadaaa... wait... What about the school fees? A HA.... I bet Mr. Luhar never thought of that. However, all was done in goodwill preserving the integrity of his family name. Mr. Luhar also promised on free education for Girls... but looking at the state of his state... he might have mistaken the word 'education' for 'molestation'. But yes, everything was done in goodwill… so it does not matter… As such… Boys will be Boys. And why do we care? We are safe, right?

Oday was born on the 5th of September 1991. Although he had the minutest respect or even appreciation for any teacher. Nor any teacher had for him. Nevertheless, they behaved very nicely with him since he was buying them all. The only time teachers were rude with Oday were in class 10th and 12th because then the Board and not the teacher was the one at the receiver's end. Politics in his veins had indeed made him a natural erratic businessman. Because of what he had seen during his childhood, Oday always thought that everything came with a price tag. And his righteousness meter was set aloof from what the average human records. Maybe because of his genetics. But mostly because he was conditioned to wrong so much that his mind's framework could never accurately differentiate between right and wrong.

Except for the fact that he had millions of rupees of royalty money at his leisure disposal and had no interest at all in the human exploits, Oday was just like a normal boy in his early 20s. His lust for more had predefined his ventures, although his standards were too high. But just like any other guy his age, Oday could not escape the wrath and melancholy of love. The concept of love was monopolized completely on 'choice' for him. His uncle had once told him that 'Man continues to fall in love… till the fall kills him'. But he had also always preached 'Murphy's Law$_2$' down Oday's brain consistently. Therefore, relentlessly after many natural warnings of 'break-ups', Oday predominantly gave in to his erroneous perceptions of his uncle's sayings, and went on a diligent scout for 'the one'. This was one of the most prevalent of the few things that Oday ever did.

A doorknob turned, a door thrashed, and Oday rushed in to jump on the sofa beside Arjun to say one of the most non-startling things ever said by man "She left me Man…"

Arjun camouflaged his nonchalance, paused the PlayStation and turned to Oday to say the most common yet the most highly recommended phrase in this scenario "Don't you say…. That Bitch".

"She left me man…. Now what will I do with myself man… And worst part…. She took EVERYTHING from me…" Oday said as he wiped his tears.

Arjun thought, "What did you ever give to a girl dude? Except for your virginity to Reena… which indeed you have taken back a gazillion times" and then said, "I never took Ashida for such a bitch."

"Who Ashida?" Oday asked negligently.

"So not Ashida… then it must be that girl you met at the bar… Amaya."

"I met Amaya at the Golf Course… and Sumedha at the bar…" Oday said.

"Then that girl you met at your dad's party… wait that was Ashida" Arjun said ambiguously.

"Wait… Ashida was the one at the party… you're right… she is a bitch," Oday said.

"Then who's the girl who dumped you?"

"Ohhh… Shalini Singh… can you imagine she left me because she saw me kissing Ashida… and then Ashida slapped me too… Now I recall that I met them both at the party… You know what… Them both are bitches," Oday said.

"Shalini Teja Singh… the daughter of Rana Teja Singh the billionaire… and the sister of Kunwar Madhao Singh the Don… You left her?"

"Technically she dumped me… but I like the sound of that… and why are you giving me her resume… I already know that… her dad is a small investor for the Ityadi Party… Dad always tells me," Oday said as he started crying again.

"Don't worry man… I will try to contact her… I'll try to fix it… she'd come back to you man… and this is a family matter too."

"What do you mean come back? Should I dump Elena now?"

"Who's Elena?"

"She's my current girlfriend," Oday said.

"This asshole," Arjun thought.

"I'll call her anyway… before things go turbulent," Arjun said as he walked out of the room with his phone. Oday wiped his tears, fidgeted and whistled for a while in search for some occupation… He then grabbed the PlayStation controller kept on the sofa and started playing.

Outside the room….. Arjun had been appeasing Shalini's assistants to reach her directly. But they had not been very helpful. They completely acquiesced to the fact that Mr. Rehman (Arjun's Alias) was calling to have a business-based conversation. The problem lied in the fact that they did not understand the relevance of their mistress Shalini on the other end of such a discussion. Arjun finally convinced them that this was regarding a surreptitious attempt of Shalini to impress her father and brother by making a brave and bold attempt at the Business Universe. So if they were not able to contain the stealth, then they might have very well given their resignations then. The passive threat alarmed the Assistants and they immediately reached for Shalini.

"Madam… Mr. Rehman is calling regarding business…"

"Who Rehman? What Business?"

"What is she saying?" thought one of the assistants… they both stared at each other and somewhat agreed through a gentle nod that this must be their mistresses' forced indifference to maintaining the integrity of her covert plans.

"It is for you Ma'am… we don't know anything else…"

"Give it to me then," Shalini said as she grabbed hold of the phone.

"Hullo! Who is it?" Shalini asked.

"Ma'am… I represent Mr. Oday Luhar… I heartedly apologize for any misunderstanding," said Arjun.

"Misunderstanding? He kissed that bitch right after he bade goodbye to me," Shalini complained angrily.

"No Madam, you get it all wrong. There is a mistake… She kissed Oday… he was reluctant on kissing anybody but you… And I really hope that this misperception might not lead to some trouble between the two families…. I mean professionally."

"If you are vouching that much for him then I might just fade out those ideas… yes… but he really has to work to get me this time… tell him to meet me at my father's Aliganj restaurant tomorrow at four in the evening…"

"Yes Ma'am… Affirmative," Arjun said as he hung up the phone.

"Affir What? Anyway… I am going to need a new addition to my wardrobe… Shantiiii… inform him to ready the helicopter… I am leaving for Delhi ASAP…" Shalini said as she kept her phone down.

"Your father will need a reason miss…"

"Absence of Vuitton and Gucci from Lucknow is more than a big reason…" Shalini said.

Arjun walked inside the room where he had left Oday, looking up the notifications on his phone "Dude I got you another chance with her… Don't screw up this time." Oday was nowhere to be found.

Suddenly Oday rose topless from behind the sofa "That's nice Man… I owe you one."

"Yeah… don't mention it… hey why are you topless?"

A girl also rose from behind the sofa.

"Hey … you are Ashida right…. Yeah…" Arjun said.

"Yeah… Hey…"

"So… What's up? What brought you here?"

Oday's ignorant expression or what is commonly known as a poker face gave in the scenario to Arjun "Ahhhhhh… now I understand… at least lock the front door man…"

Thus, Arjun left the room "Damn that bastard… that lucky bastard… and here I was starting to care about him and his family."

*   *   *

Inside a private chamber of the Shalini Intercontinental Luxury Restaurant sat Arjun with all of his nerves tending to leave his body… desperate to find the appropriate lie. Things could not have gone wrong with Shalini. Rana Teja Singh was the heir to the throne of the state Rajputana. His political influence was even greater than that of Aditya Luhar. But the real power was his Money. And it came from his business, which was expanded all over the country. From Textiles to Mining, from television to contraceptives, name anything, and the Shalini Corporation Ltd. had a tag on one of those. The Magnus Primus of these was his monopoly in monopoly… that is Casinos. Teja was a prevalent shareholder in almost all of the Casino outlets in the country. The easiest solution to convert black money to white is through casinos. Thus, his casinos formed the centre of all money laundering in the country, which further linked him to the country's Mafia. His son Kunwar Madhao Singh controlled Teja's foreign outposts. Rumour was that the son exceeded his father in influence on these Mafias. Mostly because he had like one foot in Dubai and the other in Japan. Overall, the family had money enough to buy a state for themselves… or better… Michael Jackson's boots and gloves at the auction. And had enough power that with their help U.S.A. could have actually won a war after 'imposing sanctions'. The Luhars needed them more than anything. Senior Luhar was soon going to make a move towards the Union Government. Without Teja's help not only would that move would turn a drastic failure but also he would end up losing his control over his beloved U.P…

"Who are you?" came Shalini's voice.

Arjun looked up to see the shining beautiful face, with glimmering hair, talking in front of him.

"I'm …. I'm," Arjun stammered.

"Let me tell you who you are… NOT Oday… this table is booked for us today…"

"I'm Arjun… his friend," Arjun stood up and said.

"So where is he? I am ready for the apologizing and all," Shalini said.

"Yes… I heartedly apologize for my friend's errs…" Arjun said.

"You will… wait… he is not coming right? I knew it… that fake bastard."

"No No… Oday had to…. Run some family errands… He was most persistent to come… but I told him that I would apologize for him instead… as such I will do anything for my best friend… so please Miss… This should not be a family matter, I request."

"Oh! So that's it. You fear that I might tell on you all to my father and he might take back his support, right?"

"That… and I also don't want to hurt a girl's feelings," Arjun used his witty intellect.

"Aww... but that doesn't change anything... I want Oday on his knees BEGGING for me to forgive him."

"I would do anything... just forget Oday... I would do anything to reciprocate the damage."

"You'd do anything? Okay," Shalini said as she sat down.

"What now?" Arjun inquired.

"I bought a new dress for the night... I would feel bad if I used it for nothing... so let's have our date and dinner," Shalini said.

"Wait... this only happens in movies... you literally don't wear the clothes you've worn once... you are really rich... so okay... let's date," Arjun said as he smiled surprisingly.

"Yes I am rich... let me show you..."

Shalini called up the waiter. "Tell me I'm very beautiful... I'd pay you lakh rupees."

The waiter came up and took it as a joke and so did Arjun.

"Where are you going... okay... here... take this lakh as advance and a lakh more if you say it," she said as she took out a bundle of thousand rupee notes from her bag and raised her hand towards the waiter.

He came, grabbed the money, and said, "You're VERY beautiful madam".

"Here you go," she said giving him a lakh more.

"I'm rich... I'm rich," The waiter shouted.

"So where were we?" Shalini asked.

"I was saying you're very beautiful..." Arjun said in awe.

"Hahaha... you're very funny," Shalini said as she laughed.

"No seriously... where's my money?" Arjun said in jest.

"Stop It... I can't laugh anymore... so anyway... your drink is over... so is mine... let me tip the waiter and let's go to my place... we can talk better there..."

"Wait what… you're still going to tip him… Did I tell you that you're VERY VERY VERY beautiful?" Arjun continued his jocular remarks.

"AHAHAHAHA… Stop it… let's go," Shalini said as her two guards came and stopped Arjun from following her.

"No… he is with me," Shalini informed her guards and they apologized and stepped back.

They walked out of the building to Shalini's car.

"You've got a personal Ashton Martin?" said the dumbfounded Arjun.

"No… these are butler's cars."

"Wait… you've got a personal butler… and he's got an Ashton Martin AND a Merc… wait again… what do you haunt the road with then?" Arjun said all startled.

"That's it… I do not stay on the road much… I fly," Shalini said as a Helicopter flew over them towards the building opposite of the road.

"YOU'VE GOT A PERSONAL COPTER? Why do you need these cars?" Arjun lost his senses and gazed at the incredible sight in astonishment.

"I can't walk across the road in these high heels…" Shalini said.

"Whoa… and I thought Oday is rich… You're like… Richie Rich[3]," Arjun said jocundly.

"Ahahaha. Yes… I am…" Shalini said.

"Do you have a mountain full of treasures? Like the Mount RichMore[4]? Something like RanaMore?" Arjun asked.

"I don't have that… But we do have a small castle where we keep our old jewellery," Shalini said.

3

Arjun Trivedi was Oday's childhood and only true friend. He was the only son of the renowned and revered University Professor Nitin Trivedi. Thus, it was naturally imperative that Arjun was an ingenious fellow himself. And so he was. The very reason that the Luhar family had a strong affinity towards him. Arjun and Oday became friends in standard fourth, Oday's second one that is. Oday once testified that Arjun's entrance in his life had contributed a lot towards Oday's academic survival. That and the bribes. But Arjun was a prevalent figurine there. Maybe because helping and aiding other beings was a concept alien to the Luhars. Therefore, not all the exploitation of Arjun at their hands was reciprocated well enough by sufficient commendations; but the few he received seemed like a little too much on a Luhar scale.

Senior Luhar had entrusted his son to Arjun and his father. Arjun's father was not very fond of the Luhars, yet he had always been very accommodating for those whom Arjun had outrageously and consistently backed with his word. There were educational and other illuminating sessions of lectures with Arjun's father which went rather unnoticed by Oday's inadvertence for the fact that he trusted Arjun a little too much for his grasping and executing powers and moreover his capability to handle Oday's life more perfectly than anyone else. Unlike Arjun, Oday had never imagined a time without Arjun being in his life. How could he have? Arjun was his tutor, physical instructor, chef, butler, PA, Manager, Driver, and the holder of as many portfolios as you can imagine. All because of this condition called the 'Can't say No' syndrome. Whenever anyone turned towards Arjun for some aid, he could not refuse. Somehow, the need to help became the greatest gravest motivation towards making friends. Thus came Oday in his life. Arjun knew that those who were oblivious to their own pitiable condition and the need for someone else's help, need the most of that help. So helping Oday in his exploits and ventures always left an amusing residue inside Arjun's head and heart. This symbiotic relationship made them the most peculiar of all best friends.

Anyway, getting back to the subject… after finishing school, Oday and Arjun went to the same law school given to the Luhars' persistence. By this time, their bonding could not have been broken by their incompatible virtues. Arjun's flawless acumen and Oday's dubious void. Neither of them needed to learn law, though. Arjun being an intrinsic lawman while Oday being unheeding to its existence. And neither of them wanted to be lawyers. It was just a case of scouting the easiest place for Arjun to haul Oday's close-to-dead-weight along with him, without himself lagging behind. So Law it was. A little easy for Arjun, not so much for Oday (What was anyway?) but did guarantee their co-existence. As such, Senior Luhar had assumed the responsibility of being Arjun's career sponsor. So Arjun did not mind. But a sycophant he could never be. Although his little lectures of negative reinforcement to Oday were always tagged with arrows of insults reading, "I only do it for money"; but it never affected Oday... since both of them somewhat knew that Arjun always loved Oday as his best friend. They could never find out 'why' though. As Arjun always said "There are things we Pundits can do... rest we leave to NASA". Oh, Yes! 'Pundit'. 'Arjun Pundit$_5$'; that is what all who knew him called him as. Mostly just 'Pundit'. It was like a double-ended sarcasm reeking of covetous-casteism as well as the fact that Arjun was not as nearly as physically gifted as the legendary 'Sunny Deol'. Arjun's expressions of disregard for this seemingly a misnomer were not very true to his inner acceptance of elitism. He really liked being called a 'Pundit'. But he always wore a frustrated, ignorant façade. He could never accept that something or the other could please him and ended up criticizing the most acceptable of happenings just for the sake of idiosyncrasy.

So coming back to their unbreakable bond; Oday had often been told that it was better if he was named 'Karan$_6$'. It was so deep a friendship that there were often media coverages of them hanging out together... although the objective was more inclined towards a sting operation to reveal the exploits of the prince... but yes they were important as bros too.

All in all, the two were inseparable. They were a natural testament to the fact that not only love but friendship also knows no boundaries or prerequisites. No level of physical or mental bribery is required for two people to become friends or even brothers.

The word 'brothers' makes these remarks seem a little sexist, right? Sometimes practical disparity between males and females when pointed out are mostly perceived as sexist.

Every guy has that one friend he is ready to do anything for and vice versa... and that other friend is naturally compulsorily a guy too. You know where this is leading to... you also know that IT ALL CHANGES WHEN A GIRL ENTERS THE SCENE.

Oday's inability to comprehend human feelings and lack of commitment on his side whenever it came to a girl were great factors aiding to their friendship. This led to a massive emergence of guilt from within Arjun's heart. Then a whisper sounded from within his conscience... a whisper of self-importance... which said, "He needs me... I don't need him... that's the reason he always comes out clear in these matters". But the news he was going to break to Oday was still difficult. Arjun had been living with Oday for a long time. A sudden confession of abandonment might hurt the immature Oday. But Shalini had insisted that Arjun did that ASAP. Yes, Shalini and Arjun. It had happened. Within a week itself, they both had collaborated almost as good as the folklore couples. The chemistry between them could have very well been called 'true love'. Thus Arjun was there sitting with a dumbstruck face as to how he must approach Oday with the news. Oday was busy watching a Japanese Anime called 'One Piece$_7$'. One of the favourites of them both. Not that it made anything easier. So Arjun started with a casual tone "Dude... what do you think will happen when one of the straw hats$_8$ falls in love?"

"What do you mean? They already are in love with their aims and all."

"Like I mean Goku$_9$ and Chichi$_{10}$... Vegeta$_{11}$ and Bulma$_{12}$... Naruto$_{13}$ and Hinata$_{14}$... like I mean you bond with somebody that you protrude out together from the rest of the group... So what when Nami$_{15}$ and Sanji$_{16}$ like fall in love and... well Luffy$_{17}$ and Hancock$_{18}$ fall in love?"

"That's an interesting point man... but don't ruin it all for me... I hope this never happens to such an awesome anime… I can't even imagine any of the straw hats separated…" Oday said.

"Exactly… they'd separate out right… but man is it their mistake that they'd separate… Love Happens man."

"Somebody's mistake… maybe Oda_{19}'s…. I always hated the writer… although I loved his work always. Now let me watch it," Oday said ignorantly as he turned the stereo volume higher.

Arjun rushed in front of the screen … "Hey" Oday said irritatingly.

"I am leaving Oday… you're on your own from now," Arjun said.

"What? Why?"

"I have fallen in love with Shalini."

"Love… wait Shalini…. And love… like Gwen $Stacy_{20}$?"

"Noooo."

"WAIT… NO NO NO… you found your Merry $Jane_{21}$… and that too in some Shalini?"

"Not some… it's the same girl… wait… not the point… I am leaving man…"

"But what about the PS4 black Fifa 15 Ultimate $Version_{22}$ I ordered for us?"

"WAHAAAAAT?"

"Kind of a surprise I had planned for you."

"That is… actually tempting… but man… this time I'm leaving man."

"Go then… live with her in her small house with no facilities… when you miss all these luxuries… don't come running back…"

"Actually… she's kind of a billionaire."

"You know what… I am leaving too… I'm going… I'm going to exploit my US Visa and then go and have a single Bachelor's party in Malibu."

"Good for you man… Time for me to leave…" Arjun said as he went out.

Oday sat down on the sofa lamenting over the past few moments and then he clicked on the play button on the remote and the anime said, "I will never leave my nakama (friends)".

"You say that… but you don't mean it, do you Luffy?" Oday said as he picked up the remote "You bloody hypocrite fucking bastard… tomorrow some girl is gonna have her chants over you and you're going to run away drooling, Luffy… and you too Zoro$_{23}$… I hate you all you morons…" he threw the remote at the screen, which fortunately and whimsically did not break.

"Fucking Chimpanzee Glass$_{24}$… or whatever it is called," Oday said as he sat down and continued to watch the anime.

4

"A cold?" Arjun spoke on the phone "How... wait what.... ALS Ice Bucket Challenge[25]? No, it was rhetorical... no I know what ALS is... I know what the challenge... no stop... wait... where is he?"

"Let's go Arjun... dad' reach by 2... it's already 8:45..." came Shalini's voice echoing through a seemingly outer hall. Arjun was sitting on a HUGE bed inside a somewhat girlish-themed room.

"Just a sec darling..." He shouted to Shalini "Is he there?" he continued on the mobile phone "Eating a lot of junk? .... Skipping on workouts? WHAT ELSE? No... The pain must be killing him... I told him not to skip on medication... at least not the Arthritis... okay message me as soon as he opens his door... I'd talk to Sir if it gets out of hand... I should have known better. Okay I have to go now. Thanks Ashish... I owe you yet another one," he said hanging up the phone.

"Maybe it is time you let him go Arjun," came Shalini's voice who came into the room.

"...Yes it is... I guess," Arjun murmured as he put the phone in his pocket and left along with Shalini.

* * *

Oday sat in a gloomy corner of his bedroom. It had been more than a month since Arjun's departure. He had been trying to tackle with that sudden development. Overall, his various attempts to get his life together had only dug his trepidation deeper toward Shalini as well as the concept of love.

Oday had been meditating... a lot... He had been trying to follow all the things in accordance to the verdicts of Arjun. After a fruitless week of self-abnegation that is. But yes, he's also trying to conjure up a plan to bring Arjun back into his life. And as innocently diabolical, as ever... he believed that he could impress Arjun back into his life... to his sorrow, Arjun was not around to witness this cute stereotypical attempt at blandishment. Arjun had completely been conditioned to the idea that it was better for Oday to learn survival on his own. But this was a concept far beyond Oday's imagination. This excruciating reality had made Oday do something, which he had not done in a long time... THINK. And this thinking had brought along all kinds of sadistic, lethal and even suicidal thoughts in the little brain of his. He had tried everything... well, actually he thought he did... and just like every other teen or colligative suicide-attempters he believed that it was the last resort. And he somewhat believed that it was something that would catch Arjun's attention. He had not yet weighed in the situation of him being somewhat isolated in his house due to a party rally of his father for the upcoming central elections. He would be segregated from receiving any kind of aid when he committed that folly. Therefore, he went for it. He sat with a dingy expression and a curious mind. He had googled it twice to be just more confounded since he could not find the 'safest' way to die 'easy'. Answers ranged in a diversity – Some quick Cyanide Poison, shooting yourself in the head, laughing to death, dying of a heart attack like some Jerome Carpenter[26], Head-Bursting by applying too-much pressure on the toilet-seat, listening to Justin Beiber's songs for too long, becoming a prominent Game of Thrones[27] Character and then just waiting to be loved by the audience, Etcetera. All of them most probably assured not instant but definite death. But he chose the classical cutting wrist with the blade technique. Good god, no one ever told him that its effectiveness was merely an Urban Legend and most of the survivors who ended up in jail happened to be there because of this overestimation. But there he lied. In a puddle of crimson red blood. Oday had committed suicide. His last few moments were an evanescent view of a text on his phone as well as the fading sound of his telephone ringing.

*   *   *

A dark space... Oday opened his eyes to see nothing. Then beams of light appeared across the space to reveal an endless pure-white corridor. Oday rubbed his teary translucent eyes and got up to look around. He turned around to see an African-American foreigner standing in a white suit and clutching a lit Cuban Cigar between his teeth. The man was kneeling in a cool posture on absolute nothingness. He looked up to Oday "So you're up then eh?"

"Who.... Who are you? What... Where... I was ... What happened?" Oday questioned all confused.

"I am a death-reaper Martin Messorem... nice to meet you. Raj was busy so he called for me... he said there was some emergency and to look into it... so what is the emergency then?" The man said.

"Raj?" Oday asked.

"Oh... You might know him as Yamraj..." Martin said.

"YAMraj?" Oday asked even louder.

"Oh yes! I forgot… Mr. Oday Singh Luhar… have you ever heard of something called the Near Death Experience? Well you are going through one right now. Now there's just two ways from here… you convince me enough to let you die… or you convince me enough to let you live… I'm a neutral party…"

"Near death experience… wait… I died… YES… I remember dying… and that's it… is this afterlife or something?"

"No we'd discuss the afterlife later… and you're not dead… well not if you survive this… thus the term 'Near Death Experience'," Martin said.

"So what's happening here? I don't understand anything."

"Okay… I was told you were quite a dumb person… but let me elucidate… I am a death reaper… like your Yamraj… we reapers handle the elite work of soul transport to the holy garden of verdicts whereby the judges and the 12-man jury sit to choose your path to either of the tributaries. You kind of are given hell and heaven there."

"Hell and Heaven… they're real?"

"Yeah they pretty much are… but nothing too flowery in heaven nor too infernal in hell… heaven's all about meditating and going around along beautiful sceneries… and hell is like a rock show… with pretty much literal head banging and instead of wrecking instruments they like wreck souls or something… but yeah that's pretty much it… look at me telling too much… So coming back to you Sir. I have been told there is some DEWS around… DEWS as in Dissatisfied Elysium Wandering Soul… now the thing is we do not carry dissatisfied souls without a proper briefing… but any normal reaper could have done that… I was specifically sent for my good counselling skills. I have heard that you've had issues… Issues so meaningless that they surprised even the high Angel of Death … Tell me it's not true…" Martin said.

"What isn't?"

"I've had lovers… I have had friendless… I've had exam-failures or career-failures… but you're like a rare breed."

"Rare breed?"

"Tell me Oday… why did you commit suicide?"

"I lost my only friend."

"See if that was it then you'd not be having this conversation with me. I can read the face…. You did commit suicide because of some other reason… tell me."

"Okay…. I did it because… I felt like I had nothing to do…"

"AHAHAHAHAHAHA…. I got tears in my eyes… So it IS true… you're a different one… so I believe you're quite equipped with money AND girls… what made you think you had nothing to do?"

"It's like… It's like… well when Arjun was there he used to be like… I don't know… he said I did… it was always like that… I never had to do the thinking on my own… I never had to think of what to do… And I lost that…. I'm not getting the word… the … wait… motive."

"Ahhh!" Martin said as the corridor swiftly overturned to a different scenery.

"So you're one without motive… I see… and I find that you're still pure…"

"Pure? No wait you get me wrong… I have had many…" Oday said arrogantly.

"Pure not as in like you're celibate… I'm talking about your brain… it has not been programmed by human influence yet… you are not just a different one… you might as well be the one… let's go Oday," Martin said as he started walking along the corridor.

"Go…. Where to?" Oday asked mumbling as the ground shook.

"Where else? To meet God," Martin said as the scenery changed again to a mountain.

"God… as in THE God?" Oday asked.

"Yes yes… you got the right one… He must be waiting by now… follow me … he sits up that waterfall…"

"Wait… THAT FAR?"

*   *   *

A huge waterfall accompanied by a short brown man sitting on a rubber floater roped to the mountain. Oday could still not believe that his majesty God himself sat in front of him.

"A rudderless boat… Have you ever seen it Oday?" God said as he got up and grabbed the towel beside him.

"No… Sir I haven't."

"Oh no… Keep back the honorifics… especially the 'Sir'… the Imperials art yet to knight me… just call me God… or G-dog if you want to make it sound like cool," God said.

"G-dog?" Oday asked a little surprised.

"Yeah… Okay … forget it… So… A rudderless boat… It is directionless seemingly… yet it has the natural direction of the waves… It goes where the water takes him… When a rudder is added to it then hands might lead it against the waves to their private destinies… but alone… the boat shall follow the waves… the destiny of the sea…"

"Yes I get it… what's your point God?"

"G-dog… Ahhh… see… These waves are like my teachings… but human beings have their own rudder always… they go where they want to and only once in a while is there a destiny similar to mine… You… Oday… are the rudderless boat… you might think that you're capable of nothing… but that's because you lack motive and intention. You have not been defiled by the intent of man. Whatever you have done till now… right or wrong… it was what you emulated… those whose emulations become their way of life lose their purity… but you son… you still have what others have all lost… even your friend Arjun. He is righteous in most ways but even he is not completely idealistic… You my son have not lost your genuinity," God said.

"Gen… is that a thing?"

"Yes... it is... you killed yourself because you had no motive left... All motive was that of your friend... so there was nothing wrong with you... in fact you're better off without it... I can give you motive... but there'd be difficult terms..."

"But you said right... I'm dead... I killed myself... what can I make of it now?"

"I AM GOD... I can change it... and with flattering terms too," God said.

"You can change it... wait...Difficult or Flattering ... decide it first," Oday said.

"Kind of a hybrid... but I must tell you that this is your only chance at it again... Imagine having a motive... One of your own for a change... You have just one chance... Sign this document and I will read you the terms..." God said, handing down a small piece of paper with a pen.

"That's the contract...I'll sign it right away..." Oday said signing with Gods magic pen, which then disappeared along with the document.

"So... here are the terms... You Mr. Oday Singh Luhar from now on have a power... I took you for a superhero guy," God said.

"What like Superpowers... amazing... what powers?" Oday said.

"That's the thing... Any powers you want..."

"Any powers... this is getting better..."

"Yes... but any powers you already know of through some movie, book or other piece of art... not an imagination of your own... and only for one hour each day..." God said.

"Wait what.... Guess it works me... this is supercool too..."

"But here's the thing... you can only be one superhero per day... and once you choose the time... it'll start immediately and exactly end in one hour… and within that time you'd have to help at least five people."

"Help… what kind of help?"

"Any help… it's inclusive of every help… there are controls which I'd tell you if you enter such a scenario but till then you're better off without them…"

"What if I couldn't choose a hero in time?"

"You'd automatically be made to choose one within the last hour of the day… the more you stall the lesser the time you get to help people."

"What if choose not to help?" Oday asked.

"Oday… you know hell right…. Martin must have told you it is a rock show… It is… and they do break souls there… but the only difference between their torture and earth is that on earth people die… here this thing is eternal…" God said.

"Okay I get it…. I get it… I'd help… I'd save like someone's cat falling off the tree or something…" Oday said.

"Now I am going to send you back… You are hereby completing your NDE… You would wake up soon… I am going skinny dipping now… Martin will take you back…" God said removing his clothes to instantly jump down in the waterfall.

"OH GOD…" Oday said.

Martin suddenly warped behind him and grabbed hold of his shoulder "Seriously…. Right to his face" and then they both disappeared.

5

A waiting room inside a hospital. Arjun sobbing in one centre seat, alone. He then recalled how he had planned to surprise Oday by a small visit just to boost his morale that Arjun was still his best friend and he still cared a lot about him. But as soon as he had entered the room he had seen the red-turned marble, probably the most horrendous sight he had seen in days. Oday had committed suicide. Arjun had immediately called for help only to find that no one was around in the house. He had then carried Oday in the car he had come in to escape media criticism for if he had called an ambulance. His bloody clothes and hands made him question his stand in the scene… the righteousness of his firm resolve to make Oday independent, along with himself doing some amends in life related to exploring 'love'. Just when Arjun was about to break into tears, a band of nurses gushed inside the room shouting, "Who is Arjun Trivedi… Arjun Trivedi…"

Arjun was caught aback and stood upright and said "I am" as he wiped his face.

"Come with us," they said as they turned and rushed ahead followed by Arjun. He entered the I.C.U. seeing just green all around with idiosyncratic pipes and machines.

Oday had woken and was lying down on the bed. He turned his face covered in breathing-apparatus.

"Why the fucking hell you moron… you bloody bastard," Arjun shouted as he was shushed by one of the nurses.

"I'm so fucking relieved now man… although I'm also very pissed…" Arjun whispered.

"Hey dude! Did you know that most people who cut their veins survive because veins are like easy to find… but there are some special veins buried deep inside which are hard to find… it's hard to join their cut so the people die when they get cut," Oday spoke in a Darth Vaderish[28] voice.

"They are called arteries… and I am now scared what you might do next… I see by the way that you are quite tranquilized," Arjun said.

"There was this weird guy who asked me when I first woke up that do I do Drugs or something… I was going to be honest but then I thought that he would inject more drugs in me to bring me to this state… so to evade the harms of like extra drugs... I told him that I have already had my fair share," Oday continued.

"That explains much…" Arjun said as his phone started to ring.

"Hey Pundit… I had the weirdest dream by the way…" Oday said.

"No time for dreams," Arjun said going out of the room receiving the call.

"I saw God… and this Martin Guy… wait… DON'T GOOO," Oday said as a nurse came inside with an injection.

"Next time say Hi… and ask him that when I get the money for that necklace," the nurse said as she poked the syringe in the intravenous opening.

*　　*　　*

With an acute, downcast expression, Arjun stood in a large hall inside Oday's Mansion. He was on a telephonic conversation with Shalini. "Okay... but this'll be hard on him...Bye... Love you," he said as he hung the set and hesitantly and slowly stepped ahead towards one of the rooms. He slowly pushed the door to see Oday silently lying down on the bed with a Laptop over his stomach.

"Oday... Yaar... what should I say... I mean how should I say this?"

"You're going right? Come on Pundit..."

"Yes I am... and I am really sorry but I have to," Arjun said.

"No ... Come on Pundit... I am okay with it now. No problems anymore..."

"Yes I know but still I want you to learn to cope with them... wait... 'NO' Problems?" Arjun asked.

"Yes... I have had the realization that I attempted suicide not because you left me... but somewhat because you were the one who brought motive into my life. With your absence, I couldn't create any for myself. So that's what I need to do... I need motive... the only alternative to suicide..."

"Is this Oday Luhar talking to me? You're someone else man... you replaced your soul or something... what the hell happened?" Arjun said.

"Ahahahaha... yeah... something like that you can say... I told you... I had the wildest dream... maybe my subconscious is not that dumb and had speculated all this much before I could... but being close to death... I was brought close to my subconscious too... and there I saw the thing lacking in my life... It was not you... you will always be my best friend... It was always me..." Oday said.

"Dude... I am gonna write an article about this... forget 'brain camps'... cut your wrist and be illuminated... No shit man..." Arjun said.

"Yeah... no shit... So anyway, you are leaving... Take some other car... the location of the keys is better known to you... this one is all bloody and everything... So we bid adieu then mate..." Oday said in a theatrical voice.

"Yes... Rehman Chacha is home and I have told him that you slipped and cut yourself with a tap in your bathtub... I have explained all the medicinal schedule to him... listen to him from now okay..." Arjun said.

"Okay Pundit Ji... I will... Anything else..."

"Come here you bastard," Arjun hugged Oday.

*   *   *

"It is the hour," The voice reverberated inside Oday's head... waking him from his innocent sleep.

Oday got up in a startling fright... just lying back down he heard the same voice again. He became scared. After a few seconds, his curiosity opened up his speech "Is anyone there?"

"You've already forgotten the deal child... the hour has begun... defaulter you are... now the minutes you waste are being penalized... select your hero now," the voice continued in a heavy baritone.

"My hero? Wait... is this a continuation of that dream or something... (pinched himself) Ouch... This is real... how can this be? It means that deal was real too... that God, heaven, hell, and Martin.... God I'd faint."

"You've 56 minutes and 28 seconds at your disposal... which means in exactly that time we'd dispose of you," the voice continued.

"Wait... no... wait... I would choose.... It was a superhero right... so any superhero? Okay so Television/ Movie or Comical... okay Comical... Manga$_{29}$ or Comics... let us say... Comics... DC$_{30}$, Marvel$_{31}$, or Raj$_{32}$ ... this is confusing man ... wait a sec... okay DC got the old legends... Marvel got the new legends... and Raj is just national integrity..."

"Choose Already."

"Marvel... Marvel... okay... I choose... Iron Man$_{33}$."

"Okay..."

"Wait... just okay... not something like "Your Wish shall be Granted"" Oday said.

"You have 54 minutes net... 5 people... we're counting..." the voice disappeared with an emergence of light inside the room.

Oday was still lying on the bed.... "What now... Hey... I am neither Iron Man nor Tony Stark... I don't feel like a Genius Philanthropist... although I'm a billionaire playbooooooyyyy," Oday shouted as he started floating in the air. The light reappeared, embraced, and succumbed to Oday's body and suddenly a red and golden suit started appearing around his body.

"Ahhhhhhhhhhhhhhhhh" Oday started screaming. As soon as he reached close to the ceiling, the light seized and he fell down just to thrust right above the ground. His face was still exposed.

"Always wanted to say this...," Oday said as his iron helmet secured his face. "I'm Iron Man" Oday spoke up in a robotic tone as he flew out breaking the window.

6

"We're flying low, aren't we?" Arjun asked the co-pilot sitting in front, himself sitting in the rear of Shalini's helicopter.

"The weather turned on us Sir" the co-pilot replied. Arjun was heading towards Mumbai. Shalini had invited him over for dinner with her father. The venue was the esteemed Taj Mahal Palace in Mumbai. By now, Arjun was moreover accustomed to these luxurious tantrums of the Royal Family. It was a long flight to Mumbai with a halt at some Shalini Enterprises' Private Landing zone in Bhopal for refuelling. A long journey indeed. Arjun unzipped his backpack to bring out some recreational refreshments. He saw two packets of Lay's- a Spanish Tomato and an American Onion. "How we used to debate over which one is better!" he thought as he grabbed the Red packet… He started chewing down on the chips one by one simultaneously checking his mail on the phone. He suddenly got a ping on whatsapp. It was from Oday.

"I need your help like RIGHT NOW…" the message read.

Arjun started to type "Dude… I'm like miles away".

Oday replied, "I know… you are flying in the vicinity of Allahabad."

The pilot corroborated that yes, they were close to Allahabad.

Arjun became curious but before he could inquire, Oday sent another text "I know you'd ask how do I know… but let me clear this out by saying that you know when I always wanted you to like Tomato… well I hate it when you're finishing my flavour off without me… and yeah… Glance the lookout."

Arjun looked outside all terrified. He saw nothing but the darkness of night. Suddenly a metallic face appeared in front of him to shock him out of his seat. Oday knocked on the window "It's me… open up."

Arjun opened up the door with an expression of tremendous awe. He calmed down the pilot and the co-pilot at first. Then he spoke up "What in heavens are you doing in this Iron Man suit?"

"Long story man… But in short… for the next 32 minutes… I am Iron Man," Oday said in an Iron Man voice followed by his helmet shuttering up.

Arjun stared at Oday all confounded.

"I am Iron Man… ehh? Okay let's forget about that and before you pinch yourself… I tried that… this is NOT a dream. Something like I met God and he bestowed this power upon me… but there is a catch… and you need to help me with it… I need to 'help' five people… Now he was not very elaborate about 'help'… and I don't comprehend the concept very well. And yes… if I am unable to do it within the next 31 minutes then I'm like dead…"

"You're FREAKING ME OUT HERE…."

"No No… don't freak out… You're the only one who can help me help people," Oday said.

"You're not helping Oday…"

"I know that Pundit… that is why I need your help because I cannot help myself help because I never helped myself learn the concept of help…" Oday said.

Arjun gazed at Oday and then screamed, "HELP… HELP".

The co-pilot nearly turned his head back to get another shocker of his life. Oday said "Ohhh… I am just the Pizza Delivery Guy… Modern Tech and all…"

The co-pilot turned back with a laugh and said to the pilot "Just when I start to accept it… I get a whole new shit of 'rich' with this family."

"Okay… Pundit… I'm Dying… and you are the only one who can save me," Oday calmed Arjun.

"How… How do I do it…? What do I need to do?" Arjun said perspiring heavily.

"I have got like half an hour to search people in need of some kind of help…. Five people to be exact… and I need to deliver on that help."

"I need to search people in need … I need to think straight…" Arjun said and then took a minute to think (tapped the shoulder of the co-pilot) "You need any help in there?"

"Sir… A piece of that Pizza would be lovely," the co-pilot said.

Oday sat with his poker face staring at Arjun who replied "It was worth a try man… (to the pilot) Lower the altitude… I need to glance the streets for now."

"Sir… that's not possible… We're flying over the Yamuna River…"

"God Darn it… lower us anyway…"

After a minute of scouting a possible person-in-need… they reached the Yamuna Bridge and finally found a person attempting suicide by jumping over... Arjun advised Oday to wait for it. Oday almost lost his patience but to his advantage, the man took an early decision and actually jumped... Arjun gave the green signal and Oday flew in and caught the guy. He brought him inside the copter whereby Arjun told him "I am God and this here is my Angel... I don't want you to die just now... I have a purpose for you... live till you realize it..." and then asked Oday to drop him off.

"That was some quick counselling... I mean here I was going to give some pity lecture to him being myself a suicide victim... survivor I mean... I guess it is better that I saved him... we don't want another guy with powers do we?" Oday said.

"We don't have time for all of this... from the time you declared we have like 21 minutes," Arjun said as he requested the pilot to head for the Allahabad city.

"Now don't disturb me Oday... let me concentrate with these not-so Hawk-eyes... There (Arjun pointed at a person trying to light a cigarette with a lighter)."

"Yeah... His lighter is not working... and he is getting no stores on the highway... I'd just use my thruster to light his cigarette," Oday said as he flew in.

"No you Idiot... You've to make him quit," Arjun shouted but his voice was unheard by Oday with all the loud Copter sounds.

"Sir... let me help you with that," Oday said as he used his right hand thruster to completely burn the cigarette as well as a part of the man's lips. The man started screaming and fell down all frightened.

"I'm sorry about that sir..."

"Please don't kill me... I won't smoke... I won't drink... I won't take drugs anymore..."

"Wait… what do you mean?"

"I would lie down and ask my wife for forgiveness… I would never take my children's school fees to serve my habits… I'd ask her to lift the curse…"

"Man… you're like wasted… I'd have a drink or two but I need to rush back," Oday said and returned to Arjun.

"What happened?" Arjun asked.

"He quit smoking or something… we still got four…" Oday said.

"What… how did you do that? It leaves three then…" Arjun said.

"Three… but how?" Oday said.

"Don't ask… (to the pilot) hurry ahead."

They entered the city and hovered slowly and scrupulously hunting the streets in accordance with Arjun's directions. Arjun guided Oday to help a stranded car out of Mud and save an old woman from a raging bull. It was the last couple of minutes. Arjun instructed the pilot to fly over to the 'Chowk' area of Old-Allahabad.

"Come on Pundit… I am dying… I don't feel it yet but I am… Why are we in this uncivilized place?" Oday said as they reached their destination.

"Okay … wait… let me see," Arjun scanned with the help of binoculars.

"I see it… that guy just picked that other guys pocket… I'm gonna beat him up," Oday said.

"No wait…" Arjun grabbed Oday's arm.

"It's like 1 and a half minutes to my demise… this better be good…"

"How much money do you have to yourself right now?" Arjun asked.

"Like some 60k... Now don't start on about carrying more money than I need..."

"No... for the first time this is good... Go bring him in... Don't look at me... GO," Arjun screamed.

Oday brought the thief to the copter.

Then Arjun started speaking to him "I believe that you have lost your trust on the system Sir... seemingly from your actions... but we'd like to inform you that humanity might have died... but divinity is not... This is your guardian Angel... He'd right now give you 60 grand Rupees to fight off the financial crisis you're in... And tomorrow he's going to come over and give you the keys to your auto rickshaw... but only if you return that guy's wallet and promise to never repeat this act ever..."

The man broke into tears and brought out the wallet he had stolen "I promise... you're a God."

Oday stared at Arjun through his helmet who then said, "Oday... will you?"

Oday got up and said "Wait... it is in my back pocket". He struggled a little to bring out his wallet and gave out all the money inside to the man.

"Thank you... Thank you."

"Now we'd drop you off... and return that wallet... remember we're watching... you'd receive your means of livelihood tomorrow morning," Arjun said as Oday flew the man down and returned to the copter, barely making it before the suit sublimed off his body.

"Just in Time... And I didn't die too" Oday said.... "We two make a pretty heck off a team man... by the way Pundit... I heard you are meeting her father or something... I guess I'm tagging along then..."

"Yes you bloody fucking bastard… you're tagging along and explaining the whole thing to me…"

"It's a long story man…"

"It's a long flight … (to the pilot) let's hurry ahead… (to Oday) you may now start," Arjun said.

7

India is a secular country. It has always been so. Since the beginning of time, India has accommodated and entertained men, women and Gods of all religions, races, cultures, sects, castes, creeds, countries, continents, planets, galaxies and Universes. The Persians, the Chinese, the Portuguese, the Greeks, the French, the Romans, the Arabs, the British and The Hindus, the Muslims, the Sikhs, the Christians, the Jews, the Buddhists, the Jains and the Rajputs, the Pundits, the Mughals, the Pathans, Etcetera, everybody has had some important place to share in the History of India. Indeed... the chronology of this history testifies against the word 'United'... but let's just say to sum it all... India can indeed be called a 'Unity in Diversity'. It is as if the whole Universe had a consensus that if there is a haven for all, it is in India. Their haven became our heaven... The beauty of Persia... the Handsomeness of the British... Indians didn't have to reach out for them rather they reached out to us. However, the euphony of the British accent came to a sorrowful discontinuation... Boohoo. Moreover, with that came an end to the foreign conquests in India. Indians had finally decided that it is no time to be friends with benefits with the Sly Foreigners...

but friends without benefits with the Indigenous leaders. They were now no more slaves to the invaders and had been illuminated. They had now decided that from now on they would only serve a corrupt, scandalous and sadistic power if it were Indian.

The constitution of India was…. Well… constituted. The leaders had taken a firm resolution to right the wrongs of history. The victims of injustice… those who came within their horizon of sight were all provided with perks… as ladders… to reach where they should humanely be. But there were a few left off. And those who had reached higher and those already in the high seats started to reflect signs of elitism. A little trench of political jealousy and good command over influential extempore oration aroused the remnants to form political rebellions. Thus started the Civil Cold War in India. Take away everything from a man and it leaves just his identity… the place where he belongs. And man is very possessive about this identity. Therefore, the paras in the Constitution increased in geometric progression… amendment after amendment. 'The Scheduled Tribes, Scheduled Castes, Backward Class, Other Backward Class, Minorities' and much more kept being added to it. However, one fateful day… when man saw that no water could extinguish this inferno… he gave up… he could no more conjure up some euphemistic synonyms for the newly emerging sects. So he added that one word… the word that'll give way to the most intense political tussle ever… 'Etcetera'.

The concept, at first did not receive that good a reception. Soon innovative heads started appearing to the frontline politicizing it using idiosyncratic improvised methods. This gave rise to Aditya Luhar… a businessman who was a mere pawn in the political structure of the majestic Indian Democratic Union which had been ruling the centre for about as much time as India had been free from foreign rule... the only other rival being the Indian People's Union although hardly a parallel. Aditya squeezed his way through these Political Giants to found his own little space for practicing this devil's cult. Even before the advent of 'Etcetera', Aditya had been formulating his marvellous debut into politics. He had been making plans all along to quit the party where he stood less than a little chance of ever getting a ticket. He was just there to learn. But he had been planning his escape for long. It took Andy[34] nineteen years to escape Shawshank[35]... Let us give at least the apt eleven to Aditya. Yes... after eleven long years... the day had finally come. Aditya had completely decided his political propaganda... 'Etcetera'... OR... 'Ityadi'. His initial departure was not that highlighted... but after he gained popularity... questions were raised on his past with the Democratic Union.

His political Agenda? He had learned three very important things at the Democratic Union...

1) A man alone is a Sceptic... Put him in a group and he becomes Gullible.
2) Poverty is power. If the poor are with you... never let them go... and never let them be rich.
3) If you see a shoe shinier than yours... then lick it. This will bring more shine to your own shoe.

These three may very well be called the three laws of Politics. Thus, he started his propaganda.... He located the most ignored poor localities of the state of Uttar Pradesh and made public addresses. His primary object of speech was this 'Etcetera'. He acquainted them with the reservation system and how it aided a select few. And he made them realize this hope that 'Etcetera' had brought to them... this hope of Identity... this hope of Unity... this hope of 'Ityadi'. This gave birth to his party called the 'Ityadi' party. The best part about his party was that it was not specifically oriented towards a particular group. He could somehow convince anybody and everybody that the 'Etcetera' represented them... be it Hindu or Muslim... High Caste or Low Caste. With this vivid emergence of the required nuance, it took him just three short years to overthrow the two casteists having a catfight over the regime of Uttar Pradesh. He had accomplished the dream of any aspiring politician. But his sight was fixated over the Union Chair all along. He had been ruling the state for about seven years when it happened. The elite Democratic Union was overthrown by the People's Union. And literally overthrown. They had gained an absolute majority... a thing only heard of in political Urban Legends. All because of whom... the backbone of the People's Union... Rana Teja Singh.

Rana Teja Singh had been the centre of all the political gambles of India. He had been a supporter of the Democratic Union for long... but after his son came of age... he suddenly switched sides to the People's Union. The IDU knew that the tables had turned and soon their era would see a dreadful end... Aditya knew it all along... that the dynasty of the IDU had ended and they were merely surviving because of the Rana and as soon as he realized that Rana was going to withdraw his support, he left the party.

The day Ityadi withdrew its support from the IDU... Aditya came to the Rana's notice. Aditya was merely a small politician at the centre with the Ityadi Party being in the lowest cadre of ministers. The Rana believed that there was a balance in business... lawfulness should equate lawlessness...

and his lawlessness had overtaken his lawfulness by a huge margin… thus he needed to further his political influence… he needed the IPU to win the upcoming central elections by a humungous margin. Even an absolute majority would not work… The world should see that not only the citizens… but the ministers too would flock to the shoulder where Rana rested his arm. He needed a coalition government… one that isolates the IDU majorly and signifies their political demise. Rana knew that being the ruling party in Uttar Pradesh… the Ityadi had great influence… Therefore, he met with Aditya and they had a deal. Aditya gave his full support to the People's Union. And so it happened… The Democratic Union was abandoned on the political front. Rana Teja Singh was received as the country's saviour. But he had not yet entirely grasped the unfathomable narcissism of the Senior Luhar. Aditya was just trying to pave his way through. He was making his future plans. He had no more interest in the state government… moreover, he never had any at all. He had nothing to risk; as such, his move towards the centre couldn't possibly compromise his grasp over the state. He had the trump card on his side… a successor… Oday Luhar. At least he thought so. But he knew that Oday was nothing without Arjun…therefore, he had ensured that Arjun was always there as his navigator.

Things were changing now although nothing had come to senior Luhar's notice. Aditya was ready to put Oday forward but he did not know that Oday wasn't. He was just waiting for the Rana's permission. With his bitter diplomatic skills, he had convinced the Rana that the government at the centre owed more to the Rana than he received. He had made him believe that with the Luhars… The Shalini Corporation and Enterprise would not only emerge as an unparalleled power within the public as well as the private sector... but also the Rana himself would receive irreprehensible influence and jurisdiction over the world politics. The Rana had been looking forward to laying the ground for his able successor Kunwar Madhao Singh to reach even greater heights and possibly create a chapter of history. Aditya made him believe that he could create a history book itself.

Aditya had the power of imagery. He could please a man by quoting his exact fantasies through imagery. So if he wouldn't have been a politician then he could have very well been a pornographer... he had the vision... although he lacked the quality. Nevertheless, even if he failed in the porn industry... he would get a direct entry into the Indian Film Industry and that would strangely lead to the revival of his pornographic career as well. Sounds Impossible... but Indians make it possible. So coming back to the reality where he does lesser harm to the people specifically to their eyesight by being a politician. Aditya had almost quenched all of Rana's scepticism making him witness one of his public addresses. The way people lauded at his verdicts... Rana was flabbergasted. He was mentally ready for the switch to 'Ityadi'. Aditya had somewhat revived the relevance of the Rajputana in Uttar Pradesh and within the Ityadi just to gratify the Rana. New methodologies had already been devised to defame the new Prime Minister and the People's Union. All was set for the action to take place.

Then the illest of Omens set foot in Delhi. The man who was feared even more than his father was. Kunwar Madhao Singh.

Madhao was not the common sceptic. His greatest weakness and strength together lay in his ego. He could compromise any amount of men and money just to satisfy his ego. There were factors affected by as well as channelled his ego viz. his family name, family reputation, his own pride, his own taste, his mood, Etcetera. This made him very unlike his father who was renowned for being a mastermind businessman and diplomat. It was because the Kunwar was highly selective in his settlements that Rana trusted him more than anybody and didn't proceed with anything without his approval. So the Kunwar was called for. But Kunwar didn't want to meet with Aditya or his elite party ministers. He wanted to meet with Oday.

Kunwar always believed that 'Present is worthless… Future is Destiny and past is a lesson for the Future'. And it was the future he could foresee the future he believed in. That is the future whose roots had been laid. And unfortunately, for Aditya, the future of 'Ityadi' lay with Oday. So Madhao wanted to have a face-to-face conversation with Oday…. Just the two of them. He wanted to check the authenticity of the Luhars as well as the potential of Oday as a leader. Thus, the meeting was set. Senior Luhar had been informed. However, Oday was nowhere to be found. So Arjun was informed. Coincidently right when he was having a chat with Rana Teja Singh.

After the formal dispassionate conversation, Arjun retired to the room he was given in the Taj Mahal Palace. Shalini was staying with her father at her father's Bungalow. Arjun stood in front of the mirror gazing at his agnostic self… kind of stupefied by the happenings of the past few days. He was still not able to digest all of it and was somewhat questioning the righteousness of his decision to stay in this vicious circle. Suddenly Oday appeared behind him out of thin air and startled him to fall down. Oday had his right fore and middle fingers locked at his forehead. He was wearing an orange dogi uniform with weird symbols on the front and the back.

"What the hell man? Why the hell did you surprise me like that…? Wait A sec… Was that…" Arjun said as he helped himself get up.

"I am the hope of the Universe. I am the answer to all living things who cry out for peace. I am protector of the innocent. I am the light in the darkness. I am truth… ally to good, nightmare to you. I AM SON GOKU$_{36}$…. And yes that was Instant Transmission$_{37}$," Oday said.

"What the Fuck!" Arjun said.

"Hell yeah… See this (raised his hands) I call upon the trees and the water (interrupted by Arjun)."

"You are fucking Son fucking Goku. You son of a bitch… Why the fuck are you here? To brag… because I can fucking guarantee that that's working like a charm," Arjun said.

"Duh… I need your help again… Okay… forget spirit bomb… you got to see me transform…"

"You Transform?"

"Yes… I practiced… I'm like 20 minutes late because of that though."

"Then we don't have time for it… let's go… and after that I'll tell you something very important."

"Okay I'd straight go to the highest level then…" Oday said.

"What… SSJ3$_{38}$? You got to be kidding me man… That's like super cool."

"No Man…. SSJ God$_{39}$" Oday said as he took some kind of a pose.

"Noooo…. Hell Noooo… and wait… Not inside here. And you still haven't told me anything about how you got this gift… Maybe you skipped the idea that even I would want this," Arjun said.

"Okay… After this we got to have a chat about that as well as the thing you're about to tell me. Okay then let's go," Oday said as he grabbed hold of Arjun and again pointed his two fingers at his forehead to disappear that very instant along with him.

ITYADI

PARTY

8

"Okay.... I haven't seen him myself... Shalini is not a 'family' type... but I have heard that he is a very frightening fellow. So be careful.... And Oday.... Don't fuck this up," Arjun said as he pushed Oday inside the lounge.

Oday drifted ahead slowly scanning the room for Madhao. He then suddenly saw a seven feet tall guy with biceps larger than his own chest, waving his hand as if asking Oday to come to him. Oday got stupefied. Then suddenly a young and short girl pushed Oday, to run and hug the tall man. They both passionately kissed. Oday regained his bravado and turned to wave the sigh to Arjun. As soon as he did, he saw a white, small and fat fellow in a Tuxedo standing behind him with a pensive expression.

"Are you the one they call Oday?" He asked in a hyper nasal Voice.

"Yes... so (is dragged)"

"Okay... let's go to our table (they both sat) ... (to the waiter) Two Long Island Ice Teas and A Mojito... and also a Blue Lagoon... (to Oday) ... And what do you want? Do you drink? Of course you do... (to the waiter) Make those two Blue Lagoons," The man said.

Arjun had sneaked behind a panel at an audible distance from the two.

"So what's your age, height, weight, sexual orientation, Religion, caste, race, Political Point of Views, etc.? HAAAA.... Just kidding... we already know all that... So what is your size...? Naah... we know that too... Naah. Just kidding... Ahahahaha... So what are you going to eat today?" The man asked.

"I'd love some Biryani."

"Chicken sandwiches it is... So Oday what do you do for a living except for being born in your family?"

"I... I..."

"Do you have a girlfriend? Or all those girls merely your keeps?"

"I...I..."

"It is kind of gloomy inside here right... Let's get the tunes changed around here...What's your favourite genre of music?"

"Hip Hop."

"Rock it is ... (whispered something to the waiter)"

"What the..."

"Fuck... The word you are looking for is Fuck... Complete your sentences... You don't want to come out as hesitant do you? Fuck... is what will happen to you sir if this interview of yours doesn't go well... Fuck is what we'd do to your Ityadi if you fail today... Fuck is what we'd do to your dad if we find that there's more to you all than you let us know today... Mr. Oday Luhar... remember... Fuck with us... and it'd be your last fuck ever."

"Interview... I thought I had a meeting with you."

"No... you have a meeting with Kunwar Madhao Singh."

"Wait... what do you mean? Who are you?"

"I'm his PA, GM and CA... Aryaman Mirza... Pleasure is all yours (shook his hand). See... meeting with him is like Osmosis you know... You need to go through a semi-permeable membrane and for that you need to be crystal clear water... I am that membrane and you're supposed to be that water... Let's let me be the judge of that though."

"Excuse me... What does that make your Kunwar then?" A voice came from behind Aryaman. He turned to see Arjun standing. "Arjun?" Oday stood up. "Wait... In Osmosis, water diffuses from a clearer to a dirtier medium... That sounds like your Kunwar is already so very corrupt..."

"Who the fuck are you? You cannot talk about Kunwar like that," Aryaman said.

"I'm not only the PA, GM and CA of Oday Singh Luhar but also his brother and his best friend. You mind your tone with him Sir. And why does your Kunwar sound so perverse? So... Fucky? Why is he not here? What is more important than this...? By the way, the Luhars have proven themselves quite very convincingly to his father... And I've met the Rana himself. He expressed his trust in the Luhars... so why the hell is this Kunwar so cheesy? What's his problem anyway?" Arjun said.

Aryaman stood in awe gazing behind Oday... A tall and handsomely goateed and well-suited man stood behind Oday with his hand resting on Oday's shoulder. He came out of the dark "Ohhh we are not fucky... we maintain our celibacy standards sir. The thing is ... My father is a little innocent and Gullible. Moreover, Dumb... He always needed someone to look after him... So I came into the world... and ever since I've been doing his dirty work for him..."

"Sir, why are you here?" Aryaman asked.

"I don't fuck everybody and anybody Sir" Madhao said as he gestured Aryaman to sit. "The thing is... a lot many people fucked with my Father before I was born. Then he fucked one and everything was solved… Since then whoever fucks with him… I fuck em back."

"Once? Don't you have a sister?" Oday inquired.

"Yes Yes… Shalini… that reminds me… Aryaman… Tomorrow I want to meet this Arjun guy whom Shalini is dating. Inform him to be ready," Madhao said.

"Hey wait… Kunwar… Your… Hi-g-hness. I am Arjun," Arjun said.

"ZZZZZ…. He knows who you are… Not your time. I would call you a car. You need to leave because they are leaving too," Aryaman prompted.

"But I'm here… we can do both the meetings today… it's like killing two birds with one stone…" Arjun said.

Madhao immediately took out a huge pistol from his pocket and pointed it to Arjun's head "I'd L-O-V-E to kill this bird… It sings and sings and sings even after me woe for silence so much…"

Aryaman calmed the Kunwar down. He regained his shallow expression and then smiled at Oday "I'm leaving. Follow me… And yes… bring your friend along."

Oday was frightened at the display of domination. Arjun said, "I don't want to go… You can take my leave…"

"But what about Shalini?" Oday asked.

"Yeah… Thanks for reminding… (Grabbed his phone) I am going to dump her… I love nothing more than living," Arjun whimsically remarked.

"Oh No No!" Aryaman said "Kunwar wouldn't have shot you… don't worry."

"See… he was just scaring you… now please come with me… Because I don't know about you but I am scared," Oday said.

"Okay… You lead the way Aryaman," Arjun said.

"Yeah yeah… The Kunwar doesn't kill in public places," Aryaman said.

"See… the Kunwar doesn't kill in… wait what?" Oday asked.

"Wait a sec… where are we going?" Arjun asked.

"To one of the Shalini Enterprises' Offices. The Kunwar wants to give you a field trip," Aryaman said.

"Offices… so there'd be employees… Huff," Arjun sighed in relief.

"No… I sent them back home… Kunwar likes isolation. We're getting late. Let's move," Aryaman said.

"Good Lord we're so dead," Arjun expressed his nervousness.

"But wait, what about the drinks?" Oday asked.

"Oh! None of us drink mate," Aryaman said.

"I do," Oday said.

"No… You don't…" Aryaman stopped and winked towards Oday.

*   *   *

Oday and Arjun walked inside the so-called office trading post of the Shalini Enterprises. They had been silently following the other two for a while now. The uncertainty of that imposed silence was excruciating, tempting as well as terrifying. The car in which they had come had a chauffeur-secluding black-panel. The windows were all idiotically filmed to disable even those inside to glance the outside. The insides seemed like another DC masterpiece with noise-cancellation edgings. Their smartphones had been confiscated prior to being escorted to the car. Therefore, they had no idea at all where they were right now. The raddled, overworked and solitary semblance of the place projected the idea that it was not one of the active lucrative outposts. But God knew what happened around there. As when the two walked in, they could notice small droplets of what seemed like blood on the tin-containers and jute-sacks. Aryaman composed them by suggesting that it was probably from the animal skin brought in to tan. But he also conjectured them to keep a hold of their thoughts and not do away with them immediately. As such, it was merely a suggestion and not a deterrent on their innovative imagery. They walked closely behind as Madhao slowly gave directions towards different parts of the area walking backwards with a lucid excitement. Then they suddenly stopped in front of a small wooden warehouse. Madhao asked Oday and Arjun to walk in as he opened the door. The light from the lamppost a few meters behind them reached out to the first few flight of the downward stairwell. After that, there was not even a Tad bit of light. Oday gazed back at Arjun to look for some gestures or signs for absconding the scene. But he was just as pale. Oday gulped down his dry throat, looked up for a second like a genuine brand-new theist and shivered forward. He started walking down groping the railing. "You too," said Aryaman as he gave a gentle push on Arjun's shoulders. Arjun followed Oday. They both arrived in the dark basement still struggling to find each other shouting 'You There?' and 'You're fine?' even after leaning on each other. Heavy and swift footsteps followed them down. A loud clap and the lights went on. It was a huge basement godown and on close-observation with their shock-induced blurred-vision, Oday and Arjun found almost a dozen people standing in rows doing absolutely nothing. "Surprise" they all shouted.

"Oh Ho! Cannot escape the pleasantries... You two... these are the people who 'officially' run our northern exports and imports. Well unofficially, they do much more. Our InfoTech and innovation department has flourished so much recently because of these people. Shalini Enterprises has taken it upon itself an immense technical and moral responsibility. Lucknow is going to be the hub of political idealism soon. You must be thinking 'What? How? Where?' Okay... let me explain. As you know, the last few decades have been the renaissance of technology. We at Shalini Enterprises... earlier Swastika Enterprises... believed in 'Making is Believing'... be it a God or a piece of craft. Now technology is a piece of craft. But as you can you see... renaissance is not only the advent of new knowledge but shedding the old one. Man started unlearning what he had learnt in all these millennia. Although he had already relied on 'Get it done' over 'Do it yourself' for centuries, yet even the recreational value of getting your hands dirty was slowly dying out. Digital replaced analogue. The reality saw a transition to a virtual world perceived as the ideal reality. It was not about technology anymore. That mere word couldn't sell now. There arose bastard businesses who exploited this scenario. One of them became the richest man on earth selling something virtual. The world became a fool's market. The impossible always had intrigued man... rather idiotically. Well... What can you at most do with a talking-singing bird... you can't shoot her with a catapult over shielded pigs... that too thrice in one go... Can you? They could... and what not? As such, it curbed the sadistic nature of man to an extent... now he could satisfy his urge to kill on the video-game screen. It seemed like a new thing at first. Then I realized that they had just taken a lesson from history and historical businesspersons, that is from different religions, cultures, priests, etc. They... Who are they? Well my point is not the ignorance of man. My point is that politics is serving its own ends by supporting the wrong technology. All that hypocritical transparency... the talks about 'Digital India' and all... well it is just misusing the lust for virtuality of man... shading him from the dark truths. All the shit about banning and barring... well there are deep secrets behind it. It is the primary principle of all bastard businessmen. This way they keep the layman happy and the elite happier. But... Sir... none there be a bigger bastard than I am... So here... at this godown... we collect... compile... process... and HACK.... But not like the 'WikiLeaks' or 'the fappenning'. They merely crack... We don't just illegally gain access to illegalities of the 'noblemen' ... we damn them for that... by rendering them powerless in its regard," Kunwar Madhao spoke as he moved around in circles around the warehouse observing all of his employees and then turned back to Oday and Arjun.

"Wait... I was caught at 'What? How? Where?'" Arjun said.

"So yes, I was saying. Under my father's reign, who is more of a Utopian, Shalini Enterprises found its way in the usual virtual world. When I came of age, I took over this department. I realized that I can enjoy the perks of hanging on to these mountainous political giants floating high... but I can enjoy more by bringing these giants down and standing as the one giant alone... You know what we do here. Let me give you an example... One of the techsperts hacks into the Server of the Subject1 and takes command of his IP address and VPN... using which he hacks into the Server of the Subject2 taking over his primary account. Now the data is mirrored against the RTI declared sheet... all the other server info is erased... The subject2 is now clear as crystal and the Subject1 is conspicuously projected as the mastermind. Now what happens? Subject1 is taken as

Subject2 for a successive routine. This is just one of the few things we do," Madhao said. "Well in case of money… we can't launder to that extent… It is all money unaccounted for… So we just erase its existence. Cause if we reveal the blacklist and their assets then the political system would come down leading to anarchy. What we need to do is just convert the impure into pure. Purification of the system. We are still small-scale… but this is the vision I have for Shalini Enterprises. You must be wondering how I pay off these men? Well my father is a rich man… He can afford anything…."

"So you're like… a Phil…" Oday said ignorantly.

"A fucking Philanthropist…. And you come off as a sadist…" Arjun said shockingly.

"You're right…. I am always fucking…" Madhao said.

"So how do you do it?" Arjun asked in desperate curiosity.

"Okay… every single one of these people you see were handpicked from top Indian Engineering and Sciences Institutes… they are all super nerds… and along with that they were all pariahs. I just made a simple deal. They could all have been successful entrepreneurs if left alone… but I gave them an offer they couldn't refuse… a bomb they couldn't diffuse? The bomb of friendship. They all needed the company of social-equivalents as well as the joy of fieldwork more than anything. And the work they do… it is nerdy… but in a cool way. You want to know what they do?" Madhao asked.

"What?" Arjun and Oday asked simultaneously at the same time.

"Okay… I will try to make this short… The Search-and-Haunt department over here (pointed to a bunch of men and women) constantly sits on the network to locate an appropriate convenient target. They do that by speculating and estimating the wrongs about the target. Then investigating it with their own methods and sponsored spies. It is not as easy as it seems. But these people specialize in computing and they are DAMN FAST with this. Then come the compilers... they... as you can guess... assemble the data and make a list of prerequisites. They submit the report to their engineer aides who in turn simulate the subject's defences and locate glitches and lags to be exploited. Then come the coding department... They prepare the required codes up for one click execution. The settlers also help isolate the area from technical adversaries and hounds. So... all in all... we have a good setup going on here," Madhao said.

"So why we are here then... why are you telling this to us?" Arjun asked.

"Okay... the thing is till now all we have taken down is the small guns... the turn is to face the big shots now... but to bring them down... we need way more than what we can offer... We were, until now, merely warming up. My next target... it is big."

"Big? As in tall/huge/giant?" Oday asked.

"Big.... As in so fucking big that if we try to fuck em now they won't notice... and if they do... then when they fuck us back... we'd not be left anymore..." Madhao said.

"Who are they?" Arjun asked.

"The Indian Democratic Union.... And the revered mother-son couple of Sabrina and Raj Gautam," Madhao replied.

"The GAUTAM FAMILY.... ARE YOU FUCKING CRAZY? HOW THE HELL WOULD YOU DO THAT?" Arjun rebelled.

"Well.... That is why you boys are here... Actually, I need just Oday but since you come free in the package...

rather mandatory… You can tag along… So Oday here is the so-called Prince of U.P. The IDU is moreover ready to prostitute itself to anybody who offers help. And I believe that your father has decided to meet up with Raj for a possible alliance at the centre. Many other IDU nomads have taken refuge under the umbrella of the comfortable Ityadi. You sir being the prince can exploit the perks to my preferable convenience. The IDU is breaking… there is no better time to end its era permanently. But seemingly, deposed and powerless IDU still bags a greater punch than most competitors out there do. There are many business giants pillaring the party…. We are to first bring them down… but the blacklist is very hard to prepare. Only when we find loopholes can we then fill them up. I need to have first-hand info regarding the donations and alliances… as well as all the negotiations and dealings of the IDU prince," Madhao said.

"But how would we do that?" Arjun inquired.

"Well… we have two princes on our side don't we…" Madhao replied.

Oday stupidly stood with a blank expression as Arjun said, "He means you and him idiot."

"ME… WHAT WILL I DO?"

"Sir…. You… as were destined to… would take charge," Madhao said with a smirk "And yes… Aryaman would be available to you during emergencies… you can contact him through CCTV," Madhao said.

"We do not need surveillance into your assistant's life," Arjun said angrily.

"Oh no… Chatur Champakdas Tilakchand Verma… C.C.T.V…. He is Aryaman's assistant… He is available to you ALL THE TIME…" Madhao said.

"So…. What we are doing here is fun, joyful, ecstatic, next-generation, philanthropic, majestic but unfortunately not lawful. We have not been able to change that you know… Aryaman would do the needful for you. You'd be taking over from dawn tomorrow as the Secret Executives of Shalini Info-Techs," Madhao said.

"WHAT??? What can we do? We're not even lawyers… which happens to be something we are supposed to be…" Arjun said.

"Oh… I know your history you geek… You aren't lawyers but you are law graduates. And I believe that lawmen know the smartest way to break the law, don't they? And with Oday's political influence… I guess you both shall suffice," Madhao said.

"But you have more influence than me," Oday said.

"No… My father does… and he doesn't know an icicle about this. So… any questions?" Madhao said as he took a step on the stairwell.

Oday startled and asked, "Yes… I wanted to ask… Aryaman Mirza… What kind of name is that? Is he Hindu or Muslim?"

"Ahahahaha… Buddhist actually," Madhao said as both Arjun and Oday widened their eyebrows staring at Aryaman who in turn was standing with a blissful expression and a nasal humming.

"You Mr. Trivedi? Any questions?" Madhao asked.

"Yes…. Where do I get a glass of water?"

9

"So I cannot trust him? Should I quit working with him then? I get chills every time I think about him. And I don't feel like revealing myself to him," Oday spoke to God.

"A man honest towards his job is to be trusted. And dishonesty is a job. As long as he is honestly adding up to his dishonesty... That requires some punctilious camouflage. A man too honest ABOUT his dishonesty... he can be trusted the most... trusted to deceive that is," God said.

"Beats me. I don't trust him," Oday said dubiously not even partially grasping the sardonic philosophical rhetoric. Evidently, God had a bad sense of humour... since this was not the first time man had failed to 'read between his lines'. The benefit of doubt was with Oday, thus.

The object of this heavenly conference was Kunwar Madhao Singh and the subject was his suspicious aura... while the objective was to devise the best way for Oday's survival. Oday was a part-time superhero... a fact that was to be withheld from the reaches of Madhao and likes. God's hold on the subject clearly testified against his tri-pseudonyms of 'Omni's. It was never his mistake. He had always preached 'If man ceases to acknowledge the omnipotence in me... maybe one day he'd find the omnipotence within himself... Omnipotence... it is the basis of all three of them'.

Madhao, at first, seemed like the typical businessman. Money, he had and thus fame naturally had an exclusive grasp on him. But to what end? Fame, maybe in five or six countries. But world-fame was never his predestination, although that was what he loathed for the most. And his ongoing ties were never going to get him on top. Idiosyncrasy is the mother of all Pre-eminence and renown. Madhao was an illuminated fellow. He had a distant foresight and thus a very different plan in his hand all along. For coming to the forefront, he needed to bring down all hurdles. Doing it along the way seemed to be an obvious and mundane plan. He wanted to clear the stage way before the performance. And the greatest hindrance in his way was the Democratic Union and Sabrina Gautam. He knew that coming to light could have been done simply by doing it simple and different. He never seemed that nefarious, though. He was using whatever was within his power to keep it in the vicinity of 'legal' boundaries. A wise man always finds his way out... but the wisest uses all the resources to find the best and fastest way out. Oday was the resource he wanted to exploit. The pillars earlier bolstering the majesty of the Gautams had now fled to the Ityadi... the haven for all the immigrants. They all saw business and future in this party because it was the only one, which had outrageously and marginally defeated the IPU on the state front. And unlike the IPU, the Ityadi needed support so it accommodated all who came to its doorstep.

Until now, Oday had not come out of his closet to the political front. Thus, there was no prior stereotype held about him. With the intellect of Arjun, he could have easily won over the trust of all the IPU veterans and thus form a great mole in their system indirectly. Also with Sabrina rushing to the king of U.P., Aditya Luhar, if Oday could display his political persona before that then he could definitely be a part of the successive meetings and hence shower the first-hand info to his techsperts to look into.

Madhao being a shrewd and taciturn businessman was not as trusted as his father was. His father... was kind of the godfather of the currently degraded underworld. It was all because of his jurisdiction over the Gambling business of India, somewhat coordinating most of the country's money laundering. People trusted his father by default. Even the IPU was full of people relying on the Enterprise for their survival. Although officially the IPU had turned against all policies of the Enterprise since it had openly supported the IDU in the latest elections.

But Rana was not the only supervisor of the illegalities. There were other big guns too. Madhao sought to bring these counterparts down by quashing the illegalities carried on under their supervision and hence removing the anchor holding the leaders to them. In the end, they would all seek asylum under the Rana... the only certified Godfather. They would also feel very obliged to him since he would be the master of all their nefarious records. So one sign of treason and they would be brought down in an instant. And when the Rana would retire... Madhao would be the successor to this hidden dynasty of his. The puppeteer to the largest democracy of the world. That was his plan.

* * *

Oday had been a compelled do-gooder part-time superhero for quite some time now. With Arjun's help, he had finally taken a few steps forward in his party structure.

But with all the rush of being a diplomat and a superhero, Oday didn't find time for anything else. So didn't Arjun as well. But unfortunately, Arjun had fallen in love with Shalini… even graver was the thing that he had made a commitment to her. And consistently dodging his meetings and dates with her was not working well for him. 'Bros before Hoes' only works for those who haven't fallen in love. For after that, it is 'Love before ANY-FUCKING-THING ELSE IN THE WORLD'. Arjun feared Shalini might break-up with him if he didn't give a good reason for his upcoming ventures. But this wasn't his greatest of fears. He feared more about her coming to know the reality and telling the Kunwar who in turn would chastise them by impaling or decapitation. What he feared the most was that if Shalini came to know of it all from a third-party source then she might penectomize him for dishonesty. Therefore, he decided to take the brave task upon himself.

"… Then he tied them all up, went close and farted in their face shouting 'Hulk$_{40}$ wind'… So he completed the fifth task, returned the Bag of old-notes to the bank, and came back… Phew… that's all…" Arjun said as Shalini stood gazing dumbly at Arjun's face.

"I got lost at 'God gave him powers'…. Wait a sec… This hulk thingy happened today?" Shalini said.

"Yep… just like before I came to you… You can watch the TV if you want… if you don't trust me…" Arjun said wittingly pressing on the ending part of his statement.

"No… I trust you babe…. But… what you say is… I mean…" Shalini said as Arjun switched on the Television.

"Yesss…. Channel 507… Yes… Times Then it is."

"Studio-This creature which seemed more like the fictional character hulk, today, saved a central bank from being looted. Our experts are at the scene… Moving to Ajay

Gupta reporting from Lucknow at the Union Bank Branch.
Yes Ajay.

Reporter- As you can see the old notes were being
collected over at this branch office from all the other
branches. The government plans to dispose of them but
before they could do so these miscreants attacked the bank.
But to the bank's aid came the 'green monster'. Let us ask
the receptionist herself. Yes, did you see the monster?

Receptionist- Yes... I did... he was green... green eyes.
He looked like the hulk from the Avengers. We were all
afraid. But he helped us.

Reporter- Word is that while going he farted on the
robbers' faces.

Receptionist- Yes he did... and he said 'Hulk Wind'.

Reporter- Thank You for the details. As you heard this
new 'hulk' has just helped capture robbers. Is he a coincidence
or is he related to the other special sightings of these heroes
who are hiding amongst us? And why are they helping us?
Reporting from Lucknow, Ajay Gupta, Times Then.

HQ- Thank You Ajay. 'Who are these heroes?' would be
our topic for debate number one on the NewsHourAndAHalf
Tonight. So joining us would be Sanju Jha, Meena Lekhi,
Sambit Patrakar, Gaurav Bhatti and Ajay Aloknath. Who
are these so-called 'messiahs'? Why did the hulk help us?
And why did he fart? Arlub wants to know... we ALL want
to know. So keep watching Times Then for more updates.
Thank You," Arjun switched the TV off.

"It is true" Shalini uttered shockingly.

"Yes it is darling," Arjun said.

"I wanna see it for myself then... Where is he?" Shalini
said.

"Well as I told you... just one hour per day. Come with
us tomorrow then," Arjun said.

"Okay… Deal… and yes… Arjun," Shalini said.

"Ahun?"

"Still…. This is no excuse for you just coming daily just in the night with a condom," Shalini said angrily as she left the room.

"Balls Man…" Arjun said.

*   *   *

The preparations had been made. The room gave out for the meeting of the three political giants of the IDU, the IPU and the Ityadi. Sabrina had taken a detour to her constituency for an Intra-Party emergency meeting to devise plans to put a check on the emerging exodus from the IDU. Thus, Raj had come in her place. This was highly condemned by the other two since Raj was infamous for his immaturity and low intellect. Representing the IPU was the state minister Rajat Singhania. Rajat and Aditya had been on good terms because of their common support to Rana Teja Singh. Rana was equally fond of both the parties but he had realized that the IPU had more of the battlefront in their favour, thus supporting them would only bring down the IDU. Ityadi was yet to be a major National Party. Although on the state front, it had no parallel. It was due to the outright support of the Ityadi in the Union elections that the IPU could win almost all its constituencies from the state. The Ityadi somewhat vouchered the victory for the IPU. And it was due to the overwhelming victory in U.P. that the IPU could win with an absolute majority. Thus, Rajat and Aditya naturally supported each other's ventures. But they hated each other reticently. Scorned each other's success because Aditya wanted the Union seat… and Rajat was somewhat aware of that. They had always tried tactful ways to predominate over each other in the eyes of the Rana.

Both the parties had another common propaganda. Their keen desire to see the downfall of the IDU and the Gautam dynasty. But Raj being there was both a good and a bad news for the parties. Good... because of his profuse gullibility... Bad... since he hardly was updated with his party affairs. They were all contingent on the off chance that he just might offer what they were looking for... an unofficial alliance. Or what can be called exchanging certain seats in the Union as well as different state ministries, which might serve their both ends. It was all about the survival of the IPU for the IPU... and for the other two, it was all about bringing the all-powerful arrogant IPU down to making low-scale dealings merely for survival. So the meeting started. Oday, after various requests and consistent proposals to the fellow participants, was finally allowed a witness to the meeting. Arjun accompanied him. Raj and Rajat had come... only with their pilots and Z grade security guards. The venue was an old Luhar Farmhouse completely scrutinized for any breach of security or anything, which might compromise the objects discussed. All the phone lines were uprooted and the windows covered up with wooden plies. The area outside the house-door, until the main gate, was all covered in a tent. After all the black-tinted cars entered the tent, the main gate was also covered with an over-cloth. There was no space to peep through the tent because Black Cat commandos heavily guarded all the corners. Oday and Arjun waited for all the others to enter the room. As they did, Arjun gestured Oday to stand up and greet them all with a recessive handshake. Oday did so. Aditya also came in and Oday touched his feet (as guided by Arjun). Oday rarely did that and thus Aditya sat down with a smirking expression. Rajat and Raj sat down on their respective sofas. The room was so wittingly arranged that the large television to be used for presentation just faced Aditya. And the others had to turn uncomfortably or had to stand up and turn completely to glance it. Even the Central table was kept beyond a hand's reach from them. But they couldn't have complained for they had heavy royal sofas whilst Aditya and his team just had plastic chairs. Heavy… so that they could not be shifted by a single person. Nobody other than those certified by the three leaders was allowed inside that room. After Aditya requested his guests to sit… Rajat took one of the two sofa chairs even though he knew what Aditya meant to convey.

Raj… although oblivious to this minor stratagem… spoke up to Arjun and Oday "Will you two young fellas help me turn my chair to the other side…"

"Oh! I'm sorry Raj… these two are…" Aditya said as he was interrupted by Raj.

"Young… and I'm all about youth empowerment… Come-on… Flex those biceps for me… I am sure adrenaline rushes through your core just like me… Come on," He said as both Oday and Arjun got up to shift his sofa sidewise.

Rajat sat dumbly on his sofa as he thought of shifting it on his own but gave in because it was too much trouble. He was rather ashamed as to why a dumb-wit Raj could think wiser than he could. All had taken a hold of their chairs when Aditya spoke up.

"So… my dear friends… We are here to find common grounds where we can aid each other… On the political front, we shall ever remain adversaries… But we can formulate methodologies for our future bouts. What I propose is an idea, which shall benefit us all. The political turbulence in the constituencies where there is almost a dead-draw of supporting voters… well it causes a lot of damage… On both the state and Union level. Therefore, we are here to exchange certain such sections so that our territorial control is divided with fine lines and peace can be upheld. Starting from Amethi… Raj's territory we should make plans for the entire major zones. Here on the screen (switched on the display) you shall see all of the Union Election death-battles. That is due to uneven jurisdiction in those areas. We need to capitalize the businesses centralizing on the chosen and agreed party representative. All the human-mediums shall be shared and discussed. Then we would move on to the states… Well Uttar Pradesh should be left off to my authority since I hold the strings to its core. No offence. But during the Union elections… from hence I shall stand singular and support in coalition to whoever offers a better deal. I'm just doing business mates… no offence," Aditya said.

"You get Uttar Pradesh and we let you come to the Central Front… I believe you are edging your ends more than we expected…" Rajat said.

"Sir… with all due respect… In this highly competitive world, there is no survival without edging one's own ends. And he is offering timely help whenever need be. The IDU needs support more than ever…. And the IPU needed it… and he provided it when approached. There is no dubious hidden plan here. Everything that the greatest technical collaborators of the Ityadi have collected is on that screen. You should really see what he has to offer. You would definitely appreciate it sir," Arjun remarked.

"Who are you… young boy?" Rajat asked.

"Well whoever… he has you asking questions to stall for coming up with a suitable argument in your mind… Definitely the kind of man we want here," Raj said.

The meeting went on like that for an hour or so. And after it was over… the guests were escorted to their respective cars. As Raj walked out the carpet setting, he halted to greet Arjun goodbye, saying "It was nice meeting you… looking forward to more…". Oday made fun of him by saying "He is Sooooo horny for you dude." As the guests departed… Aditya approached Arjun.

"That was… though not surprising… yet a wonderful conversation that you made there… I would definitely want you to be there in the future meetings… All I want is for you to train Oday accordingly. He also needs his say in the conversation, right? I mean…. just saying… he is the heir to the throne. I am sure you'd be his faithful and ever-diligent general. He needs you to win. He definitely does. So you both prepare accordingly. Okay son? So… I will take your kids' leave now. Bubye," Aditya said as he left in his car. Arjun stood gazing as the tent was brought down. Somewhat speaking aloud 'Nobody important left to hide.' He walked back to Oday and said to him "I just got fucking owned by your dad…"

"Well what did he say?" Oday asked.

"A lot of diplomatic things… but it all sounded something like 'Shut the fuck up and let Oday speak… HE is my son, not you," Arjun said.

"Oh… don't mind it… he is full of shit sometimes… He has some trust issues. But I am sure he trusts you. Hey… on the positive note. He did mean to say that you're in for further future meetings… right?" Oday tried to console Arjun.

"Oh Fuck it… let's go help you play hero on the world…. After that, I have a date with Shalini… and this time … I CANNOT BE LATE…. AT ALL," Arjun said and they both got into Oday's car.

10

"Oi! Pundit… I have this next-level idea about my next super-hunch. I wanna be Naruto… Again…. I mean your idea of choosing low-profile heroes was fine. But dude, last time I could only use the combo of Shadow-Clone$_{41}$ and Rasengan$_{42}$… This time I will RasenShuriken$_{43}$ the shit out of some nitwits… What say mate?" Oday said as he rushed in through a huge corridor leading to Shalini's room. To his embarrassment, he caught the couple in the act.

"What the hell! ODAY…. GET OUT…" Arjun said. The couple tried to regain their modesty.

"Hey Hey Hey… I am sorry… You called me in the evening saying she is coming along today as well," Oday self-consciously closed his eyes.

"Oday Luhar… How dare you enter without knocking? It is a GIRL'S room… in fact HOUSE," Shalini uttered ferociously.

"I am really sorry about that… I was too excited. So you are both coming right?" Oday interrogated.

"You didn't let us get to that sucker," Arjun wittingly remarked.

"Shut Up Arjun!" Shalini got up, threw the pillow at Arjun, and went inside the changing room.

"That was a nice one (winked). But dude this is way more important than you two cuddling inside a blanket..." Oday said.

"You go wait in the hall... we would follow soon," Shalini said as she came out wearing her robe.

"Okay... but before that.... KNOCK KNOCK," Oday said.

"Not the time and place Oday..." Shalini said.

"You are supposed to say 'Who's there?'" Oday said.

"Okay... Who's there?" Shalini said impatiently.

"Oday."

"Oday who?" Arjun asked.

"Oday who is kind enough to give you 10 mins to finish off... Okay then... Kudos... I am waiting," Oday said as he left the room.

"He is so full of himself... so bloody fucking over the top..." Shalini said furiously and turned to Arjun "What are you looking at?"

"Well... we just have 10... let's get going then..." Arjun teased Shalini.

"Go to hell... I am not in the mood..." Shalini said.

"Oh! Come on babe..." Arjun said.

"As if you'd last that long..." Shalini said offensively trying to intimidate Arjun's man-ego.

"Don't be so mean babe... Okay... let's go out to him then," Arjun said disappointedly.

"Well we are going out... I need a shower," Shalini said.

"Okay... I am going to the dumbass... You come as soon as possible," Arjun said as he came down the bed.

"No... You are joining me..." Shalini said as she went towards the washroom.

"Oh.... Kay... Yeiiiiii," Arjun smirked and quickly followed her inside.

*　　*　　*

Tragedies change a person... for the better or worse. But overseeing your tragedies to realize the tragedies of the world... well, it mutates the person. Evolves him into a singular, majestic and somewhat absurd being... Absurd, because the tendency to look beyond your own horizon makes you deliver ...than expect. You don't find the time to find your own problems leave it be battle them. The darkness of the world becomes yours to reckon with. This is not a reversible change. Once initiated... there is no looking behind.

Optimism and Pessimism are not merely about the half glass full or empty. Those are just the outlines. Funnily, though... it is about the thirst. The contrast between the two is that of hope. Optimism is completely about hope. Whilst pessimism is about quitting before trial. A thirsty optimist would drink the glass hoping it would keep him alive. The thirsty pessimist would panic about the small amount of water he is left with... would nevertheless drink it... but the lack of hope would eventually kill him. Throw the 'Why's at the neurologists. They would acquaint you with the scientific behaviour of the 'Placebo Effect'. Hence, we conclude that the most important of all things is Hope. That is what we have all learnt from the constant quoting of the story of Robert Bruce and the spider.

There have been many illuminated and evolved beings in the past who could look beyond their wants... succumb to just their bare minimum needs and foster the ailing world around them. The great Mahatma Gandhi... Nelson Mandela... Gautam Buddha... Etcetera. There was one thing common amongst them all. They could look beyond themselves and be witness to the oppressions of the world.

History is a testament that such beings surface up every time the global turbulence gets out of hand. And time was paving its way to another one.

*　　*　　*

Shalini once again hiked along with Arjun and Oday on their fantastical adventure. Rather Arjun and Oday hiked along Shalini in her bulletproof helicopter for their adventure. With the help of Arjun… Oday was easily able to finish off four of the five tasks… Three of them was just catching pickpockets and the fourth was escorting an accident victim to the hospital. They were scouting the city corners for nefarious activities. They were easily able to locate a bunch of people overpowering a young man and beating him black and blue. Oday instantly intervened, took the lot of them down, and rendered them unconscious in no time with his 'Ninja Skills'. He went over to the young man to help him up and look for some serious injuries. He got up, thanked Oday, and limped his way out of the dump. The chopper picked up Oday and they all made their way back happily, celebrating yet another day of successful missions.

On reaching back at Shalini's place, Oday and Arjun wanted to play Xbox on the big screen in the hall. So Oday went to pick up the console from Shalini's room who in turn was scrolling through the channels to reach 'Zee Cafe' since it was time for the new episode of 'The Big Bang Theory[44]'. Oday suddenly asked her for the second remote and hence she halted her scroll and went to look for it in the drawer. As she did… Oday started gazing blankly at the screen. A random News Channel was on… Shalini was intensely going through the drawer as suddenly she was startled by Oday shouting "What the Fuck…. Arjun… COME HERE… NOW."

Shalini turned around immediately inquiring 'what is it Oday?'

"No…. this is not true… No," Oday murmured with his face turned pale.

Arjun rushed in and inquired the same. Oday pointed at the screen. "Breaking News. Eight years old girl was kidnapped… brutally raped and then murdered… Her body was found near the Lucknow Junction Railway Station about an hour after the kidnapping. She was travelling with her family when a person allegedly kidnapped her. Here is his picture as retrieved from his wallet."

"Is he? He can't be," Arjun said in a frightened tone.

"Keep Watching," Oday said.

"This picture was submitted to the local police by the five pursuers who claim to have chased the person as he carried the little girl from the train to an isolated area near the station. Two of them being the girl's father and Uncle themselves. They say when they arrived they could not see the girl with the man and presumed he had hidden her somewhere. So they started beating him up to tell it to them. But moments before he was about to give away the girl's location, another unknown ally of this man appeared and took the five pursuers down, aiding the man's escape. We do not have much information on them. The wallet was retrieved from the site and it just contained a picture of the kidnapper who was chased. Not even an hour after this incident, the mutilated body of the young girl was located close to the station junkyard. The police are investigating the site and are looking for the paedophile duo all around the station premises. The posters have been…" Arjun turned the television off.

Oday stood numb with his eyes widened as a teardrop fell from them …. Then he suddenly passed out.

*   *   *

An ambulance speeded through the main gate of the 'Suraksha' Hospital… the Medical Chain of the Shalini Enterprises. The door thrashed open as Arjun and Shalini came down. The ward-boys rushed to escort the stretcher carrying Oday to the Intensive Care Unit where he would be examined. Arjun and Shalini closely followed until the ICU door, which was in-turn a terminus for visitors. Shalini called up her brother for assistance as Arjun took various peeps through the circular glass on the door. Shalini asked Arjun to inform Oday's father… although Arjun revolted stating that crowd and media would definitely accompany the Chief Minister… and between informing a father about his son's ailment and disturbing the decorum of the hospital and many more numerous patients… the righteousness meter weighed more on the latter. Arjun was also not in agreement with Shalini on calling her brother… but since it had already been done, he could not have helped it. Two major reasons… Media conspiracies could talk unimaginable shit regarding the two elite families of the Luhars and the Singhs and their recently emerging apparent partnership and also could raise questions on conspicuous intimacy between Arjun and Shalini. Some might also question the succession of the Luhar throne if Oday passed away. There was no time and place to bear with media idiocy. But the second reason was more of importance to Arjun. There were chances that people might come to realize Oday's powers… maybe the doctors and in-turn the Kunwar. That was an uncertain risk he didn't want to take… but since Shalini had already done the deed, he couldn't have helped it. The ICU door slowly opened as the doctor, the intern and the nurses came out. Arjun approached the doctor "How is he?"

"It is not good news. He is the same as you brought him here. He is in a shock-induced coma. I had only heard about such mental traumas. Never witnessed one. This is a rare case... We have no leads to work on here. He has a stable heartbeat so there is no question for Cardioversion, CPR or ECT. There is no injury to reckon with. We just need to be patient," The doctor said.

"Isn't there anything that can be done?" Arjun asked desperately.

"We have done what we can," The Doctor said.

Shalini stepped up to the doctor and said, "Hey... keep trying okay... you know who I am right?"

The doctor stood blankly since Shalini had so rarely frequented her father's set-ups that nobody was acquainted with her face.

"She's my sister..." came a bold voice as a bunch of commandos walked through the corridor towards the ICU. They spread out to give way to Kunwar Madhao Singh.

"Kunwar Sir... You... here... then she must be Madam Shalini," The doctor freaked out.

"The man inside is Oday Luhar... the son of the Chief Minister Aditya Luhar.... Get working on him to get him working ASAP. You will have all the resources you need. The speed and quality of your success shall be considered greatly in the future," Kunwar Madhao commanded.

"Yes Sir... Hey Siddhesh... Shift him to the Special Ward... vacate it now. He is CM sir's son..." The doctor's inner sycophancy arose.

"There is no need for that sir. A better air conditioner is not what Oday needs right now... I'm quite sure... and I reckon you shouldn't disturb the other patients," Arjun said.

"Tell me what you need Doctor..." the Kunwar asked again.

"We have tried an adrenaline shot already. But I believe nothing below an overdose directly to the heart would work. But I would need recommendation from a Government Medical Officer... and also a Risk Certificate of his parents," The doctor said.

"Okay. I am onto it. I will inform his father," Kunwar said.

"Can we go and see him?" Arjun inquired.

"Yes Sir... Of course, you all can definitely come inside."

"Shift him to the observation ward. The ICU should have space to accommodate others in need," Kunwar said as he walked by typing through his smartphone.

Oday was wheeled out to the observation ward whereby Shalini and Arjun accompanied him beside his stretcher. Arjun was lost in thought of wonder. He was recalling the last time he was there with Oday. The infamous 'suicide' that only they two remembered. It was not the same hospital but yes, the scenario was almost the same. Arjun beside an unconscious Oday... giving no signs whatsoever of recovery. He was thinking as to how heavy Oday might have felt when he saw the news. Arjun was feeling a part of the guilt as well. The depression was also similar to last time. Thus, while summing down the contrasting similarities between the two incidents Arjun came across a very important point. He was reminded of the most import key-phrase that Oday had used last time. 'Meeting with God.' He got up from his chair feeling all enlightened... and just as he did, a loud scream came across the hospital "WHAT HAPPENED TO MY SON?"

11

God works in mysterious ways. Everybody has always said that. History is a testimony to the greatest mysteries being held confidently by the most discernible of objects. Da Vinci always said, "Simplicity is the Ultimate Sophistication". The answers to the biggest of questions are always very simple. God works in very simple ways. But simplicity sometimes is rather too less of an answer to us... that is why we are still searching for the answers with all of our science which just took Gautam Buddha forty-nine days of meditation. What was different... what did he do that was so aloof from the rest of them? Well... for firsts... he chose to relax rather than flex... he chose to keep relaxing and think as simply as possible and he got answers to all those mysteries. But such answers are not satisfactory for the general masses. They need more. Well the grasp of the Placebo is way beyond just the medical field. Tell an obese to go walk it out... he probably wouldn't... but tell him to go up the stairs of some insanely high altitude temple to pray for his well-being... he might do it indeed. But the current badge of the Dharma gurus... those narcissistic, prejudiced, greedy, illiterate and arrogant bastards... they exploit the innocent crowd. There was a time all of this was done just for the benefit of the gullible crowd… Like "Leave alcohol… Allah condemns it…" made it much simpler than "Leave alcohol… it kills you" … and "God abhors fornication" was much easier to impose than "Fornication is unethical and immodest". These enlightened leaders used the path of fear of that 'complex answer' in the minds of the ignorant masses for their own benefit… Like the Great Mohammad, the Buddha, Christ and in the modern day world our very own revered Mahatma Gandhi. They were all prophets indeed.

God's ways are very simple. He created the initial four and then all he did was have faith… yes… faith. God has faith in us. And… yes… four… Well, the answer is simple yet again. What when they were two and had two kids… a boy and a girl… what then? Once again… unethical… God never vouched for incest you know. So times passed by and new generations of over-smart assholes came by who complicated things in geometric progression. Soon God realized that his real Prophets were fading away amongst the frauds and he had to level up his game. In the past very rarely had God been urged to provide 'Superhuman' capabilities to some chosen ones. This time… the intensity of the powers endowed was also much more. Entrusting in a human… with all those distractions at his end… so much power… well, he went overboard for sure. But he was ready to take a chance.

*   *   *

Martin Messorem was again entrusted to escort Oday to the one and only God. Although Messorem was this time, and for the first time not told about his target. He came to the reception to inquire about his subject and the floating woman pointed towards the 'DEWS waiting room number

786'. Martin opened the door to find a man crying intensely with his head buried in his laps… sitting on a bench.

"Hey… Hello there… I am Martin… a death-reaper. Who are…. Oh this is a first… you are a…" the man lifted his head. It was Oday who stopped crying and spoke up "Dissatisfied Elysium Wandering Soul… I know," He wiped his face.

"My My… Oday Luhar once again. What brings you here?" Martin inquired shockingly.

"I am a murderer…. A rapist…" Oday said with a devastated expression and dialect.

"Hold on a second… calm down there… you know my payroll doesn't have me meet the same soul twice. So tell me the whole thing along the way. I am quite very busy today. Let us go to the Paradise Restaurant. Get up… let's go," Martin said as both of them left.

*   *   *

Martin escorted Oday to the door and then bid farewell as Oday stepped in. There sat God on a mat in a Seiza position having some three-course Japanese meals.

"Oh… you got yourself into quite a trouble there Oday… isn't it?"

"I don't deserve such ability Sir… I mean Your Highness…. Your Grace… I don't know… GOD… send me to hell… I don't think I can do it anymore… I deserve damnation or whatever it is you call it," Oday said.

"Take a kneel on the mat Oday. And order something. It is on me. Do you wanna drink something?"

"I can't take it… I have killed… Please… I demand my punishment…. My condemnation."

"Relax Son… Tell me, what would you have?" God said as Oday sat on the mat.

"What's the menu Sir?" Oday asked.

"Ask for anything you desire," God said.

"Even intoxicating drinks?" Oday inquired.

"Son… everything intoxicates… the differentiation was made by man not me. Some are there for the taste… some for the health and some for being light… everything has its addiction and side effects. So… order anything," God said.

"I would have… a mango shake," Oday said.

"Okay… you heard it Sameera… Get started on it… our guest deserves his shake… So… Oday… until we are waiting for it… let us get talking again. Let's start from the beginning. I want to start over as we first met. So… who are you?" God said.

"I'm Oday Luhar, son of Aditya Luhar. I'm a law graduate and currently I work as a part-time superhero and a full-time unemployed spy for Kunwar Madhao Singh. My best friend and brother is Arjun Trivedi. I have… have the blood of an eight-year-old on my hand… and the right to justice…. (Cried) the justice to her family…" Oday said while breaking into tears.

"And I'm God… so calm down Oday… so… you have a thing for Mangoes huh? That is nice," God said as Oday took a hold of himself.

"You know who else had a thing for mangoes? Vijay… I will tell you the story of Vijay. Vijay had a family of all males. A father and an elder brother. Vijay's father was a successful businessman. A gold vendor… do not confuse him as a jeweller… In those times, Gold vendors produced mass coins and took royalty from the king for the production. So yes… Vijay had a thing for mangoes although his father was allergic. His brother Vishesh had always warned him about bringing the fruit nearby the house. Thus, Vijay always took to eating them at the orchids themselves. One fine day when his father had gone on a trip... Vijay brought back a dozen mangoes and enjoyed the meal storing the rest. His father returned that night when they all had slept... earlier than planned. Intrigued by the juicy pack of fruits on the rack, his dad had a bite or two... giving in to his spiritual ignorance. But biology overpowered him and he died of swelling of larynx and resultant suffocation. The brothers woke up next day to their shock. Vishesh beat up his little brother and blamed him for the death. The laws of the first-blood succession endowed the riches of the father on Vishesh... Vijay was banished by his brother... away from any access to the father's possessions. Vijay requested just for two things... his father's body and the packet of mangoes. The now arrogant and selfish elder brother granted the younger brother's wishes. Vijay buried his father's body in an open grassland outside the village... even though the villagers proposed ritualistic cremation. He ate all the mangoes and also buried the seeds all around the burial site and the one his father had eaten exactly at the burial site. Vijay stayed in a hut nearby the grassland. The plants grew and gave their first fruit within five years and slowly went on to become full-fledged mango trees. Vijay nurtured them, protected them, and distributed the mangoes freely. The villagers offered Vijay a place in their town although Vijay refused and said that he had to live for his father... always pointing at the centre tree. Meanwhile, his brother had become a well-to-do tradesman and was now also an owner of diamond mines. But his brother was being overshadowed by Vijay's emerging fame. Therefore, one day he conspired and just when Vijay had gone for a morning stroll into the jungles... all the trees were set on fire. The villagers were famished… Vijay came back and tears fell from his eyes as he saw the trees turn to ashes,"

"Then?" Oday inquired curiously.

"Then just as the villagers had started sympathizing for Vijay… who had been just sitting there watching the fire… he suddenly got up and picked up a mango which had fallen away from the tree. He ate it and went to the centre to dig up a little soil with his hands to bury it again. The villagers were confounded at the weird step taken by Vijay. They asked him and he replied 'The ashes shall be good fertilizers. They shall never die. He shall never die'. The people slowly went around lifting their own mangoes and did the same, saying 'you can't possibly eat them all'. This time with their help… an orchid as huge as a forest… with trees healthier than last time… was formed within the next ten years. Just as the phoenix that rose from the ashes… the trees were reborn. Within that period Vishesh had passed away from ailment… he died with three kids and a lot of property… and his kids would grow up to be just like him… a successful businessman. Vijay… after many more years of rejoicing his paradise on earth… finally gave in too. He had vindicated himself from that burden he had carried all along by reviving his father's soul for the next eternity. He passed away sitting beneath his father's tree which he believed to have held his soul. He died smiling. The villagers erected his figurine but due to lack of skill they could not give exacting definitions and thus the statue's face didn't resemble him. Rather it resembled no one. It could have been rather blank. But in their hearts… forever… they remembered him… as The Mangoman…" God said.

Oday sat in front of God in awe… somewhat realizing the aspect of the story that God was trying to present to him.

"So Oday... let's start again... Who are you...?" God said with a blissful smile on his face.

"I'm the Ma..." Sameera "Here's your Mango shake" interrupted Oday.

Oday gulped it down "This is amazingly tasty,"

"I know, right?" God said.

12

The doctor raised up the large syringe in his hand filled up with some strange fluid. He tested the needle with a small push of the piston and dramatically moved towards the marked spot on the chest of the unconscious Oday. Arjun and the rest waited and witnessed the intense scene from outside the glass lookout, almost in slow motion. Arjun had been trying to delay the shot just for the sake of his presumed meeting of Oday and God. But Aditya stopped giving into Arjun's lame reasons and compelled the doctors to go with the adrenaline shot. But just as the doctor got close to Oday... suddenly, the pacemaker and rate-monitors started fluctuating. The staff paused for a second... and inhaling deeply... Oday got up... to everybody's astonishment. None of the staff could hold him down and he broke free and rushed towards the door shouting "Arjun... Arjun". As he reached the door, it pushed open and there came the senior Luhar.

"Dad...You" Oday said as his father hugged him tightly.

"Yes... me... I was worried sick son. But apparently the reporters outside had much more questions to ask," Aditya said.

"It is highly recommended you keep to the bed… we would examine you" the doctor said.

"There is no need doctor. Just escort him to our convoy and we shall take him home," Aditya said.

The doctor instantly pulled Oday back and the nurses laid him down on a stretcher. Aditya led forward into the corridor. Arjun and Shalini stood there worried.

"Hey Arjun… Dad can I have a second with…" Oday said.

"Some other time Oday… let's go home for now," Aditya said.

"But dad just one sec," Oday pleaded.

"I said… some other time. Let's go," Aditya said as his assistant opened through the corridor end-door revealing a swarm of bodyguards and stopping dozens of reporters.

* * *

A Pitch-black night with the polluted faded sky of Lucknow… unveiling only the few brightest of the stars. Somewhat resonating with the competitive world of today… well, pollution of the sky… pollution of the mind… it ruins it all indeed.

"Why are you so worried? He knows better you know…" Shalini said to Arjun. They were both on the rooftop of her Bungalow.

"It has never been this late in the day. I am sure something fishy is going on… I mean he would be clueless without me. And I am sure he has met God yet again… I need to know what's up…" Arjun said worriedly.

"Madam… Sir… your friend… you must see this…" Shalini's butler came up the rooftop through the escalator.

"Oday? Is he back? What happened?" Arjun said.

"No… but Arlub has something to say about him," The Butler said.

"Oday is on Times Then?" Arjun widened his eyes.

"Not exactly him Sir," The Butler said as all of them left for the hall.

On the news channel, they saw Arlub talking about a mining accident in Tamil Nadu whereby two-hundred and fifty workers were trapped inside an unstable mine since thirty minutes. The mining coordinators had raised their hands up and the reason for the accident was unknown. Until a man dressed in a cave dweller attire appeared and pushed open through the rocks saving the workers from inevitable death. The reason for the failure was instantly revealed as the workers explained seeing layers of magnesium along the rock surfaces and also smelling methane, all which was not reported in the assessment. They were saved from a devastating conflagration. The man made a video of his heroic act and the workers' and engineers' complaints and handed it to the on-sight media in a flash card. F.I.R.s were reported against the Officers and Engineers responsible for the Negligence and False-Assessment.

"That is definitely Oday… but why the fuck… and how the fuck did he reach the South? And why the fuck is he He-Man$_{45}$ all of a sudden?" Arjun declared his query.

"But it is a good thing right? That he was able to complete the day's quota. I mean you were worried about that earlier I guess," Shalini said.

"He is not following the pattern. I mean this is different. This is large scale," Arjun said.

"Yes it is," Kunwar Madhao walked inside the hall. Everybody shut their mouths instantly.

"I wonder… he was earlier seen at most saving banks and all… And that stunt he pulled up with that paedophile…

I mean it had me wondering whoever this idiot is… he is a fucking dumbass idiot… damn it that was redundant. So Yes… I was here to ask you love birds. Where the hell is Prince Luhar?" Madhao said.

"Oday," Shalini said turning to the television screen displaying first person view of Oday playing hero. But interrupted by Arjun's angry eyes. she turned back to her brother "We d…on't know where He is."

"Then who does? He is mostly with y'all. That idiot ran from his home today. Tomorrow is an official meeting of his father and Rajat Singhania. I want him there. I thought I would notify his lazy ass regarding this. Tell me if you get to know anything about him. Meanwhile, I have some important work in Bangalore. I am leaving in an hour. Cheerio. And yes, Shalini… it is Okay for him to drop by all the time but you do not get pregnant before marriage… that is if you do want to marry him. If no, then DON'T get pregnant," Kunwar said.

"Brother… you are embarrassing me. Go now," Shalini said as the Kunwar left the house.

"That moron… Marriage shit… already… can't take it…" Shalini said.

"We have bigger shit on our heads right now. Can you ready a jet darling? ASAP? We are heading to where that nitwit idiot is," Arjun said.

"Then you should come upstairs man… it is like chilly as fuck here," Came Oday's voice as Arjun and Shalini turned to see Oday come down the central escalator.

"You…. The fuck is going on here? I'm so confused," Shalini questioned.

"Bro… you were just there…. How?" Arjun asked.

"I'll tell you all about it… Let's sit on it," Oday said.

"Get us the best Single Malt in the Cabinet," Shalini said to her butler.

"Shalini... Ammmm... Make it a Mango shake for me," Oday said.

* * *

"............. And she brought me the Mango shake then. And that is not it. The story was just a eulogy for me to adhere to. Then after the meal, during the walk outside, he told me about my chance at exoneration from the guilt. He told me that I was to take as much help as possible from now on as things were going to be huge... actually affecting humanity... All in all, he gave me a purpose. And yes... Pundit... Also an Upgrade. Or should I say, Upgrades," Oday said.

"Upgrade? Like what?" Arjun asked curiously.

"Well... for firsts... the boundation of 'helping' five has been removed. Now I can myself play hero at will... since as per his understanding I have finally realized the true capability of this gift," Oday said.

"That is like awesome bro... No more worries now, right? We can take weekends off... and what about the time boundations?" Arjun asked.

"Well that is there... I can just be hero for one hour Of course. But yes. It is a total of one hour in the day. I can play hero all throughout the day for a total of an hour," Oday said.

"COOOOLLLLLL... so now tell me... How did you reach the South in no time as He-Man? You took a jet or what? And did you get like Spidey sense$_{46}$? If not, then how come you reached like half an hour after the incident," Arjun said.

"Whoa Whoa Whoa... Hold a grip to your questions man... Okay... simple answer... the last and the most import upgrade. I can switch," Oday said.

"What do you mean you can switch? Wait a second… no…. Anyone you want?" Arjun asked as Oday nodded in agreement.

"Don't tell me that's how you… What combo did you use?" Arjun asked.

"I ran as the Flash$_{47}$ for like two minutes and then got bored of it and went Goku," Oday said.

"Instant Transmission huh…" Arjun said.

"Yep. You got me bro… And yes about that Spidey sense. Sorry to disappoint you mate. I just opened the TV… caught the news. And there's where I got an idea too… You two… will be my sidekicks from now on okay… Finding trouble for me to solve…" Oday said.

"You still are a jerk you know sucker," Arjun said as Shalini walked out of the washroom in her bathrobe "Sidekick… Not so much."

"Come on… Shalini… you get to travel EVERYWHERE…" Oday said.

"I can do that whenever I want," Shalini said.

"But this way… it would be adventurous because you would never know which place is next… and yes… we would go shopping after that… And Arjun can lift all your bags… Pretty Please…" Oday put forward his generous request.

"Okay… what would you need then?" Shalini asked.

"I don't know. Ask Arjun. I just know I need you two. Arjun here is the technical guy… ask him…" Oday said.

"You are not James Bond$_{48}$ okay that you will need equipment or anything… Basics require just a chopper and twenty-four-hour access to news. Basic smartphone with good 4G can provide that. Just in case, we would have him (pointed to the butler) for emergencies. And yes, one last thing… Oday… What do you mean by everywhere?" Arjun said.

"We are going Global man… and yes… last but not the least… Pundit…Call me The Mangoman…" Oday said with sparkling eyes.

"Fuck off mate… I'm not using that word," Arjun said.

* * *

A tall dark man in a black suit stood beside God "Why do you trust him so much?"

"He has been set on the right path… the path of the right. I think he'll suffice. His guilt consciousness is enough to see right from wrong… and his immaturity will make him not think twice before taking the rash instantaneous steps needed to deal with the wrong. The right choice indeed," God said.

"Why do you think he'll not fret… that so much power will not make him go over his head?" The man asked.

"He has a do-gooder friend… As I said… I think he'll suffice" God said.

"He should," he said as huge white wings came out of his back… strangely dissolving the suit around it yet not tearing it. "Or else I will personally deal with it… (Took out black aviator glares from his inner pocket and wore them) and as you know Sir… regardless of anybody else… I always serve my purpose," he said and then flew off.

"Yeah Yeah… be sarcastic… for interrupting your job twice… but don't forget who made you Angel of Death in the first place. Hey… Mritunjay… Finish off this week's work before taking a detour," God said in a low-pitched high intensity and high decibel voice.

"Yes I will," Mritunjay replied fading off in the heavenly skies.

"This rude idiot… Sameera… get me a Mango shake… and make it tasty… like you did for Oday," God said.

"Don't order me around Sir… Oday was a special guest. You may be a regular but don't forget I am the owner. I feel some respect is due here," Sameera sonically remarked from inside.

"Hey… what… I'm the … owner. Of like… Everything," God said.

"Don't you get started with that again Sir."

"I'm sorry. Just get me that shake," God gave in.

13

Finding a more definite heading for the future, the trio, or let's say the duo with the complimentary girlfriend, furthered its adventures by hunting for more large-scale incidents. Shalini's Butler was keeping a close eye on the television and newspaper and was all-ears to radio broadcast to hear such incidents, which required miraculous aid. He was also to set priorities as to which task to finish first. With Oday's newly gained abilities, he could easily warp from place to place wherever required. But in the end, he was just one man. And, strangely enough for him, he had too much on his head to be worried about. Playing hero was an important task he had been entrusted with, but it was entrusted to his covert alter ego. So he couldn't spend much time just preparing for his heroism. For the entire world did not know how busy a man he had actually become. Too much delivery was expected from him. Especially by Kunwar Madhao Singh. And in the Kunwar's eyes, Oday had already procrastinated much over his job. The Kunwar had sent strict notification for the two to report at the Northern-Trade office for a briefing. Shalini accompanied them just in case things went south for the two. The workers became conscious as soon as Shalini entered the premises... they were not sure if the Kunwar would approve of it. Shalini was okay with the work going on there, after Arjun told her about it. She was really happy about the philanthropic activity… but as soon as Oday used the word 'illegal'… she caught aback and got angry. With whom you might think? Well… when we have the Universal Boyfriend at our hand… then why should a girl be angry with anyone else, right? So yes, she got pissed at him… and with the boyfriend, the best friends are always a combination package. Hence, she went and sat in a corner hoping for Arjun to come and console her. But before he could… entered Aryaman and Madhao.

"Well… I see you have been missing appointments… meetings… what the hell you think we do here? Aryaman never missed one. I gave you our best. CCTV… you couldn't even exploit him to your best. You know we had never gone a week without a job… and now it has been three. When I was in Dubai… I thought that I can run this hidden business better by being myself here in person… but I guess coming here and trusting you fools with this fucking job makes me a fool myself. Three weeks without a corrupt, scandalous leader falling to my grasp. There is not much time before the next elections you know? Four years shall pass by fast. There are seventy sets of three weeks in four years… and you lost one. I hope you don't lose anymore. Aryaman here is leaving for our workstation in Dubai. You Sirs… should get me something before he returns. A lead at least. And report back to him," Kunwar said.

"But we already submitted a list of all the Vote-Seekers of Rajat…" Arjun said.

"It is not enough…" Kunwar said.

"That mine…. The accident we heard of a few days ago… It was being controlled by the IDU… I believe if we push through the mining database under it, we shall get more such dealings… And the ones in the North especially," Oday said.

The Kunwar clenched his brows and questioned Oday "What do you mean? How do you know of this?"

Oday recollected himself thinking he had nothing to offer Madhao as a perfect alibi for the information. And just as usual… Arjun came to his rescue "The NewsHourAndAHalf constantly shows that it was an IDU thing… that mine."

"NewsHourAndAHalf… are you fucking kidding me? That contemporary conspiracy theorist and his wannabe news channel? You bringing me that as a factual evidence… you two boys did go through puberty right? Okay then… get me something concrete… and I have recalled some work to do… see you later," Kunwar said turning around… and Shalini was standing behind him.

"You… Are… Here… Welcome to our Trading post… getting acquainted with business are we miss?" Kunwar said in a faint voice.

"Don't try that hard brother. I have already been told what goes on here," Came the angry baritone.

"Oh… Did these two?" Kunwar became agitated.

"Don't you dare say anything to them or else I'll have dad pay a visit to this place," Shalini said.

Being angry with the boyfriend and the best friend didn't change the fact that the girl won't defend them. Instead… For her… the final judgement was at her jurisdiction and no one else's. And once given… no one else could say anything. She would support him against all. And history is a testament to the one rule… that if your woman supports you… no one can do shit to you.

"I see then… Now if you're here… you should know that I do it all for good. And after years of effort, we should finally accept that good doesn't always have a legal way to it. So if you can… then don't come in the way… think like a nationalist… and help if you can. If you have heard a word of our conversation, then you would know that these two need help. Okay then. Kudos. See y'all," Kunwar said as he left.

"Okay you brothers from another motherfuckers… time for me to leave as well. And you too Lady Shalini," Aryaman said and then kissed Shalini's hand and went away.

"So…" Oday said. The three turned around to see all the people standing in front of their cubicles waiting for further command.

"What next then?" Shalini asked.

"I don't have anything… the last report we submitted… I have just that," Arjun said.

"We have all the info regarding that sir. We just await further instructions. Kunwar had told us to take orders just from you," said one of the Compilers.

"From me?" Arjun asked excitedly.

"No… him," the man said pointing at Oday.

"Huh… So… Mr. Commander… What next?" Arjun whimsically questioned Oday.

"Well… I just have that mining thing," Oday said.

"Sir but the Kunwar said it wouldn't suffice."

"The Kunwar isn't your boss man anymore is he? He himself made us… no, Oday right here your boss… so you would do as he says?" Arjun said.

"Yes… you will do as I say… or what I ask Arjun here to say to you… Okay?" Oday followed.

Arjun immediately conjectured that Oday was asking for his help. Oday had never been the commander types as such. So Arjun took the job.

"Okay… But people… we need a full insight of all IDU hidden networks and servers. Keywords "Mining", "Mine",

"Cave", "Mine-workers", "Mine-Accident". If some code, Binary, Decimal or any kind of code… which relates the word 'Mine' then push for more information. Get to work. Search and Haunt. Meanwhile, the hacking team, all of you collectively will search for and break-through all private and suspicious party and related servers. You have one hour to give me your first reports. Collaborate with each other to find loopholes. Get working then," Arjun said. He turned around and wondered why Shalini was gazing at her nails in such an emergent hour.

"They need a pedicure… So I am going to get busy as well. Bye then. See you boys," Shalini said and left.

"People… be sure to look around in all the southern states. Look for mails from IDU workers to privatized organizations and engineers," Arjun said.

"On to it Sir," Said one of the programmers.

"Sir we have a suspicious activity in Chennai," one of the programmers said.

"Already? What is it?" Arjun said as the two went close up to the woman's system.

"It is a heist Sir. There was an informal visitation to the Chief Minister's residence in Chennai. And we have a black server having a combinational lock in the form of hexadecimal coding of musical octaves," the woman said.

"How do you know it was informal? By the way, what's your name again?" Arjun asked.

"Sir I ran through the records and that day the residence did not host any meetings. I even ran the confidential records through the RAW's server. No leads there. And the CM was not there. And my name is Ananya."

"Okay… so now what?" Oday asked.

"The octaves… here… Yes… locked on… 6163636964656e74… that is Accident. The incoming text on the mobile phone connected to this private server. It says "Make Up for the Accident." Searching for more," said a geeky man sitting beside Ananya.

"Amit… Uplink to the CCTV access through the CM residence Chennai… 1500-1600 hours around day before yesterday. Get clear statics and run them through the record. Also get me the street cams around the residence," Ananya said.

"On to it…. Ammmm…. Yes…. Found them… Uplinking. Running through the records. It is some Sriram Vijay and Harish… People… Look through the telephonic conversations of the phones connected for first person keywords "Sriram" and "Harish" and assign accordingly. Update the records," Amit said.

"Updating Emails,"; "Updating Phone IDs"; "Updating Credit Card Info and transactions"; "Updating Bank Info," Came different voices from different cubicles. A resonance of keyboard strokes for about a minute and then they all shouted in co-ordination "Done. On the big screen now." The big LED started displaying.

"Sriram Vijay… a worker for the IDU since 1982. Has been a stringent employee as well as employer. Not much is on record for this guy. He has been running the dirty work for the IDU in the shadows. His recent bank transactions show a large amount of credit from a source, which mediates between him and our other guy Harish. Harish is a freelancer who has been to prison several times on the issue of human trafficking. Getting workers in mass from villages on heavy contracts of low-wage servitude is his new way of getting his work done… after the media-revolution in the country. They had a meeting in one of the rear halls of the CM residence… the issue is apparently the very mining accident. The car that Sriram came in belongs to this guy (showed another picture). Zamaanat Khan. He was an engineer onboard the board of engineers in the mining project. He is the primarily proclaimed culprit for the negligence causing the accident. Also, the labourers working in the mines are reportedly unprofessional and were hired in masses from some distant tribe. I suspect Harish has something to do with their illegitimate documentation. So these two have definitely something more to do with the accident. We can get much more if we push," Ananya said.

"Okay…. That… I apologize for asking…" Oday said.

"That is… Awesome…" Arjun's amazement surfaced.

"We can push for more… but we need a groundsman," Ananya said.

"How can we help you? We'd do anything," Arjun said.

"Not you sir… No offence but Mr. Verma has more professional experience," Amit said.

"Verma… oh wait… CCTV…" Arjun said.

"Yes Sir."

"Okay then… I'd get in touch with him… You people carry on the good work. And you can have a round of applause for yourself. Come on," Arjun said as everybody clapped.

"Also one more thing Sir… the tribe is reported to have about three hundred and fifty number of people being provided employment. About hundred have no record what so ever. The local media-report regarding the mass recruitment shows about two hundred and twenty-nine men and a hundred and seventeen women being recruited. Whilst those recovered from the mine… they are reported to be just two hundred and twenty-one men and twenty-nine women. Eight men and Eighty-eight women are missing. Nobody knows of this," Ananya said.

Arjun looked at Oday "Would you come with me for a minute?" dragged him to a silent corner and then whispered to him "You saved the women too right?"

"Yes … I did… what about it?" Oday replied with a counter-question.

"And all of them were old?" Arjun asked.

"Strangely… Yes… but how do you know of this?" Oday asked.

"Shit… Guys…" Arjun turned and screamed, "I need you to search again… search for suspicious exports… containers large enough to hold eighty-eight women. Also, search high-value suspicious money transfers. I believe we have some sexual slavery issue," Arjun said turning all the employees pale yellow.

"Is it sir? We are on to it…" Amit said.

"What about the eight missing men?" Oday said. Arjun zoned-out in deep thought and wonder.

"Also… Haunt through southern hospital servers for illicit organ trading activity. Look for anything… this is critical issue at hand…" Arjun said.

"Found something Sir… There is an unofficial docking and loading of a trading ship around Kochi. The Ship's satellite server shows a conversation between the Captain and the dockyard official regarding the pass. Although we checked through the Permits and no such off-route pass-by was approved or even proposed," Ananya said.

"Where is the ship heading for?" Arjun asked.

"For Abu Dhabi Sir," Ananya said.

"When is the pass-by?" Arjun asked.

"Ammmm…. Today Sir…. In 2 hours," Amit said.

"In 2 hours….in Kochi," Arjun said looking at Oday and then continued to the workers "And do you have any leads on the organ thing? Look for kidney trades. Around eight-sixteen. Make a radius from Chennai to Kochi and circle the area up... swipe it for kidney transplants... and bring it down to just the suspicious ones. And also check unidentified morgue entries," Arjun said.

"On to it sir..." Ananya said.

"Oday... would you go beep Shalini? I would not call her. She gets angry if she has to pick a call during pedicure," Arjun said.

"Okay I would," Oday said as he left.

"Sir... we have a lead... Five hospitals along Bangalore and Mysore have eleven suspicious organ transplants. Nine Kidneys, one heart, and one bone marrow. From fake sources," Ananya said.

"What about the morgues?" Arjun asked.

"Sir... about 3000+ unclaimed unidentified male bodies in the radius," Amit said.

"Of course... unreported deaths are not enough... Keep looking for it. I have some errands to run. Would be back in three-four hours. I would be meeting CCTV along the way. Okay?" Arjun said.

"Yes sir... We are on to work. Just one more thing sir. Now that we know of this possible human trafficking... what now? We can't do anything about it right?" Ananya said.

"We unfortunately can't... do what, take a break all of you... don't get overworked... See you all then... Appreciate the effort," Arjun said leaving the basement.

14

A lonely dockyard in Kochi. A ship slowly and silently floated along to anchor near the loading terminus. The engines had been shut down. The top deck of the ship showed no crew. The dark of the night probably hid them well. A mechanically controlled ramp motored down to hinge at the dockyard pavement. A black SUV... with black-filmed windows slid down the ramp to the dockyard and stopped near a blue shipping container. Three doors opened slightly and similarly-well-suited men, in black suits and shirts and red ties, came out. At the same time, Oday and Arjun teleported behind the dockyard building. They were oblivious to the presence of the other people. Oday had switched back to normal, just to save his superhuman quota. Arjun peeped to see four men standing at the four corners of the container, presumably securing it. Suddenly, giant tongs came down a crane and clutched the container. The people were somewhat trying to make the least possible noise, seemingly avoiding unneeded attention. Arjun started devising his plan of action and dictated it to Oday. The container, meanwhile, was lifted up in the air. After about a minute of Arjun's narration, Oday got up, and with sparkling eyes, he disappeared. In just a span of about 3 seconds, five unconscious men were bundled beside Arjun. Their face was covered in skin coloured masks, just revealing hair and eyes. Eyes were in turn covered with black glares. Before Arjun could wonder much about their idiosyncratic façade, Oday, who was playing Quicksilver$_{49}$, reappeared with lifted collars. He somewhat stared down Arjun expecting a 'Good Job'.

Arjun asked, "What about the black car?"

"Oh Yes… I somewhat forgot," Oday said, "Let me take it down wait."

"Do it fast idiot. And I'm checking up these guys meanwhile," Arjun said.

"Yes boss," Oday said.

"Wait a sec… Are you sure they have passed out?" Arjun said in a trembling voice.

"Yeah Yeah… I knocked them out for sure," Oday reaffirmed confidently.

"When did you do that? I didn't hear even a hair moving," Arjun ambiguously questioned.

"Well I took them like two miles up the town and knocked 'em out and brought 'em back," Oday said.

"Whoa… Improvisation Buddy. Almost a good job," Arjun said.

"'Almost'??? I fucking nailed it," Oday said.

"Oday… The car," Arjun reminded him.

"Oh Yes," Oday said as he disappeared and reappeared near the car. The car had all its doors closed. Oday opened the front door and there was nobody inside. He turned to look around and the car beeped and burst up into flames. Arjun fell out of shock and Oday reappeared in front of him "Just by a millisecond man…"

"The fuck man… this was not part of the plan… Definitely not a part of the plan," Arjun recollected himself.

"Did you check them up?" Oday asked.

"They got nothing man. Not a piece of paper or pen on these bastards. No script. I clicked their faces though. Three guys and two girls," Arjun said.

"No shit man. I might have accidently molested one of the girls... my Indian mind set didn't expect a girl to on the front, you know?" Oday said, as suddenly the crane started moving and stopped above the dockyard power station.

"I have got to finish this up," Oday said. But just as he was preparing to go super again, the crane loudspeaker spoke "I know you're there. I have been kind of following up to you. I know you are here to fuck with my work again. But before you try to do so, I have to warn you. That I have to just push one button to land this fucking container over the live current. I know you know what is inside that metal. And I am sure you fucking philanthropist do not want no shit inside being fried. Right? So... I would want you to come right in front of the fire. And reveal yourself. Tell me who you are. So I can name your grave."

"What the fuck are you going to do now?" Arjun asked Oday.

"Get me one of those white masks. Now," Oday said. He wore the mask and walked straight towards the crane, right by the fire.

Oday shouted, "You can't possibly see my face from there. But I would tell you who I am. I am... The Mangoman."

"The Who?" the man questioned.

"The fuck... what the hell is this sucker doing?" Arjun said to himself.

"Not the Who... The Who is although one of my favourite rock bands," Oday said.

"What the fuck. You are not fucking taking me seriously... I am going to count until ten.... ONE."

"What you haven't heard Behind Blue Eyes?" Oday said.

"TWO."

"THREE," the man said as speaker started fluctuating.

"Listen to it bro. This is awesome," Came Oday's voice through the speaker as the song started playing "No one Knows what it's like... To be the Bad Man."

"That's it. I'm done...," the man said inside the crane bunker as he pressed the button to drop the container. Instead of dropping, the crane vanished into the air. The man, expecting some light show, got up from his seat. Oday appeared in front of him.

"Hey... What was your Plan B?" Oday said.

"I'd kill you," The man said as he pointed a gun at Oday. He pulled the trigger multiple times but the barrel was empty.

"Okay... believe it or not... all your six bullets are in a safe place. Two thousand kilometres away. And yes, you have a bad sense of time man. You should of have said TEN like five seconds ago. Never mind. Because your time is up," Oday held the man's hand and disappeared near Arjun.

"Where is the container idiot?" Arjun asked.

"Man... a good combination of Iron Man... Superman and Goku. And yes... It is safely away from here. I'm going to neutralize the ship now ok?" Oday said.

He turned towards the ship to make his move and as he did, he heard a gun being loaded. His ignorance, this time, had beaten him. And before he could turn, the shot was fired at him from his blind spot. Oday was pushed away from the line of fire. Arjun had fallen down to the bullet.

"Pundit. No," Oday screamed in agony. He caught Arjun as he fell.

"You..." Oday walked up to the shooter. The man fired a bullet, which pierced through Oday's heart, later to come back out. The injury self-healed and Oday revealed his metal claws$_{50}$ and impaled the shooter immediately. The shooter fell down. A whole new pack of armed people had come down the ship trailing the blast noise. They were scanning for the attackers who had intervened their plan. Meanwhile, Oday was thinking of means to fix the issue at hand… that is Arjun Dying.

"What should I do Pundit? Tell me?" Oday asked restlessly.

"Ahhh (moaned)… you need to disinfect and cauterize," Arjun said faintly moaning and struggling to keep his eyes open.

"English Pundit… please," Oday said as he hurriedly tried to plug the bleeding.

"Okay… become magneto$_{51}$… now. And pull the bullet out," Arjun mumbled as he fiddled in pain.

Oday waved his hand over Arjun's abdomen and the bullet floated out of there.

"Now what?" Oday asked.

"Now. Pick up a metal object. Heat it up and iron the skin into the wound…" Arjun said.

"That's too much work… Ahhh… I know what to do…" Oday said as he waved his hand over Arjun's abdomen again. And this time within seconds, Arjun's injury had healed completely.

"What was that?" Arjun asked as he regained complete consciousness.

"Dende$_{52}$… DBZ$_{53}$… come on man you no true Otaku$_{54}$," Oday said.

"Heal our buddy over here as well. Cannot kill anybody. And quick. Before those guys come here," Arjun said.

Oday started healing the unconscious guy but before he could completely do it… the man woke up and groaned in excruciating pain. The other fellows heard it and started approaching the building's rear in formation. Oday knocked the man down midway the healing and took Arjun near the power station.

"What now?" Arjun asked.

"Man. I am starting to feel all that mind of yours is being slowly transported to mine. Just step back and look."

Oday went to the power hub, held the live wire, and seemingly absorbed a bit of the power.

"Have you ever wondered that the word electrocute has the words Electro$_{55}$ and Cute? Well. For now, I'm both," Oday said as he raised his hand to release lightning streaks, which knocked everybody in the dockyard down except for Arjun and Oday. "You killed them?" Arjun asked.

"No no... I just acted as a human Taser Gun," Oday said.

"There must be some others on the ship right?" Arjun said turning to Oday who had his middle and forefingers fixed to his forehead.

"I sense a few.... So now for the final part."

Oday widened his eyes as a wave erupted from him rendering everybody on the ship unconscious. Even Arjun fell down.

"Oh shit... I forgot about you completely. Arghhhh... My bad... But Conqueror's Haki$_{56}$ is badass man. Sad that you are not conscious to see the after-effects," Oday said and then carried Arjun over his shoulders.

Oday indulged in a session of soliloquy "Let's get the container back... I should inform the police... What else would Pundit do? Ammmm... He would also inform the media... yes... Let's see what they have to say about it."

* * *

"India wants to know… Arlub wants to know. Why didn't the police or the leaders have a hint about this huge trafficking racquet? And if they did… why didn't they act? Were they bribed? Were they forcefully silenced? Or are they working for the ISIS? Watch in the NewsHourAndAHalf Tonight… "India drifting towards an ISIS territory"" Shalini switched the television off.

"Hey Darling I'm back… CCTV had a little too much to give. Have to give that guy much credit… He is fat… normal middle-class looking person. He is like the perfect undercover guy. I guess Oday and I can take a lot of time off… owing to him. He has called us both again to hand over the data he collected. For now, we just know that his mission was successful. Let's hope he found the culprit," Arjun said.

"Don't bloody take Oday's name in front of me," Shalini said.

"Oh forgive him already. He has apologized so many a time," Arjun said.

"He can apologize as much as he wants. I am not forgiving him. For god's sake… I twisted open my lipstick and there was a bullet… instead of a lipstick… and in all of them… Have you ever experienced that? No right? Then you wouldn't know…" Shalini said as Arjun controlled his giggle.

"Oh babe… Come On… (Held her through her waist). Forget about it already… He is just a kid… and you got like two dozen more from Guerlain right? Forgive him… he saved my life…" Arjun said.

"Okay… but for the last time… he can't act funny anymore… because you know what? He isn't," Shalini said.

"Yes he won't. Nothing that hurts my babe," Arjun said as he came close to her.

"Promise?" Shalini asked.

"Yes... Promise," Arjun said holding her cheeks to kiss her.

*   *   *

"Yes I'm almost there. Yeah sorry to keep you waiting... I know Kunwar never... I am not the Kunwar... What do you mean I cannot ever be? No, Fuck You.... Yeah... Hellooo?" Arjun said loudly keeping his phone down.

"Sir... to the Indranagar restaurant then?" The Butler asked from the driver's seat.

"Yes... Or wait... Let's pick up Oday first from the CM Mansion... turn around then," Arjun said.

He picked up his phone again and called Oday "Yes... Sucker... Come down. We are to go... yes... NOW."

*   *   *

Oday and Arjun walked inside the restaurant to find it filled with young couples. But CCTV was nowhere to be seen. Arjun got a call on his phone.

"Yes... what inside... wait you mean inside the kitchen? The Fuck you doing there? Okay we are coming in..." Arjun said and then led Oday inside the kitchen.

There he glanced his eyes across the room to see just the uniformed staff. Suddenly one of the chefs turned behind and said "Hello Sirs... Your data is in this pen drive (handed the pen drive)."

"How'd you get it though?" Arjun asked.

"That Sir is there in the drive itself..." CCTV said.

"Tell me something At least. Did you find the man at the centre… or At least some group to look from?" Arjun asked.

CCTV came close to the two and whispered: "That is an information for some other place."

"Okay then… Thank you, I guess. We shall take your leave then bro," Arjun said and went and grabbed the doorknob.

"Yeah Yeah fuck off now the two of you. And come again if you need some help," CCTV said with a sudden dominant persona.

* * *

Arjun and Oday entered the Northern Export House and met Amit and the rest of the team. Arjun passed over the pen drive for further analysis. Ananya took and plugged the drive into the main system. The screen by default opened a video-

"Hello… I am Chatur Champakdas Tilakchand Verma and the following contents are to be only seen and analysed by Oday Luhar and Arjun Trivedi and their most trustworthy aides. So if either of you two can come up to the microphone and say "YES", then I'd move up to the contents. If it does not happen in the next 30 seconds, then this drive would self-destruct."

"All of you… move out then… fast… All of you all…" Arjun said.

Everybody lined up to move outside the basement.

"Hey… Amit and Ananya… stay with us here. We need some technical help as such," Oday said.

"Okay," Amit and Ananya said.

"YES," Oday said as soon as everybody had left.

"Okay. Times up… Kaboooommm… Ahahahaha. Just Kidding. Got Ya. I am not James Bond you know. And as such how much can you program a 4 Gigabyte pen drive to do," CCTV spoke in the screen.

"This jerk," Amit said. "He never changes," Ananya said.

"I know you must be thinking this jerk never changes. But ignoring compliments… moving on… so yes. I streamlined all the organ-trade thingies, all the trafficking thingies, and all the people you gave me. Sriram Vijay … Harish… and Zamaanat Khan… they form a vicious triangle… and not since today… since past 6 years. I could gather all the data on these people and I am transmitting it to you guys for the hacking and everything. It is not easy to bring these people down. Because there is somebody at the centroid of this vicious triangle. And this somebody is like a shadow. He orchestrates the whole business and I believe he is bigger than what we imagine. It is not just this business but he runs about almost all of the drug trade that Sriram handles as well. He sets up the plan. The roots. These idiots are just the branches. The sleeper-cells. My guy followed Zamaanat up to a mansion… after his police statement that is. He said that there was some meeting with some politicians there. I figured he was planning his clean slate. He clicked all the pictures and everything. I had everything on Sriram and Harish already. But this guy Zamaanat seemed too deep an ocean. The mansion had too much security to get bugged. So I asked my guy for the residential address. Maybe I could have forwarded it to you guys and you could have done something about it. Get it cracked or something. But that was the biggest shock ever. I ran the address through record… just for some time-pass and look, what I found. The house is in the name of Arjun Trivedi's girlfriend.

Shalini Teja Singh. I was all confounded and full of shit. So I bugged Shalini Madam's room. And what I heard was most shocking ever. What the context suggested was quite astonishing. I would just like to say congratulations Oday Luhar on having those powers. I hope you use them well. Well going around the world and playing a superhero isn't as easy as it sounds (everybody stared suspiciously at Oday). And the philanthropy and compulsory secretiveness required me to keep silent about it. Kunwar Madhao is though pro Philanthropy… but yes, I respect secrecy. I hope I have not said it in front of people whom I'm not supposed to say it in front of. Okay then moving ahead of my inarticulation and finally regaining a sense of responsibility, I searched for more and found that the mansion, for now, has been given to government lease. It is a kind of VVIP rest house. The pictures, I am giving to you. Rest is on you superheroes and your superhackers to handle. Kudos… CCTV checks out. Over and Out."

"That Fucking Bastard…" Arjun said.

"So it is you…" Amit said nervously.

"Ahhhhhh" Oday speechlessly stood as Ananya was gazing at him.

"Yes… Okay… I'd tell you the whole thing if you just analyse the pictures first… and compile the data," Arjun said like a true Pundit Diplomat.

"Yes… but… he has superpowers… Okay Okay… we are on to it… Ananya get to the system. Do as I say," Amit said excitedly.

"Okay," Ananya said in a low-pitched shivering voice. She sat on the system as Amit guided her.

"These are all marked… see the unmarked… the usual CCTV way… yes here… This one… Ummm… No… next… next… this one is irrecoverable as well… Next…

yes… zoom in… do the magic… yes I see Zamaanat Khan and two others. This guy whose side face is covered with hands. Clear him up and get an analysis."

"Okay ten mins. I got to pee. Just a minute," Ananya said.

"I got to pee as well… I'm nervous with all the attention," Oday said.

Ananya and Oday walked down the corridor to the male-female washroom division. When Ananya came out, she saw that Oday was waiting for her.

"Why are you still here sir?" Ananya asked.

"Well I walked you down here… it won't be good if I don't walk you back right? What you call it… Chivalry, yeah… Arjun has been like shouting it down my ears since before I was born. Always wants ME to be the do-gooder. Mate… what were you made for then," Oday said innocently.

"Hahahahahaha…" Ananya laughed.

"I know, right?" Oday remarked.

"No, I laughed Sir… because you don't know you are…" Ananya said.

"I am what?" Oday asked.

"A good guy…" Ananya said with a dramatic silence to follow. The both started down each other's eyes. Then suddenly Ananya leaped across the corridor to kiss Oday.

"What was that for?" Oday asked.

"Oh… I'm sorry sir…" Ananya felt guilty for a second.

"No I meant why'd you stop," Oday said making Ananya blush. They both started kissing intensely and Oday paused for a second "And stop with that 'Sir' nonsense already. No queen put a sword to my shoulder," Oday said as they continued.

"The two of you… come here fast…" came Arjun's voice from inside the chamber. The two took five seconds to stop and then creased and tucked their clothes properly to go out.

"Yeah… We were just you know…" Oday began trying to give an explanation.

"Fucking Shut up and come and see this the two of you," Arjun said in a recessive and scared tone.

Oday and Ananya walked in front of the screen as Oday read out "Match Confirmed. Subject. Kunwar Madhao Singh…"

Oday turned to Arjun and asked, "What the fuck does this mean?"

"Whatever it is… we're in deep shit now," Arjun said.

Right across the warehouse, Mritunjay floated over a vast and deserted land, in a black suit, black shirt and black tie and black glares. He, through his telescopic X-RAY vision and long-range ear-receptors, had seen and heard everything going on in the basement.

"I see… this brat escaped the clasps of death twice. Death himself shall assure there is no third time. Your true worth shall be your only weapon Oday Singh Luhar. God won't help you in this game of mine," Mritunjay said as he jumped on the ground with intense velocity thereby cracking it. His wings then retracted back to his back. His suit strangely showed no holes.

"Behold… For I enter the arena," He said and his clothes transformed into a clerical attire. He held a briefcase in his hand.

He walked up to the main gate. Everybody was rushing to it to see the cause for the huge crater. They walked past him as he greeted them and saw nothing inside the big crack. They turned behind to ask, "Who are you?"

"My name is Jai. Jai M. Nirmal. I was sent by Kunwar to serve here," Mritunjay said.

"What are you to do?" Oday asked apprehensively.

"I mean literally serve. I will serve the coffee, tea and other food and all. Well the Kunwar figured the population of this place is increasing so he took me out of another outpost and brought me here. I know everything that goes on here so you needn't worry," Mritunjay said.

"Yes… We need… not…" Arjun said as he sceptically eyed Oday.

15

To find faith, in oneself or the other, is finding a pillar to rest on when the going goes bad. However, man seemed to have a hard time finding faith in himself or others. Hence, God sent his prophets, to be discreet yet conspicuous, human yet divine, incisive yet verbose. These people taught the world of the presence of an entity, which provides the penultimate, perpetual and eternal faith to all. He is indeed the creator and is always looking forward to providing guidance to the needy whence the need be. So those who found no faith elsewhere succumbed to the faith of this entity called God. Different sections of the world, at particular timelines, were embellished by many such faiths propagated by many a chosen prophet.

Those who were confident in their other faiths formed the cults of the atheists and the agnostics. Not that God abhorred them. God only abhorred the inhumane, and that too because he was not happy about the indirect creation of one such being. A Philanthropic Atheist is closer to God than a Misanthropic Theist. Yet the egoism of the acute mindedness of either side created a cold war between the two sects. Overall… God always showed the righteous path to all… it was for them to see and realize it… and most importantly… walk on it.

That is all about faith in God. Faith in humankind is equally important. A faith reciprocated can create history… can win wars, can change the course of mankind. Don't worry… faith not reciprocated will also do those things…. Just not in your favour. The latter forms the more noticeable of the two. See the history… From the Biblical Judas' Kiss, to the infamous 'Etto, Brute', from Ephialtes leading Xerxes behind Leonidas, to the infamous treachery of Jai Chand against the Legendary Prithviraj Chauhan (although Jai Chand was, in turn, himself betrayed by his ally Mohammad Ghori. Ha! Karma had that dog.), Etcetera. There were a plethora of betrayals during the British Raj of India itself. What if none of them had happened… that is what if the faith of the defeated/deceased was rightly placed? What if Jesus had lived? Would he have shown greater wonders? Would the Bible be longer? Or would we have lost the chance to see him rise from death? Can't say. Surely, it would have changed history. What if the Great Caesar hadn't been assassinated? The history of the Roman conquest would have changed completely leading to more or lesser number of deaths… depending on whether the conspirators were right about their presumptions of Caesar being a tyrant, or him being the just ruler he proclaimed to be. What if Jai Chand hadn't betrayed his fellow ruler and son-in-law, The Unparalleled warrior Prithviraj Chauhan? Perhaps the Islamic faith would've taken a little longer to reach India… the huge line-up of Sultans would've been a much larger number of smaller Hindu Kingdoms. For the better or worse, we do not know. Because the Islamic dynasties reunited the age-old Empire of India into one, rather than several small arrogant selfish kingdoms. What if the superhuman, known as Maharana Pratap Singh, hadn't been betrayed by his allies and brothers? What if all the Rajputs had rather allied with him? Would it have meant the historical defeat of the all-powerful Akbar the Great? Would it have re-established Rajput dynasties? The course of the world would have been majorly different. The smallest of ill-placed faiths caused the largest of ruckus in the history. Thus faith needs to be placed rightly... after the most meticulous introspections.

Now let us see the perception of the betrayal. Generally, the one victorious is protagonised above all. There are exceptions. But this has mostly been the way of man. Being the protagonist of history makes the difference for you... forever. If you were betrayed... then you gain sympathy and become a martyr. If you were party to a betrayal, then you become a hero... one who went out of his way to win for his people. For everything is fair in love and War... just for the protagonist. This has been the way it is done. Here's an example... let's talk about a war between India and Pakistan... for us, whatever we do to win is justified... even if it is using a chain of spies and double-agents. Similar is the case for them. Although it is impossible for us to realize each other's cases... well, this has been the major reason for wars after war. Here is another example... This time love... While watching love stories you always see the point of view of the protagonist. Like, let us talk about the movie 'Dhadkan'. You support Sunil Shetty as long as he is reflected as the hero... but later on, when you become sympathetic towards Akshay Kumar... you antagonize Sunil and all his efforts to win Shilpa. And in the end, you are happy to see Akshay win Shilpa. That was the director's trick to fool you into forgetting Sunil... so that you hang on to the rest of the movie. If you had rather remembered Sunil and his goodwill, then you might have seen Akshay as the bad guy. So you get the point, right?

Hence, the strongest of heroes fall to backstabbing… the largest of empires end, reason to the smallest of moles in their system. So keep friends close… enemies closer… and the loyal the closest. For to break trust one first needs to be trusted.

*   *   *

"Hey Arjun… you trust me right?" Oday said to Arjun sitting beside him in a skydiving jet.

"Hell Fucking No…" Arjun shouted, trying to be audible in the high decibel jet sound.

"Then you are the first to say hell fucking no to this parachute," Oday said.

"You guys are Crazy," Shalini said as she got up to sit beside Arjun to give him a kiss on his right cheek.

"Yes we are," Oday said transforming into the Green Lantern[57] and then held Arjun in his ring's green aura.

"You Sure about this?" Arjun asked timidly.

"HELL FUCKING NO," Oday said. He flew out of the Jet door with Arjun and then threw him upwards. Arjun traversed upwards a few hundred meters and then started accelerating down. Oday flew closely behind monitoring Arjun's fall.

"Wuhooooo…. This is nice… We are flying…" Oday said.

"We are fucking falling Moron…" Arjun said nearing the ocean surface.

"Technically… you are falling… I… AM FLYING," Oday said.

"Now that is a morale booster… Fucking catch me… (Turned around to see the huge waves closing in) … CATCH ME SUCKER" Arjun said.

Oday caught Arjun with his ring and flew by touching and cutting the water surface. He then made a green air catapult and threw himself and Arjun towards a distant, faintly visible bank. Nearing the land, the finger-ring disappeared from Oday's hand.

"We won't make it," Arjun said fearing an early fall into the waterbody.

"Hold tight for some aggressive landing," said Oday intriguing Arjun to close his eyes and clench his teeth. Arjun opened his right eye after a few seconds... quenching his curiosity. He saw that he was safely hanging by a spider-string from a large tree on a beach. He wondered how he got there... then appeared Oday who cut down the string to let Arjun fall from that short height to the sand. Oday held three swords$_{58}$... two in hands and one in the mouth.

"Three words... Goku-Spiderman$_{59}$-Zoro" Oday said.

"I guessed it... someday I will submit to my inner urges and finally kill you, you know?" Arjun uttered angrily.

"I love you too bro," Oday said sarcastically.

"So we are at (Looked at his GPS device) Mogadishu... nice one mate... got the destination right, tell you that," Arjun said.

"You don't say.... But why is this place abandoned? I heard it was quite the tourist spot..." Oday said.

"I was wondering the same thing," Arjun said clearing his trousers of the dirt and sand.

"Let me get some tech support..." Arjun dialled through his smartphone.

"Hello... Yes, babe... yes..." Arjun said.

"Shalini... Shalini is your tech support..." Oday said.

"Keep it down bro... if she hears it we are done with... (Got back on the phone) Yes, babe put him through... Yes, hello... How're you doing mate?" Arjun said.

"Cut the small talk… the clock goes tick tock…" Oday said.

"He's checking on clearance to just Ananya and Amit… wait a tick…" Arjun said.

"Okay…" Oday said. They were both suddenly alarmed by the sound of a distant gunshot. They sat down behind a small rock to glance covertly.

"Can't see shit… Let's get closer," Arjun said.

"Wait a sec… (Oday's eyes became pale white… widening beyond ordinary, hence revealing veins running beside them… all contracted hard) Byakugan$_{60}$," Oday said as he meticulously scanned the area.

"Okay… you do the good work buddy… I think I am through… (Got back on the phone) Yes… Ananya… Okay… we need your and Amit's help… This is the first time we are doing this spy with high-tech in-ear support shit… but it feels awesome. What do you mean Amit isn't there? Have you tried to reach him? Okay… that is strange. Maybe he isn't well. So getting to the point… we are finally here… and it is an empty area. I do not see any ships nearby. Nope… And there is some armed stronghold nearby… Oday is up to scanning it… Yes… Okay… so that's where he is held captive isn't he. So can you get the inner info? Yes, he is on to a field scan… to him? Okay… (Turned to Oday who was still scanning the base) I am attaching this phone to your belt buckle… do not drop it… so here is the earpiece… I am waiting back here with my phone… Go brother. Do not forget your mask. And be careful…" Arjun said.

Oday attached the earpiece, wore the mask, and then burrowed underground using powers of diglet$_{61}$.

"So everybody can hear me?" Oday asked.

"Yes," Arjun, Shalini's Butler and Ananya simultaneously corroborated.

"So Ananya… guide me inside where the ambassador is being held. I'd make it quick. I'll save time to scout for those three ships," Ananya guided Oday straight under the base. Oday emerged outside and found himself in a dark hallway. A wand$_{62}$ appeared in his arm as he uttered "Lumos Maxima$_{63}$".

There were puddles of blood all around in the room. Oday carefully dodged them whispering "Mr. Williams…. Hellooo".

Oday encountered a tied up old man with duct tape across his face. He released him from the ropes. He was the British Ambassador to India… the same one who had been held hostage by a badge of Somalian warlords who were working in coordination with some pirates. The pirates had also taken in three cargo ships, one of which was delivering oil to India. Oday recognized him and prepared for their escape. The lights in the room switched on… making it pinching bright. Oday was deemed blind for a few seconds. His vision recovered and he saw a few bunch of people standing with guns aiming at him and the Ambassador.

"We were expecting you," said the apparent leader in a Somalian accent.

"Who is that…? Oday?" Arjun asked.

"Sir?" Ananya asked.

"Me… expecting me?" Oday inquired ambiguously.

"Yes… we were informed by our Indian support of your existence. And that you might intervene our little extortion here. You see… I don't like any interruptions in our business," The man said.

"See… even you know nobody is giving you ten billion dollars…" Oday said.

"We would see about that," the man said.

"You are not making good friends you know… One Australian-American Trade ship… one American-Arabian and one Indo-Arabian… and then the British Ambassador to India… you are pissing off so many countries at once… I see you're not that smart," Oday said.

"Stop talking will you…" Arjun said.

"That's the plan… I believe collectively they can all donate ten billion dollars to our cause can't they. Tie them both up," The man said.

"So I am your hostage as well now? Think that might increase your probability of success do you?" Oday said.

"Oh No No… I have been specifically given instructions as well as a contract of one billion dollars if I kill you both…" the man said.

"Both… What do you mean by both?" Oday asked. Suddenly his earpiece started giving static disturbance and after a few seconds, his call had cut off.

"You exactly know what I mean… By this time your friend on the beach is probably dead… we cleared it off specifically for this," The man said.

"What…" the enraged Oday shouted.

Several men shot dozens of injection darts from behind him, all along his spine and brain.

"Dormicum… I made preparations you know…" the man said.

Oday fell down. The man walked up to him, held him up, and got him seated.

"Actually… I am taking too much credit… the preparations were made elsewhere because of your recent stunts. I was just handed over the plan. See Mr… What is your name…? Whatever it is… you are going to be unrecorded history soon as such… so yes where was I… I was saying that you… Sir… should really check into whom all you trust. Not that it would change anything now, you will not get any more chances. Reminds me, I have to send before and after pictures (clicked a picture of Oday). So let's see who lies behind that face," the man said moving his hand to grab Oday's mask.

Oday held his hand in between "My Name is... The Mangoman."

"The what?" the man asked.

"When Neo_{64} said that to $Smith_{65}$, it sounded way more dramatic and like powerful... Nevertheless, I am sure... you aren't ever going to be prepared for me," Oday said.

"You are full of yourself," The man said.

"You think sedative would work on a man who is made of poison?" Oday said as violet fluid appeared around his body somewhat similar to $Magellan_{66}$ from One Piece.

"What the fuck!" the man shouted as everybody fired at Oday. The poison ingested all the room's furniture along with their bullets. Oday released a poison cyclone inside that room, ensuring that none of it touched the ambassador. Then he grabbed the ambassador and teleported back to the beach where Arjun was supposed to be.

"Pundit... Where is he?" Oday walked along the rock to step on Arjun's phone.

Oday dialled Shalini's number on his phone and got himself through to Ananya. Ananya gained access to satellite-scanning and started hounding the zone for signs of Arjun.

"I found him... He is in the water... two miles out in the north," Ananya said to Oday.

"In the water? Like the sea?" Oday asked.

"Yes..." Ananya said.

"Get Him Oday... Please," Shalini requested.

"Yes... I will. You wait here sir, I would be back. Okay Ananya guide me," Oday said.

"He has been now moved to the land… or wait. Below the land surface. I get it. There must be an underwater-aerated cave. You need to dive in," Ananya said.

"I have a better plan," Oday said as he walked up to the shore and raised his hands in the direction of the water.

"By the power of Poseidon[67]…. I raise the waters of the realm of earth," Oday said as the water rose in an upwards stream all to the clouds. The seabed showed, revealing three ships closely docked. Apparently, they were intentionally sunk upright.

"The ships showed up sir… I guess they were drowned to not give away the location. I guess one of them was used to escort the ambassador from the chopper crash site to the country," Ananya said.

A golden trident[68] appeared in Oday's hand. He floated on the air moisture and came down to the cave to see that four people in diving suits were escorting Arjun, who in turn was also in a suit, to some inner captivation at gunpoint.

"Pundit…" Oday shouted.

"What the fuck man… this is a huge mess you made here… the Arabian Sea… have some respect bro," Arjun said.

The other divers removed their masks to reveal that they were all women.

"A female squadron scares me the most," Arjun said.

"Shut Up… And you stay away or we would shoot," one of the women said.

"Okay," Oday said as he warped behind the women and knocked them out with his trident.

"Just a second Pundit," Oday said as he lifted the three ships with the help of water and guided them ashore. Then he held Arjun and flew to where the Ambassador was. Oday slowly guided the water down.

"Who is he?" Arjun asked.

"The Ambassador," Oday said.

"Oh… Our Dear Ambassador… Don't you think that I don't know," Arjun said to the Ambassador.

"What do you mean?" the Englishman said.

"Yes… What?" Oday followed.

"Ask him," Arjun said.

The ambassador drew a pistol from his jacket and pointed at Oday "I'd kill you both."

Arjun sneaked up and threw a stone to his head rendering him unconscious.

"What was all that about?" Oday asked.

"Oh, I'd tell you along the way. Those mermaids were discussing him being the mastermind or something. Let's go as long as you have your share of mojo," Arjun said.

"Okay… work done for the day," Oday said.

"Is that Ananya? Ask her to get the media acquainted with all this as soon as possible," Arjun said.

"Yes… and by the way that black dude was going on about a mole," Oday said.

"What mole?" Arjun asked.

"Mole… Mole… like traitor," Oday said.

"But only a select trustworthy few know about this," Arjun said.

"Yes… that's what's scary," Oday said.

"Okay… let's discuss that over a coffee. I am soaking. Let's go," Arjun said.

16

"No man... it can't be... it must be someone else... Like that Jai guy. He just comes off as a spy of Kunwar," Oday said.

"Hey... we are not yet sure about my brother's involvement in all of this," Shalini said.

"No... we're sure. Even you said your brother handles all assets in your name. And even if it is now a mixed-sector asset, the strings your father holds in the system, just with his name your brother can influence a lot of it," Arjun said.

"But human trafficking and piracy and extortion... they don't match up, you know. Again, let us talk about the problem at hand. Our man is missing here," Oday said.

"Our recently acquainted man who can earn bigger profits by selling us off to the Kunwar. And all those three things don't match up... but go hand in hand. I mean the Shalini enterprises has businesses all across the electronics to communication to apparels. It is just about exploring different departments man," Arjun said.

"See between Amit and Jai... I trust Amit more. He would definitely be back," Oday said.

Ananya came in "Sir. The Kunwar is coming for his weekly examination of our reports. What should we give him?"

"That drug investment thing you caught. Also exposing the illegal imports to the narcotics department," Oday said.

"But no matter what... don' let them know about the dockyard thing as well as the Somalian thing," Arjun said.

"Aye Aye Sir," Ananya said.

"Yes... listen to your Captain," Arjun said.

"Yes. (Turned to Oday) I always listen to him," Ananya said and left the room.

"Hey... What makes him the captain?" Arjun said.

"No Baby Don't worry (kissed Arjun). Okay I am off to my friend's baby shower. Cheerio," Shalini said and left.

"Okay some hell of a fucking shit is going on. Villains knowing about us... Our new friend disappearing... the probability of Kunwar knowing about us...the probability of Kunwar being one of those villains.... This new spy Jai.... And people calling you captain over me..." Arjun took a heavy sigh.

"I am not going to kiss you..." Oday mocked.

*   *   *

A white Bugatti stopped beside the main gate of the warehouse and the Kunwar jumped out of the convertible in his own weird style and buttoned up his white suit to walk in. Jai appeared right before him. Before the Kunwar could question him regarding his identity, Jai spoke up staring down Kunwar's eyes.

"I am one of your workers."

Kunwar confusingly gazed up and down Jai. Jai spoke again.

"Ain't I?"

A gush of wind flowed across the Kunwar's face out of nowhere. Kunwar immediately concurred, "Yes, you work for me."

"Come inside sir. We all look forward to your field assessment," Mritunjay said. He led the Kunwar inside to the basement where everybody nervously stood in the Kunwar's wait. They greeted him at his entrance.

Meanwhile, everybody had been collaborating a report of the week's work. Arjun had asked them to hide away the human trafficking report using the smart alibi of concealing failures from the Kunwar.

The Kunwar held the file and without even glancing at the index, straight-away congratulated Arjun and Oday for being diligent at their job, and went back to his car. Everybody followed behind closely.

"Sir. I wanted to enquire about Amit. Where is he?" Oday asked.

"He left. Will send a replacement soon. Bye then," he opened the door, sat in, and drove away.

"What was that about?" Oday asked Arjun as they both stood dumbfounded at the gate, wondering about that weird event.

"That was a first timer. Kunwar never left without a clear insight of the work here," said one of the guys standing behind the two.

"Strange things are happening nowadays aren't they? All about that then... let's get back to work then," Arjun said.

*   *   *

The clamouring keystrokes perturbed our heroes, who sat on separate stairwells eating through their nails for whatever was to come. They ordered regular servings of Espressos for Jai to bring to them, sometimes even forgetting that he might be a possible spy. The whole crew somewhat entrusted the job of their technical-to-comprehensible translator as well as a general spokesperson to Ananya, because they were well acquainted with her singular segregated meetings with the two. Hence, all the work was routed to her system, whereby she compiled it for presentation. The keystrokes slowly became lesser and lesser with the general "Done", "I'm Up", "Wuhooooo", Etcetera. The last to come to a halt was Ananya's system after which she spoke up to Oday.

"Sir… We are finished. But before we start you might want to know that we found that Rana Teja Singh is in Lucknow," Ananya said.

"Okay… (Looked at Arjun) Listen to it well brother. I won't know what to do with what info. (Looked at Ananya) Tell him everything," Oday said.

"You might want to hear too sir," Ananya said.

"I'm all ears as well. Go on then," Oday said.

"So… Look at the big screen (turned on the screen-projector, dimming the lights) you remember this guy (displayed a picture of Sriram Vijay), right? Well we told you we have everything on him. What we didn't tell you… was that we were wrong. But this has not much to do with him. Just his sister. (Displayed another picture) Padmini Misra… elder Sister of Sriram Vijay. We would come to her surname later. She has been a minister in the Tamil Nadu Assembly since like ever. She has hopped back and forth the agriculture and forest departments. First, a minister under the Nationalist Party… until it dissolved under the IDU. Since then a huge asset for the IDU. She literally administered many of the illegalities of her state as well as other states. She has been famous for her dealings with the infamous Veerappan. But that relationship did not last long since her ends were not being served well… with all the Sandalwood not hers to smuggle. She was one of the most benefited people from Operation Cucoon. Apparently, she was always fond of illegal forest trade… since with just the right sources, it is always easy to get away with. Well if you do it right that is. If you sell off unaccounted fodder to make money… it is okay. But if you issue money from the state to buy fodder… and you keep the money to yourself… that is… well too obvious… and not the right way. Anyway… Padmini got married to this guy after coming to IDU (displayed another picture) Eklavya Kumar Misra. He was the right-hand man of Shiva, the biggest indigenous drug mafia in the history of Uttar Pradesh… that too back when it was united. But ironical to his name, he came to the political front by getting Shiva arrested for his illegal Acacia trade. Shiva was an IPU man… the then recessive party. Eklavya had realized that political fame could be earned easily in the IDU… so he betrayed Shiva. And that helped in strengthening the IDU stronghold in the state… which later unfortunately broke down after the intra-state caste war. And after the advent of Oday Sir's father… Mr. Aditya Luhar… there is no possible existence of any other political power. Well that's the reason all in this state are rushing to him for sanctuary. But understanding the importance of Eklavya in the system, he was soon made party free. Eklavya was an important asset in the regulation of the legal trade as well for he had taken over Shiva's empire. He soon became party-free… although his inclination always lied towards the IDU. This might be hard to listen Sir Oday… Under your father… U.P. has been a primary centre for Acacia, Teak and Shisham smuggling. Although most of the hidden Cannabis farms are now in Uttarakhand… yet some of them still lie here in U.P... All of them run by Eklavya. Eklavya and Padmini form the deadliest forest-mafia couple in India. Now here is something catchy. Aditya learned the basics of politics under a man at the IDU... called Avaneesh Kumar Misra... who is the late father of Eklavya. Now as per official OR unofficial records Eklavya and Aditya have never met," Ananya said.

"Okay... where are you going with this?" Arjun said.

"This... is for Oday Sir. Today we have a secret meeting scheduled in about (saw her watch) one hour and forty minutes. The meeting is between three parties. And this... Sirs... shall sound strange... the three parties are... Oday Sir's Father Mr. Aditya Luhar... Rana Teja Singh and Eklavya Misra. And last but not the least... we scouted through the Misra family's recent transaction history... and Sir... some of it is being streamed to Shalini Enterprise Affiliates as well as Ityadi Party workers. This is something strange. Even Padmini Misra made recent donations to the U.P. land development firm... which although is headed by the IDU... but the money will go to the state treasury of course," Ananya said.

"Okay... THAT... is weird," Oday said.

"The meeting is in about an hour and a half right? Okay... Oday... we shall leave now... Your father also might appreciate our involvement. Let us go then," Arjun said.

"But what about the black money and other assets?" Ananya asked.

"What do you usually do with them?" Arjun asked.

"We disperse the money to different clean-chit NGOs. And the assets... we just open them up for sale online," Ananya said.

"Then do that. We may take your leave. Bye then," Arjun said.

"Bye Sir... (Gave a weird smile to Oday) Bye Sir. Have a nice day and meeting," Ananya said.

*   *   *

"What do you mean we can't enter?" came Oday's furious growl as the two stood outside a farmhouse of the Luhars. They were five minutes late. The gatekeeper, who was wearing a 'Shalini Enterprise' tag, was blocking their way. After numerous attempts of gratifying their way inside the house, they gave up. They were clueless as to why... and what then? They stood with blank expressions. Then came a smirk from the gatekeeper followed by an illuminating arrogant sarcasm "The only way you could go in is if you were invisible." Arjun and Oday turned towards each other with eyebrows lifted and wrinkled foreheads.

"Yes... Okay... Maybe you are right. Thank you then. Will see you later," Arjun said and took his leave back towards the car they had come in. The blackened windows didn't allow anyone to glance the insides... especially not from the distance at which the gatekeeper stood.

"Okay... I won't be a type of invisible where I get naked. So no Hollow man or Mrs. Fantastic," Oday said.

"Sure... what about adding little extra clothes?" Arjun asked.

"What's in your mind?" Oday said.

"Let's play the dynamic Wizard-Muggle duo yet again bro," Arjun said. He pulled the hatch to the car trunk as it lifted open behind them.

The gatekeeper was constantly gazing at the suspiciously stable car with an open dicky. Arjun came out and kicked the rear left Tyre shouting, "God... you had to deflate now."

He took the spare tire out and collected the tools to start his fake repair. The gatekeeper yet again smirked... somewhat pitying Arjun. He was rather oblivious to the now-wizard Oday... who slowly sneaked from beside him inside the Farm... carefully passing through all the gates under his invisibility-cloak[69].

After about fifteen minutes of patient traversal through the big villa... Oday finally arrived outside the room where the meeting was happening. There was no possible way inside. Hence Oday took a comfortable spot outside the room where he could safely switch into another hero. He thought for a while and then smiled and whispered to Arjun (on the Bluetooth headset) "I'm going blind."

"Daredevil[70] huh... Nice one. Improvisation huh. Just be careful," Arjun replied.

Oday reappeared in a corner outside the room and started eavesdropping on the conversation. After about twenty minutes, the meeting was over. The official meeting, to put it right. One of the participants took his leave... namely Eklavya Misra.

Outside, the gatekeeper's suspicion had elevated to a great level and thus to quench his curiosity he quickly walked down to the car and asked Arjun if he needed help. He sat down and started screwing out the Tyre, which Arjun was since so long struggling to do. While doing that he realized that the Tyre was in fact not punctured.

"What the hell?" He got up. Arjun got worked up and started thinking of escape ideas. The man then bent down to look inside the car through the trunk.

"Where is the other guy?" The man asked. As he began to take his head out, Arjun tried one of the most famous stunts called the "Pulling the Trunk cabinet down on the investigator to have him pass out." The man caught the cabinet edge with his inverted right hand. He pushed it up with brute strength and drew his gun out to point at Arjun. Arjun freaked out.

"Wait Wait Wait Wait," Arjun said closing his eyes. He waited for a few seconds to hear a gunshot and then opened his right eye to see the man still pointing the gun at him. He closed it yet again, out of fear. Then after another ten seconds, he opened both his eyes. Strangely, the man seemed to have frozen in his stance. Arjun went close to touch him and found that indeed he had frozen. He turned around and there stood Oday smiling with heroic elite arrogance.

"What power is that?" Arjun asked.

"Professor X_{71} sucker," Oday said.

"But you can walk," Arjun said.

"Two words... First $Class_{72}$," Oday said.

"Nice... you are indeed learning art of innovation. What should I do with him now? He would report us to the Rana for sure," Arjun said.

"I'd do away with him," Oday said.

"No... you can't kill him," Arjun said.

"Just wait and see... and get aside. He is gonna wake up," Oday said. Both of them went and stood on either side of the man. A wand appeared in Oday's hand and the man simultaneously woke up. Oday pointed the wand at him and said "$Expeliomus_{73}$". The Gun flew out of the man's hand to Arjun. Arjun bent down to get the gun as the man charged at him. Oday again uttered "$Stupefy_{74}$" and the man fell down. Oday said his final charm pointing the wand at the man "$Obliviate_{75}$".

They laid the man down to carry him back to the gate but as soon as they lifted him up, the distant inner door of the villa opened.

"Oh! I completely forgot… Eklavya is on his way," Oday said.

They hurriedly pushed the man inside the car. Eklavya walked to the main gate talking on his phone, probably calling his car. He hung up and saw the weird site. But to his understanding… Oday and Arjun were fixing tires as the gatekeeper was working up the brakes and the chamber. He ignored it completely as his car came to the gate and sat in and left.

"Fast… let's get him to lie beside the gate and then pursue this Eklavya guy… fast," Oday said. They both carried him again to the gate and sat him down outside. Then they returned to the car.

"We have a problem… A rear Tyre is to be reattached," Arjun said.

"You go and sit… I would fix this," Oday said.

Arjun went to the driver's seat as Oday raised his hand$_{76}$. The screws and the Tyre flew around to get fixed at their place within seconds. He came inside the car.

"Magneto?" Arjun questioned.

"Nope… Vader," Oday said. Arjun sparked the ignition and raced in behind Eklavya's car.

"Okay… so what's the deal…? At least tell me now," Arjun asked.

"See… this guy has guys inside the forest okay. In the tribes and other locals. There is a tribe Sarpanch… having his allegiance to the IPU in the northern wildlife sanctuary. He has been troubling the cannabis farms across the depths of the sanctuary. There is a chemical factory nearby run by certain IPU investors. Apparently, they have a lot of money laundered into Rana's minor opposition. The Rana wants a chemical accident in the factory affecting the village too… This would kill two birds with one stone… that is… if the tribe was migrated from the accident site then it would free the trade routes. In addition, Aditya can take over the site under the state and then when declared safe… lease it to the Rana. This would strengthen the Rana's image and business even further… although it needs barely any strengthening… but this is the Rana's payment for providing incessant support to the Ityadi. Also the IPU would come to Rana's aid, which would be a dire reminder to the Political giant that their major victory was reason to Rana alone. Eklavya is now heading to a local rural bar where all his regular Gunmen reside. We need… to neutralize them," Oday said.

*   *   *

A big mesh of thin, curvy streets. Disfigured small buildings all around it. Eklavya's car stopped close to it. He stepped out to walk in through the rugged door. A few seconds later three men with huge rifles in their hands came out of the door. One of them, apparently their leader, shouted, "Mishra Sir has a tail… come out. The car is nearing." All along the balconies and doors of all the buildings, armed-people, both men and women, came out on the orders of their leader. The black BMW, in which Arjun and Oday sat, slowly drifted along the roundabout. It halted a few meters near the bar.

"Open Fire," said the leader. A swarm of bullets rained upon the car. The leader, realizing that it was a level-one impenetrable bulletproof car, ordered the men to stop. He asked two men to go near the car and open the door. They went and tried to pull open the door to no resolve. As they turned around to signal the leader, they heard the door-lock open. One of the two came near the door. The door banged open on him and he fell down. The other one stepped back and pointed his gun at the door. The one who had fallen got up again. He was suddenly pushed away by a leg. Everybody started shooting in the leg. After emptying their magazines, they took to their pockets to reload. That is when Oday stepped out wearing a mask and holding a prosthetic leg in his right hand.

"I love this newly grasped art of deception," He said and shut the door which relocked from inside. Everybody aimed his or her guns at him. The leader shouted, "Surrender to us. Mishra sir might show mercy."

Oday raised his right hand forward and said, "Take your best shot".

They all opened fire. However, after a few seconds the leader realized that all bullets were just floating in the air[77] around Oday. They all stopped again to reload.

"Quoting yet another awesome masked man called 'V[78]' from the famous book by Alan Moore... and that overly awesome movie... MY TURN," Oday said and flew in within a span of seconds to all the attackers, breaking their weapons and rendering them unconscious. The roads were clear for him to enter the bar. He walked to the main door. As soon as he turned the knob, the bar exploded into flames, pushing Oday flying through the air. He got up with a tinnitus as Arjun rushed in to help him back to the car. He backed up and started driving towards the city. They heard various gunshots and screams on their way. Arjun turned around to check onto Oday and saw a blinking red light below the seat. He stopped the car and went to get a hold of whatever it was.

"BOMB" Arjun screamed and threw it out the window. But as soon as he pressed the accelerator... the bomb went off, toppling the car. Semi-conscious… Arjun saw the petrol slowly dripping down to where the flames were.

"NO… NO… Oday…. NOOOOOOOOOO" Arjun shouted. The car went up in flames.

17

There are two kinds of people in the world... Simply put... leaders and followers. Probably some or the other intellectual philosopher might have pushed that down your throat at some point in time with the ending note of "Be the leader". Ironically... and moreover hysterically... if everyone was the leader then there would not have been any leader. It is one of the most naturally imperative symbiotic mirrored relation... along with day and night, good and evil, dark and light, India and Pakistan and most importantly Shahrukh and Kajol, Etcetera.

The follower varies from the predetermined to the gullible to the arrogant. One can see examples of the commonest follower amongst the Indian Education Set-Up with some bizarre prejudice for the Engineering Class. Teach every farmer's kid to be an engineer and there'd be a day we won't have farmers. Same goes with everything. That is just the sad erroneous system of our country and the superficial mindset. Some credit also goes to the media as well. Okay... moving on... the circumspect follower cautiously glances at the miraculous examples of the past, present and future and formulates a plan of action to adapt to the greats. Tens of Thousands followed Gandhi in the

Dandi March, but he is the one we all remember. We all remember Prophet Muhammad, maybe the first few Caliphates and few Islamic saints of specific timelines. We remember Jesus Christ… and know the names of maybe a couple of Vatican Popes excluding the current one. That is when we have been keeping up with history. But why? Let us come to the leaders.

Starting with an example. Actually, examples coalesced into one. What are the few principles common to all religions? Prayer, no adultery, the institution of marriage, no killing, reading the prescribed holy texts, fasting, pilgrimage, Etcetera. Let us go a little over-the-top and out of the way to justify the parity.

Prayer was a form of meditation which is Good for Health; No Adultery ensured civility, marriage ensured a systematic methodology for survival of the race, no killing meant regard for human life, reading the holy texts ensured literacy, fasting enhanced tolerance and resilience and pilgrimage connected each one to his roots and also gave him opportunity for recreational travel. All the religions were preached initially not as the path of God… but the path of the Good. God was just the medium. Tell a man he cannot kill, he might ignore you; Tell him God would punish him for it, he might stop, kneel and ask for forgiveness for the mere thought of it. Now the irrationalism and communal prejudice have divided man on the bases, which were just intended to unite him to moral sanity. It is high time we realize that the only two dissimilarities between religions are location and time. However, if you take religious prejudice away from a man worthless to humankind… he is left with nothing. Hence, he is very possessive about it.

So, we have already discussed the leaders and the prophets, haven't we? The legitimate ones as well as the fraudulent ones. But the legitimate leader is also of two types. The right and the wrong. Now the fraudulent leader has much in common with the wrong leader… mostly his innovation. All leaders have it. But the quality that differentiates the two is the lack of fear. The wrong leader… just like the right leader… lacks fear. Most recent examples are Adolf Hitler, Dawood Ibrahim, and Osama Bin Laden. Only the rarest of the follower species that is the motiveless follower can achieve that aim. They say to aim for the stars and land on the moon. If you add a limit… a predefined motive… and then be satisfied with underperformance, you are definitely not a leader. A leader just keeps exploiting all the resources available to serve his ends. That takes him wherever it takes him. It can be the moon, mars or Andromeda. We do not know. And good or bad, a leader is always selfish. Everybody is. Another striking difference is that the right leader gets pleasure from another man's pleasure. And the wrong leader gets pleasure from another man's pain. For either… their cause is justified for it serves their ends as well as those of their community. Hence, they are selfish for it.

The right and the wrong leader, each have their respective mononym. Let us rather call it a mother category. One is said to show the path of the light to mankind, providing hope with his guardian angels; and the other is said to show the path of darkness through his misguiding demons. Yes… the right God and the wrong Devil. These two also form another regularity amongst all the religions. The protagonist and the antagonist. They are also a mandatory dual occurrence.

Devil… also known as Shaitaan… is the name categorizing the common wrong of the world. He is known to persuade someone to wrong. That is his primary eight to five job. Compel people to be evil. Thus, just as the Great leaders who served humanity are called Avatars of God, those who follow the devil's cult are christened as demons. 'Christened' as Demons is sardonically hilarious, though. So demons... or Rakshasa... is said to be the fragment of the devil or Shaitaan inside those sadists. Yes... Sorry to say but all those exciting and thrilling Demonic possessions from Exorcist Series and Paranormal Series... in reality, such incidents are not even close to the phrase 'possession by a demon'. What the hell would a demon get by playing hide and seek with a family in a house, or possessing a teenager and self-stabbing her genitalia? Those cases, like that of Anneliese Michel, either are a fictitious exaggeration or close to the scientific diagnosis assigned to them. It all depends on self-analysis as well. If you believe you are possessed or are made to believe you are possessed, then you shall act possessed. Real possessions are so noiseless and camouflaged; the possessed would specifically never believe OR preach the presence of a demon within itself.

There are also semi-possessions whereby the victim somewhat comes to realize that there is a demon within him. Yes, there is. It is the rarest of them all. This case mostly coincides and is confused with the last kind of possession, which involves neither a demon nor a possession. Convenient-Alibi-Possession or CAP. Hereby, the claimant seems to use the excuse of split personality, the other one being that of some demonic entity, as the reason for some crime. No human can differentiate between a CAP and a semi-possession because in both the cases, the person claims to be possessed and is guilty of some crime.

Hence, we conclude, that demons do not just desire to inflict damage on a single being; they rather aim to use a medium to preach negativity in the humankind as a whole.

Common scepticism, the same that says that God is a belief and a medium, might double that Devil is the name for the evil amongst us. Yes... it somewhat is. But... if God exists... then does the devil or the Shaitaan does too? Why has religion been one dynamic yet common thing through the course of mankind's history? Moreover, why do all religions have this duality... the positive and the negative?

History testifies this dual occurrence in records. A common protagonist needs a common antagonist for balance. A Hero... must have a villain.

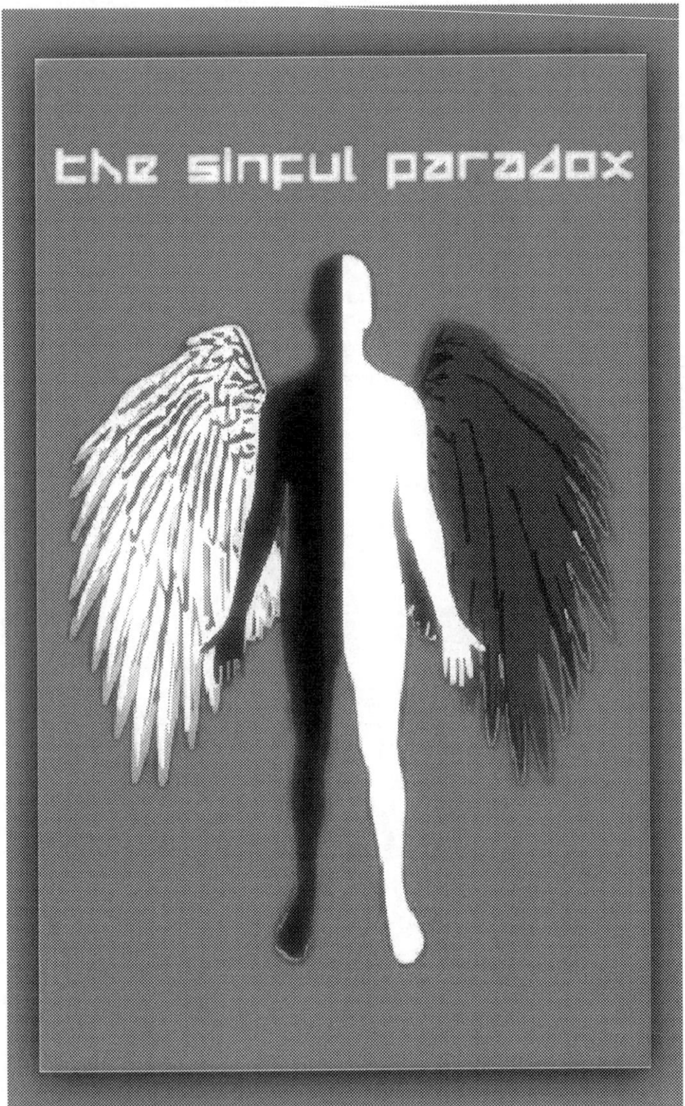
the sinful paradox

18

"OOOOOOO" Arjun screamed with closed eyes, in expectation of extreme heat and flames, to suppress the upcoming pain. He continued his loud groan for a few seconds and then faintly stopped, just as he noticed an immensely awkward silence. He opened his eyes one by one, clenching his face muscles. To his colossal joy, he was lying on a sofa, beside Oday, inside a huge hall. He got up with excitement and overflowing laughter and innately thanked Oday.

"Yeiiiiiiii…. GOOOOOO LUHAAARS…. Dude that earned you a lifetime of my servitude," Arjun said and then turned to see that Oday was lying sidewise on the sofa.

"Hey… Luhar…. Get up bro," Arjun tried to shake his friend up. Oday got up from the sofa and smiled. He then said in an evanescent voice "Arjun… we are alive…. Yeiiiiii" and then fell down revealing a huge shrapnel piercing his spine.

"Odayyyy… What the fuck," Arjun held him down and tried to pull out the triangular shrapnel just to fail.

"How did this happen??? Luhar…. This can't be……
HELPPPPP ANYBODY," Arjun shouldered Oday up and started dragging him to the room outside. On reaching there

he saw a bunch of young women sitting on sofas in a semi-circular fashion. One of them held an infant feeding on her. As soon as she saw the two men come in, she turned around in sheer shame. The others screamed in fear. From the entrance rushed in Shalini "What happened?" She gazed at the blood-clad Arjun and took a couple of seconds to identify him.

"Arjun… Why are you here?" she said.

"What the fucking hell are you waiting for? Call an ambulance will you?" Arjun snapped at Shalini.

"Hey…. How dare you talk to me like that in front of my friends?" Shalini said ignorantly.

"Shalini…. Look here," Arjun said as he gestured pointing at the impaired Oday. And just as every girl has to, Shalini strengthened her power of observation and understanding and glanced at the unconscious Oday.

"What all happened to him now?" Shalini inquired.

Arjun calmed his anger down and turned Oday sarcastically "Can you hold back the pleasantries for once?"

"Oh No! You are wasting time…. We need an ambulance right now," the fluorescent tube-light namely Shalini spoke up.

"Is your car here? I guess yes…. Get it then," Arjun shouted on Shalini.

"Okay," Shalini said as she held Oday from his opposite shoulder and escorted him out to her car. Both Arjun and Oday sat inside and Arjun closed the door in front of Shalini before she could enter. The car left, leaving Shalini alone and wondering just what the hell had happened there. She slowly walked back in. Before she entered the room she could hear loud bitching like "Her boyfriend is so controlling, isn't he?", "My jaan would never talk to me like that", "So what that his friend was dying? My babe would never snap on me even if he was dying himself."

The erratic reverberations converged in a resonating giggle of the whole lot. The infant started mewling and so her mother got up to take her out for some fresh air. As she turned, she saw that Shalini stood vacuously at the entrance. An awkward silence followed.

"Shalini. We were saying," the woman said. Shalini ignored her and made a move towards the cordless telephone. She dialled a few digits and said on the phone "Yes... I need my chopper. Yes... at her place," She hung up and turned back to the door and started walking.

"Shalini..." one of the girls said. "Ria has become a mother. Let's celebrate na," she followed.

Shalini turned around and grabbed her bag from the table. She went in for her chequebook and pen and started scribbling. She then tore a cheque off and turned to Ria.

"Take this... it's a blank cheque," Shalini said.

"What does this mean Shalini?" Ria asked.

"Oh.... This is my expression of happiness for you. I mean this is why you invited me, didn't you?" Shalini said and turned around to leave.

"Where is this cheesiness coming from? Shalini.... YOU BITCH," Ria said as she kept her child down and hurled a Vase kept on the table towards Shalini. Shalini ducked to save herself. She turned around with a furious face keeping her right hand inside her bag. She slowly walked towards Ria.

"Hey... what will you do now? Hit me? Kill me? You... you cannot do that you know? Shalini... step back..." Ria said as she slowly stepped back herself. Shalini suddenly took her hands out of her bag. Everyone got up in fear. Ria fell back. They saw that Shalini was holding her pen pointing at Ria. She was smiling.

"You need the same ink for the whole check right?" Shalini said.

Ria grabbed the pen as nervous perspirations ran down her face.

"It's an Aurora Diamante... so don't worry... if the cheque doesn't pay you At least have a mortgage. And yes... if the ink runs out I would send a stock of the Aurora ink," Shalini said and left the room.

"Ria... Ria..." one of the women said to Ria. She got up and moved her hand to almost throw off the pen. But she stopped in between realizing the value of the item at stake. The child continued its mewl behind her on the table.

"Ria... she has been crying for a while now," said one of the girls.

"Then give her some vodka and shut her up. Why bother me? I have way more important things to do," said Ria, gazing at the pen.

"Messing with Ria Mishra, the daughter of Padmini Mishra, would not go as well for you as you believe, Shalini Teja Singh," She continued.

*　　*　　*

"Please.... Tell me something," Arjun said to the doctor standing outside the ICU.

"We have done all in our capacity... And now," The doctor's sentence was intervened by Arjun "All you doctors say is that we have done all in our capacity and now only fate can save him..."

"No No... I was going to say that we have done all in our capacity and now Mr. Oday Luhar is alive but has lost mobility," the Doctor said.

"Mobility? What does it mean?" Arjun asked.

"His spinal cord is ruptured. He cannot move anymore," Doctor said.

"Okay," Arjun said. He turned and ambled for a while in a zig-zag manner and then fell unconscious.

*   *   *

Arjun woke up in the big ICU ward of the 'Suraksha' Hospital. He shockingly sat up and saw Shalini sitting beside him.

"Shalini… Oday…" Arjun said. Shalini immediately pointed across Arjun to his right. Oday was lying on a special bedding, with a hole making his wound accessible. His upper body was mummified with bandages and his face was covered with the regular inhaler. He spoke through the inhaler in a faint voice "I'm Okay…".

"Oday…" Arjun got up and then moaned, clutching his left arm. Maybe his fall had injured him there.

"Yeah Yeah… I'd be good… And fuck you for daring to join beside me in the hospital ward," Oday said.

"Bros before Hoes they said," Arjun said.

"Don't say that when your whore is standing right beside you," Oday mumbled through the inhaler.

"Who the hell you call whore?" Shalini said.

"He must've meant hoe darling. Spinal injury impairs control of muscle. He is speaking something and we are hearing something else," Arjun smartly covered for Oday. He had seemingly overcome his anger on Shalini and was back to being the recessive lover. Shalini's phone rang. She went out to receive it saying "I'm outside if you need me".

"So…. Whom do you call Professor X now?" Oday said.

"Ahahahaha…. Yes. Suckhead," Arjun said.

"Won't feel no pain no more sucker," Oday said.

"The Perks of Being a Wall, huh? Ahahahahaha" Arjun remarked.

"Jokes apart. You have a more serious thing than your best friend immobilized for life," Oday said.

"She is still angry isn't she?" Arjun spoke with a sigh.

"Yes… I mean those are the perks of being a flower…" Oday improvised Arjun's sarcasm.

"I'll be back," Arjun said and walked outside the room in his Hospital gown.

"That makes me wonder… what if the T-800_{79} had a girlfriend? Nice… these 'new and awesome' ideas urge me to take up writing man. Now let's sleep and quash the awkwardness of a soliloquy," Oday said to himself, stared at the ceiling for a while and nodded off.

* * *

The Suraksha Hospital's floors and rooms were shaken up by the sudden echoing of sirens. A dense tempestuous multitude of politicians, security personnel and reporters gushed inside the hospital through all doors. Arjun sat terrified in the corridor, hearing the reverberating footsteps from outside. He started equating a proper sentence to present before the Senior Luhar for Oday's condition. In came the horde quoting Oday's numerous sobriquets. Closely followed the complimentary slogans. Aditya passed by various emergency wards, surveying them for his son. He entered the corridor where Arjun was sitting. He slowly turned and gesticulated at his trailing followers to lower the intensity of their voices. He then walked up to Arjun and asked "Is it true?" to which the latter corroborated with a nod. Aditya walked inside the room.

"Is it you, dad?" Oday questioned.

"Yes… It is I. How did this… Okay… let's leave the questions aside. How are you feeling my son?" Aditya asked.

"I am good dad… how are you?" Oday said.

"Don't you worry son. I will get the best. Dr. Hussain is coming from Germany just today to have a look at you. Take care son. I will go talk to the doctors to escort you to our house with all facilities. You have my word son… you will get walking," Aditya said and walked outside. He went close to the door and paused for a second and walked back to Arjun. He politely got Arjun up by his shoulders and hugged him. He whispered into Arjun's ears "I trusted you…". He then left the hospital with his clique of concentric sycophants and curious media-men.

A few minutes later a nurse walked towards Oday's room. Arjun intercepted her. He took a hold of the medicine pouch she was carrying and inquired the routine. He then asked the nurse to leave, saying he would himself have the patient eat them. He then went to Oday.

"Pundit… you should really go see Shalini. She left unannounced and you didn't even pay a glance to her temper-tantrum. I really insist. Go bro."

"I am not leaving here. And let's get you up. Medicine time. Okay where is the manual for the electrical suspension bed… yeah found it. Here we go," Arjun pushed some buttons on a wired panel and Oday's bed started straightening up to help him get into a seating position.

"Now let us see… two in the morning… two in the morning… yes, evening… found it… whoa six tablets…. Okay… one by one (put the medicine in Oday's mouth and bent his neck back to let him have water) And yeah Oday… Thank you for saving us," Arjun said.

Oday gulped the tablet in a hurry and said, "But Pundit…"

"Just a second… have another one first…" Arjun said and shoved another tablet inside Oday's mouth. Oday gulped it down and said again "Pundit…".

"Yes Yes… hold back the modesty… You saved me from inevitable death… and sacrificed your limbs for me…" Arjun said.

"I didn't," Oday said as Arjun placed another tablet in his mouth.

"Yeah I know you didn't. I mean you completely didn't save my ass there," Arjun said ignorantly.

"ARJUN…. I DID NOT SAVE YOU…. OR MYSELF…" Oday shouted.

"Wait what… You didn't… then who?"

19

A sandy wasteland in some unknown corner of the world. Mritunjay stood in the midst of heavy sandstorm, surrounded by dunes in all directions.

"What are you up to huh?" Mritunjay said with his eyes closed.

He continued "Tell me about this new executive you have been hiding from me.... Because neither of us saved them.... I want to know... Is he an archangel? Is he a reaper? Is he a new seraph? As far as I saw... the chosen one had utilized his temporal slot for the day. I thought of making a move... but witnessing their foolishness I held back. I had the opportunity to rub it in your face... that I told you so... that it won't work. But some unearthly power saved the two. Who is thee who stands against the Angel of death? After the demise of Pran... the Angel of Life... there is one who can be swift and powerful enough to escape my third eye that is God himself... So who is this new power? (Waited for a few seconds and then opened and widened his eyes) ... Sanctions against me? I won't return till I expose this messiah of yours. The only choice then remaining would be me... that is death. This realm of earth entrusted to you by the kingdom of God... I guess it needs a renewal altogether. A restart… as I have held in the past few centuries. And no I wouldn't return… (Paused for yet another minute) … A death-reaper you say…" Mritunjay said.

The heavy sandstorm started coalescing together, aligning to form a desert cyclone the size of a city. The cyclone revolved around Mritunjay for a minute and then calmed down to reveal Martin Messorem standing at the eye of it.

"I, on the order of the God, am here to take you back to thy almighty's office. You shall come to heaven and retain your duties or stay here and face heavy charges. Your choice…" Martin said in a formal dialect.

"What shall you do if I say no?" Mritunjay said.

"Officially, I am to arrest you… Unofficially… I shall kick your ass… and I have beaten death either way… many a time with your client Mr. Luhar," Martin said.

"Hahahahahaha…. A mere death reaper hereby challenges the elite Angel of Death himself…" Mritunjay mocked Martin.

"The king of reapers…" Martin said and jumped in towards Mritunjay and punched him and sent him flying miles away. He then swiftly kicked Mritunjay again. He gripped his arms and pushed them, somewhat digging Mritunjay downwards into the dune. Mritunjay shouted in agony as his wings started protruding, just a few seconds before getting buried inside the dune. Martin jumped back with a grinning smile on his face. Suddenly the ground started shaking and the sand from within Martin's feet started shifting away from him. The slowly shifting particles slowly paced up into literally floating sand. The sand cleared away in a gushing wind-storm revealing Mritunjay who was waving his huge wings.

"And whom do you think dethroned the last king of reapers huh?" Mritunjay said and disappeared into thin air. He then reappeared behind Martin and took a soft vertical slash with his two smaller fingers at Martin's neck, rendering him unconscious at the very spot.

"Is there no one else?" Mritunjay said looking up at the sky.

"Wait… there is… and I WILL find out about him…" He concluded.

*　　*　　*

A huge juggernaut truck stopped by the Luhar mansion. The back shutter mechanically lifted up and showed a big wooden box, twice the size of a normal human. Also, there were smaller cardboard boxes. Two men came out from the front of the truck to pull out the wagon containing the wooden box. A black Mercedes halted behind the truck with an ambulance trailing behind it. Inside the mansion, Oday laid on his velvety bed as his orderlies surrounded him. Arjun and Shalini loudly argued in the adjoining room. The argument slowly magnified into an audibly apparent violence. Furniture breaking, Glasses Falling, Vases Falling, there were various sounds which indicated that Arjun and Shalini were having a serious go at each other. All of a sudden, the noises stopped and a few seconds later Arjun rushed in through the door.

"Your chair is here Suckhead…" Arjun said.

"Sir…" An orderly pointed at Arjun's unzipped jeans. Arjun immediately turned around to zip it up.

"And here we thought you were fighting with her…" Oday said.

The main door opened wide and a black coated man walked inside.

"Hello Oday… I am Dr. M. Hussain. Your father told me everything and your doctors have given me all your reports. I will do a series of surgeries on you which have a probability of 30% to be successful. Successful meaning you At least would be able to feel your arms and legs. After that, suitable physiotherapies would help you regain a level of mobility. Until then (walked aside to reveal a polythene-covered wheel-chair) this is the most expensive and best neuromobile in the world. It was built by Me in collaboration with Tesla and Volkswagen. It runs on all forms of automobile inputs from electricity to petrol to diesel to CNG to Hydrogen. It has an autopilot mode and can run at speeds of over 80 Kilometres per hour. Amazing right?"

Arjun walked through the doctor's side and started scanning the room.

"Oh it is right in front of you…" Dr. Hussain said.

"No… there was my girlfriend in here somewhere…" Arjun said worriedly.

"If you are searching for the girl with the unhooked blouse… then she ran out of the house rigorously trying to hook her blouse…" the doctor said.

"Oh Fuck…" Arjun said and ran out.

"But Dr. Hussain… Then I would have to have someone to operate the buttons or manually move the chair, right? Cause I cannot myself push any button," Oday said.

"What buttons?" The doctor said.

"The ones on the chair…" Oday said.

"There are no buttons on my chair…. It would be controlled by you alone… through your nervous system. For that we would have to do a small surgery. And about manually pushing… only if you allow someone to do it to conserve the fuel. Overall… all the buttons are there in your brain. But you would have to train to use them. For that we would have a simulation mode of the chair prior to ground tests. But first things first. You are to go through a series of three operations. First one is spine reconstruction. Second is nerve-mapping and third one is to install artificial nerves routing to a small socket in your brain protruding from the surface so that we could plug the chair in," the Doctor said.

"Back to the hospital already…" Oday said disappointedly.

"No No… The surgery would take place in this very room Sir… I have all the accessories in the veranda. And all my staff is here as well. So let's begin," The doctor said.

*   *   *

Politics is a very vicious business. In the ancient times, knowledge was the weapon which was extremely politicized. The knowledgeable would rule since they could strategically dominate the foolish. The fear of knowledge was so much that sometimes those foolish in power killed off the knowledgeable just on whims of their insecurities... just like it happened with Socrates. See Ravan... he had a plethora of knowledge and all he did was use it to subjugate. In the end, he was defeated... but the defeater wasn't Lord Ram... it was the knowledge passed by Vibhishan without which Lord Ram would have faced utter defeat. The lack of knowledge of the chakravyuh saw Abhimanyu's demise. Coming to medieval times, the Church ruled the west. The Bible was revered as the mother of knowledge. Although a religion built on pure thought, Christianity in the middle ages was in its darkest of phases. From the killing of geniuses like Galileo, who scientifically rebuked certain Church theories and tried to illuminate mankind, to converting Churches into brothels (They held that out of the three six-inch organs of the male body, the lowermost shall be used the most to keep one busy from using the upper two), they went to the most extreme of limits to contain the plague of knowledge. In the eastern world, though, knowledge was secondary. Although the knowledge of canons won the Mughals their Indian conquests, but the importance of knowledge had degraded. Annexation and Administration became primary. But the renaissance changed it all for the world. Knowledge had finally taken over the western world and was stretching its claws towards India. Came here the sly 'tradesmen' who sold telescopes for a dozen boxes of gold. After Aryabhata and Bhaskaracharya, the age of Indian

Science and Mathematics saw a slow degradation and hence it was easy for the visitors to gratify the public with their 'Modern Technology'. Keeping scientific knowledge aside, knowledge of war could have played an important role in saving India from slavery. The strategy of Camouflage and that of Guerrilla Warfare was clearly mentioned and also utilized by past intellectuals like Chanakya, who brought down a dynasty with his immense knowledge and also defeated the undisputed Greek raiders. But Indians were busy building the most ill-maintained one of the seven wonders of the world and also building its first copy in the state which is more famous for the Ajanta Ellora caves. Hence, by offering rusted metal for rich spices, the British looted India. Back in the west, the Churches had lost their influence. People succumbed to knowledge from other sources as well. Then the Industrial Revolution happened and the era of exploration initiated. In the modern era, knowledge of advanced sciences won many wars. Sadly, the first use of all the scientific inventions and theories by even the noblest and peaceful of scientists is always to make a weapon. US defeated Germany because of its knowledge of the German Enigma Machine and it defeated Japan because of the knowledge of the atom bomb. The two world wars boosted the exploration era and within seventy years, the world digitalized into something which seemed impossible in the very near past. The era in which the impossible of yesterday becomes the science of today.

Even in India, the IDU ruled for six decades because of the immense knowledge it had gained from its British predecessors. The only crisp added was that Indian people now didn't know that they were slaves. They felt free because their constitution read so. But constitution for an Indian became just like the Bhagvad Gita for a Hindu…

You are Hindu even if you haven't read a word of it. And this lack of knowledge helped the IDU serve its own selfish ends. Rarely did they show signs of Philanthropy and soon returned to their genetic form of leeches. They tried to overpower knowledge by imprisoning the wise nationalists, by declaring a National Emergency, by arousing riots, Etcetera. But on 26th May 2014, the dynasty of the IDU came to an end. The reason? Knowledge of Media.

Stereotypes and public-belief have been the most common friends as well as foes of the leaders. In all the aforementioned instances, the media, in whatever form it existed, used projection techniques and imageries to create certain stereotypes. And the world having a natural innate democracy instilled within, roots out the wrong amongst it and lifts the righteous to the podium. The common belief and public image always helped leaders to win battles. This was a technique most recently used by Adolf Hitler. The genesis of the holocaust was primarily on the stereotype of the Jews he had created through his robust speeches. Similarly, all other leaders also use the media to control the gullible minds and use them at their behest to win their battles. Some say the downfall of the intellectual standards of the IDU after the advent of the idiotic, immature mumma's boy, Raj Gautam, saw the downfall of IDU. But genuinely speaking, it was the well planned social media strategy of the IPU which displaced the predecessor. The modernized campaigns got wonderful receptions and the very idea of a contemporary and active party at the centre urged people to vote for them. And thus, just as a teenaged girl who uses top-angle selfies with variety of retouches and filters to receive the maximum likes on Instagram, twitter and Facebook, the IPU won. Just if the IDU had KNOWN the most obvious… or had KNOWN that sometimes the most obvious should be the obvious choice.

Aditya Luhar was no stranger to the power of knowledge. He KNEW that in the day's world, publicity was most important. Which God will you approach when you have a mob of people marching with lit up candles in their hands in protest against you? No matter how much you pressurize them, it would only worsen the condition. The more you are antagonized, the more you agonize. So it is better if you are the one they are marching for. But what can you possibly do to have them gather in your support? You haven't done any charitable work lately, have you? Wait a second… so what if you haven't. Just wait for something sad to happen. Sympathy works equally well.

*   *   *

Arjun was driving his father's old blue Ambassador. His phone started ringing loudly. He drove the car to a safe corner and received the call only after stopping. It was Oday.

"Yes Suckhead… Oh yeah the chair… now slow down already… Okay… Hmmm… I'd be there in (The phone started beeping)," Arjun said and then glanced at his phone which showed Shalini's call in waiting.

"Oday… I would call you in a bit…. Yes… What is it jaan? I was talking to Oday…. Hello… Hello," Arjun gazed at his phone for a while and then redialled Oday's number.

"Yeah bro…. count me in…" Arjun concluded and turned the ignition. His car had only covered a few meters of the road as the earth started shaking.

"What the hell! EARTHQUAKE," Arjun uttered with fear. He continued driving fast towards the Luhar's Private Mansion shouting "The end of the world…. Noooooooooooooo."

He drifted around with his car and started accelerating in the opposite direction.

"Fuck the chair…. Shaliniiiiiiiiii…," He screamed.

Within ten minutes he arrived beside the Shalini Mansion. He stepped out and carefully walked on the shaking ground. He went close to open the gate but suddenly a couple of helicopters hovered over him. Shalini was in one of them.

"Arjun? Come on up," She said as she pushed down a ladder. Arjun climbed up with a huge smile of relief on his face. He entered the chopper and said, "I came to save you my darling…" Arjun said.

"Did you? Awwwwwwwww…. I love you too… (To the pilot) Change of course. Tell dad I am not coming to Delhi," Shalini said.

"Wait… you were not coming to save me?" Arjun said.

"Let's go to Oday's place… I heard that he has some new awesome chair," Shalini said, wittingly trying to change the subject.

"Hey Answer me… Shali," Arjun was stopped by a kiss from Shalini.

*　　*　　*

Arjun and Shalini entered Oday's house. They walked inside the hall. There was no one inside strangely. A voice came from inside the adjacent room.

"I want to play a game."

Arjun and Shalini turned around to see a shadowed man on a wheelchair. The man came forward to the light to show that he was none other than our hero Oday. He was wearing his regular yellow mask.

"If only you were wearing Billy the puppet$_{80}$'s mask…" Arjun said.

"Look here… the chair has a dock for my phone. It is not only charging my phone but also connects to my phone either directly or through Bluetooth OR Wi-Fi. This is it… Salvation…" Oday said.

Shalini's butler came in "Miss… Your father has left for Gorakhpur for Earthquake relief. There are reports that the quake would have a follow-up. So from there he has a plan to go to the epicentre at Nepal."

"Nepal… this is from Nepal…" Arjun said.

"Yes sir… reports are that thousands have lost their lives till now… (to Oday) You didn't know? Your father is accompanying Madam's father…" the Butler added.

"What? I did not know that…" Oday wondered.

"But more important right now is the quake and its epicentre and a predicted after-shock. Oday… let's go to Nepal…" Arjun said.

20

A Shalini Enterprise chopper descended down in a playground of Kathmandu. Inside, Arjun prepared Oday's plan of action in the inflicted and ailing country. All around them they observed nothing but targets innately and inadvertently calling out for help.

"Oday... I have a great plan. Okay... let's begin with Anti-Venom$_{81}$. He can detect ailment right? Now whoever you believe is in greater need of help you go to them and heal them with the angelic healing from 'Supernatural$_{82}$'. That's the quickest," Arjun said.

"Okay.... Here we go..." Oday disconnected the cord from the back of his head, jumped out of the copter wearing a yellow mask, transformed into Anti-Venom and started observing the people.

"Got em," He said as he transformed back and disappeared.

"You there Suckhead?" Arjun said in the transponder.

"Yeah yeah... healed 15... 16 already" Oday replied.

"Don't try and heal them fully... Don't get me wrong. I mean heal them to the level optimum for survival. We have way many survivors than we have time and force," Arjun said.

"I am going for it again… Scanning… Got them. Wait a second… Arjun…" Oday called out.

"Yeah buddy?"

"Do earthquakes release nuclear radiation?" Oday questioned.

"Not to my knowledge… they generally don't unless caused by a nuclear event," Arjun replied.

"These people have traces of radiation in them as I can see…" Oday said.

"What? Are you sure?" Arjun asked.

"Yes mate… dead sure…" Oday said.

"Okay… So that means this place has radiation… There must be some unstable material underneath… or some source…" Arjun said.

"I see it increasing in traces… Come you guys follow me as I move along. I will heal and move forward. We have about 50 minutes to us. Let's go…" Oday said and flew in the southwards direction. A few minutes later he said "Found it… This is strange… there are multiple sources…" Oday said.

"What do you see?" Arjun asked.

"See for yourself…" Oday said as he put on his google glasses streaming live to the copter's LCD.

"There are men… loading wood onto trucks," Arjun said.

"I really don't think that is wood…" Oday said.

"What is written on those trucks… go closer…" Arjun said.

Oday walked in from the side to get a close-up on the truck's sides which read in a huge font "Shalini Enterprises".

"Oh Fuck… that's your dad's truck…" Arjun said.

"What the fuck does this mean?" Oday said ambiguously.

"Say something?" Shalini said casually.

"You... what should I say to you... Let me get to Ananya... wait a second..." Arjun said and dialled few digits on his phone to get Ananya on a conference.

"Hey... hello... Yeah Oday is here as well. Okay... off with the pleasantries. We need your help. Are you at the office? Nice... Okay... this is too much to ask of you but can you trace back the godowns of Shalini Enterprises' Woodworks back in Nepal and their Trustees?... CCTV is with you... AWESOME... Okay we are waiting..." Arjun said as the call was put on hold from the other side.

"What should I do? That is not wood we are looking at..." Oday said.

"Wait a minute..." Arjun said. The phone beeped and Ananya reconnected "Sir... as per records there are four sawmills of the Shalini Enterprises in Nepal dealing in Mountainous Wood and also Teak and Sandalwood. The only thing fishy is that there have been multiple reports of overloading," Ananya said.

"Overloading... what does that mean?" Oday asked.

"It means smuggling... they are smuggling wood sir..." Ananya said.

"It seems like wood is not the only thing they are smuggling... Oday... we don't have the time to waste on this anymore... Deal with it," Arjun said.

"Okay I am ready..." Oday said as he took his stance to make a jump inside the mill. But the ground started shaking... not as intensely as it did in the prior earthquakes but just as a minor aftershock.

"Whoa..." Arjun shouted and the pilot warned them that they needed to lift up.

The building beside the mill broke in half and began to fall down over the trucks. Oday flew in and lifted the building as Superman.

"Good Job brother," Arjun said.

"Sir… If we do not lift up now we are going down…" the pilot said.

Arjun asked him to take off as the ground continued shaking. A wire broke from an electrical hub and loosely caught on to the rear vertical rotors of the copter. The helicopter started rotating and crashed in. Meanwhile, Oday had been safeguarding the falling building.

"Are you all right Arjun… hey, hey…" Oday said in the transponder.

"Yes we are okay…" Arjun said. He saw the pilot remove his helmet revealing that he was none other than Shalini's butler.

"You fly as well? Nice. Okay… Shalini… you and him should get down and arrange for pick up. I will go and aid Oday on the ground like always," Arjun said while wearing a yellow mask.

"I am coming along…" Shalini said firmly.

"No you are not…" Arjun said.

"My chopper my rules… who made you boss anyway?" Shalini mocked.

"Hey hey… it is Mah life mah rules… okay just come along… but wear this mask…" Arjun said putting forward another yellow mask.

"Ewww…. No…" Shalini retorted.

"Ewww… yes…" Arjun replied.

"Okay I would… (to her Butler) but you go and arrange for a pickup… and don't forget to take Oday's chair along… and also get sanitizers…" Shalini said.

"Oday where are you?" Arjun said in the transponder while walking in the smoky field after the shaking had stopped. Shalini followed closely behind him, trembling with fear.

"They…. shooting…" Oday's voice came in a statically disturbed signal.

"What?" Arjun and Shalini came out of the smoke to see that the men who were just now loading the 'wood' inside the trucks were shooting at Oday without a known reason.

"Why are they shooting at you? Oday can you hear me?" Arjun asked.

"OMG! I am scared to death…" Shalini said hiding behind Arjun.

"I don't fucking know why… they just saw me when I stopped the building. I went close to see if they need my help. But as soon as the shaking stopped they took out guns from inside the trucks and started shooting at me shouting "He's the one we were warned about…"" Oday said.

"Go professor X on them mate," Arjun said. Immediately within seconds, the gunmen fell down. The three of them regrouped as Oday started scanning the trucks and its contents.

"What is it? Uranium/Plutonium/Radium?" Arjun asked.

"Hey… Mr. Science… I slept through the periods and the periodic table…" Oday said.

"We need to send this one away. Teleport it…" Oday stood beside the truck placing both his hands on it and disappeared along with it. He reappeared moments later and just as he did, the building burst into flames. A faint sound of a chopper followed.

"Is it here already?" Arjun wondered.

A man covered in flames dropped down from the balcony of the building screaming in agony.

"Oday… Mermen can use moisture from air to create water right?" Arjun said.

"Yeah…" Oday transformed into a blue-skinned merman and blew away the flames from the person's body.

He then went inside the building curbing the fire all around it. The two of them closely followed. They reached an end where they saw the helicopter hovering in the backyard of the building. In the translucence of the fumes, the man in the chamber seemed different from Shalini's butler.

"Who is that in that Kurta Pyjama?" Shalini said.

The fumes subsided to reveal that it is none other than Oday's father Aditya Luhar. Shalini saw that the well-suited man closely walking behind the Senior Luhar was none other than her very own father Rana Teja Singh.

"DAD'S HERE TOO? WHAT THE HELL… AND WAIT… ODAY… YOUR FATHER HAS A RIFLE IN HIS HAND," Shalini said.

Meanwhile, Arjun had been loitering around looking at the materials inside the mill. He found Chinese scriptures over the packaging inside the mill and also Chinese manuals on the desks.

"These are all Chinese Imports… Legal OR illegal… but they are getting nuclear material from China…" Arjun said as the back door was kicked in by Aditya Luhar.

"Well Well… If the quake was not a surprise enough. I did not expect you to be here so soon," Aditya said.

"What is this going on here? What are these radioactive materials?" Arjun asked in a heavy baritone. Shalini and Oday were standing dumbstruck in a corner.

"Well… see… We are importing them from China as per our deal from last year for purposes better known to us in confidentiality. See. But there are ethics to illegality as well. Smuggling wood is illegally legal as per the conscience of the pseudo-nationalists who can be bribed to do so. But smuggling nuclear material is not only terrifying for them but also anti-national," Aditya said.

"So to fool them… we 'guise them as wood and bribe them at the check posts and custom posts to let the wood go through. As they say, no one questions a man honest about his dishonesty," Rana said walking inside the godown with an RPG strung on his back.

"And we can't let you live since you have heard that," Aditya aimed to fire at Oday and Shalini.

"Gyojin Karate$_{83}$…" came Oday's voice as the bullets stopped mid-air and fell down.

"What the hell? They were not wrong. He is a superhuman," Aditya said in awe.

"Let's see you stop this," Rana said loading his Bazooka on his shoulder. Oday gathered his friends to leave for the staircase. Rana aimed and fired at them.

"Gyojin Karate" came another voice as the RPG stopped mid-air as well. But this time, it exploded. Oday gathered the moisture from the surroundings to keep the fire from reaching him and his friends. The air dried up and Oday fell down unconscious.

"Hey… Oday… Let's go up…" Arjun said as he shouldered Oday upstairs with Shalini's help. He laid Oday down on the leopard-tiled surface.

"What happened to you?" Arjun said slapping Oday to wake him up. But Oday lost the last iota of consciousness he had and closed his eyes. Shalini and Arjun sat worried on the roof as they heard footsteps up the stairwell.

"Oh no! We are in big trouble… Where is your butler… You better wake up…. Oday… Oday…. ODAY…" Arjun said.

21

"Six of us have been slain at the hands of he who calls himself Mritunjay," said a Grim Reaper, standing in the midst of a wasteland of the upper realm.

"After Martin… Six more. That Angel of Death…. Together we can take him down," said another Reaper.

"The human who calls himself Oday Luhar; The erstwhile prophets rebuking the very purpose of Mritunjay… he has rebelled against God's decision to create one out of this Oday creature. The survival of the Humans is always prolonged after the advent of these prophets," said a third reaper.

"We grim reapers are merely the transitional modes from the realm of mankind to this realm. Our duty is not to protect the race," said the first reaper.

"And neither is it to witness its destruction," said the second reaper.

"Help or no help… we must fight back this Angel of Death," came the consensus.

Meanwhile, the souls of heaven and hell were marching up to their respective realm HQs protesting against the growing intolerance amongst the Grim Reapers.

* * *

Arjun, Oday and Shalini entered the trade-post of the SE. The place was strangely extremely silent. Just as silent as it was when Oday and Arjun had first come there. They slowly descended down to the basement. They opened the door to pitch black darkness. They switched the lights on. And weirdly there were two clicks of the switch. They turned around to see that Kunwar Madhao Singh stood alone in the middle of the basement pointing two guns at Arjun and Oday (in the wheelchair).

"Shalini….. Come down here behind me…" Kunwar said.

"You all shall die now…I caught them father. Come out now," Madhao continued.

"Wait…whatever Jai told you is a lie…" Oday said hurriedly.

"Jai didn't tell me anything… Wait… Who Jai?" Kunwar said in a shocked tone.

Rana Teja Singh walked down the hall from the inner corridor, closely followed by Aditya Luhar.

"Oday… WHAT ARE YOU DOING HERE… (To Kunwar) Put your gun down now," Aditya said as Kunwar kept his hands down.

"Dad. Why are you here at my office?" Oday tried to act innocent.

"They cannot do anything… She is your daughter for sakes…" Aditya said to Rana.

"Kunwar… let's go…" Rana said and left. Shalini followed.

"You boys come home soon…and give me your guns" Aditya said and left, taking Kunwar's Pistols.

"Mr. Trivedi… Who is this Jai?" Kunwar questioned.

"Jai M. Nirmal… we thought he is a spy sent by you to keep a look on us… that if we are working fine or not…" Arjun said.

"Jai M. Nirmal… M. Jai… I would meet you kids later…" Kunwar said and left as well.

From within the corridor came out dozens of the InfoTech workers.

"What was all that about Sir?" asked a worker.

"I don't know…" Arjun said.

"Are you keeping fine sire?" said another worker to Oday.

"Yes… where is Ananya?" Oday asked.

"Sir… CCTV… his body was found near the Gomti River" said the first worker.

"What!!!" Arjun said in shock.

"Where is Ananya?" Oday asked again.

"We suspect something similar has happened to her. She has been missing since a day."

"Missing since a day?" Arjun said.

"Arjun talked to her like ten hours ago. She said she is at the office…" Oday said.

"She hasn't been here sir… we are sure."

"These guys know about us… It is not long now that we would be targeted," Arjun said.

*   *   *

Arjun helped Oday into the CM Mansion. There Aditya was having a conversation with the Rana inside his room. Oday asked the orderlies to leave the two of them alone for better eavesdropping opportunities.

"You don't know that Rana… Whatever your son might be saying… My son knows allegiance to only me and the Ityadi," came the loud commanding voice of the Senior Luhar from inside the room.

"Your dad is defending you Suckhead," Arjun whispered to Oday.

"Your son is a naïve fool…" Rana said.

"Hey! That sucker… I would kill him. Dad would kill him," Oday said to Arjun.

"I know… I know he is a naïve fool. But that's what I am saying. He is immature. If he didn't have that Arjun boy with him he wouldn't know to make even the minutest of decisions," Aditya said.

Arjun giggled softly and turned to see that Oday was seeing red. He paused for a second and continued "Your father is right…"

"That fool who drools after my daughter; As Kunwar told me," Rana said.

"Even your father in law is right Pundit…" Oday retorted sarcastically.

The smiles on the faces of Oday and Arjun got faded when Rana said "I stopped Kunwar from killing them then. But he is mostly right in these matters and their fate has been decided."

Arjun gulped at the sentence.

Aditya said, "YOU CAN'T KILL MY SON."

Oday sighed in relief… just to be startled at the very next couple of words which the Senior Luhar uttered "NOT YET".

Oday and Arjun were stupefied.

Aditya continued "He might be useless but not completely futile for our political front. He will be the reason for my sympathy votes… The reason I would be protagonised the most. The reason our alliance shall get the brightest of receptions… subduing the controversies put forward by the state and the union opposition. You can do as you like with him post my campaigns. That is three and a half years. That might add to my manifesto at the centre. 'DEATH OF AN ONLY SON. STILL READY TO

FIGHT FOR THE NATION'. Mind it sir; I am a man of my word. When I said that I am ready to make Ityadi the state religion of the world, I meant it. The Chinese Ideal of no religion shall stand alone. It shall become the global religion. All those centres of religions shall be destroyed. There would be collateral damages. But the outstanding balance of humans, the enlightened remnants with one religion, the Ityadi, shall aid in the survival of the humans. There won't be a God. There won't be any disparity. When we have just one religion then we have no religion. For the Ityadi becomes our Identity. Like the 'Human Being'. And we shall rule that earth. If the earth is too large and diverse to be ruled by one man, then let's make it small and uniform… and let TWO of us rule it. To achieve the aim, I shall sacrifice anyone, be it family."

"And what about that Trivedi brat?" Rana asked.

"He is the brains of my son… But his father lives across the city. Dr. Nitin Trivedi. I guess you would be interested in him. And yes. My assistant has prepared a report on the man who calls himself 'Mangoman' and his two aides. Please look into it," Aditya said as the sound of a latch was heard and the front door apparently opened. Rana Teja Singh had left. Oday turned his chair around to find that Arjun had run towards the back-gate. He followed.

"Pundit…. PUNDIT… Listen first…" Oday shouted.

"My father Oday… they are going to kill him…" Arjun said in fear.

"They didn't say anything like that… Didn't you listen… Oh! Come on, I can't even pull or push you without hands or legs… Just friggin chase you," Oday said.

"Don't chase me Oday… I have just one man as family brother," Arjun said.

"And you call me brother while saying that... Listen for once mate... I am your family as well," Oday said. Arjun stopped.

"Thank God... Okay here's the thing. Firstly, we heard them talking, right? They DON'T KNOW who the masked man is. They were there with us because of something Kunwar told them which was maybe our spying on him. But not the hero thingy. Although I am not sure how Kunwar got to know of it all. Jai not being one of his own. Reminds me, where is Jai? Wasn't there, was he? Moving on... showing up at your father's place would be very suspicious. As dad said... he needs you because he needs me. He won't let anything happen to your father anytime soon," Oday said.

"Okay... what when this anytime soon ends? Would you kill your father?" Arjun said.

"We'd find another solution bro..." Oday said.

"Okay. I get it. But secondly?" Arjun asked.

"Yeah... and secondly... we didn't hear them talking..." Oday said.

*   *   *

The Earth is small but the World is Large. Strangely, it becomes larger as we close our eyes. This is given to the 'unimaginable' and 'incredible' making frequent cameos in our dreams. The massiveness of the world often makes us question a possible unification. But only those who can comprehend the earth above the world can unite it. For them the massiveness of the world intriguingly adds to the magnanimity of this unified small Earth. There have been a few capable of bringing forth this wonder. There are also those wannabe claimants who disregard all ethics of sanity to go to the utmost possible extent to end up a catastrophic and historical failure. Don't confuse, the former authentic ones also insanely go to the utmost extent but they end up partially succeeding. Ironically, both of them are mostly simultaneously commemorated, usually to contrast the antonyms of a specific field. Noble Leaders like Nelson Mandela and Abraham Lincoln dreamt of World Unification in some way or the other. They delivered more than the bidding of one man... Unifying the races of man. The primary prerequisite for World Unification into one Earth is acceptance of symbiotic existence. But all we point out are the differences amongst us. In the midst of being a male, female, old, young, black, white, long, short, fat, fit, Hindu, Muslim, Indian, Pakistani, Western, Eastern, Northern, Southern, Blonde, Brunette, Green-Eyed, Black-Eyed, Hairy, Hairless, Etcetera, we forget being a Human Being. And the ideal of the Human Being is not merely Intra-Species Unification but also Inter-Species Harmony. The very existence of a conscience amongst us indicates our sole purpose, that is to empathize the needs of others.

A man with a gun might kill twenty, but when raided by thousands, he is but powerless. The power of the Earth is in Solar Distinction... is in its Unity. Those whose ambition is to Unite the Earth to some extent by accepting differences, empowering the essence of mankind, they would only achieve this aim. Those whose ambition is to Unite the Earth by quashing the differences, solely to empower themselves, they can never achieve this aim. Such wannabe fascist Impotent Bastards like Lord Curzon, Adolf Hitler, Saddam Hussain, Osama bin Laden, Hafiz Saeed, Pervez Musharraf, Kim Jong-Un, Abu Bakr al-Baghdadi, Etcetera might have existed. But their conscienceless approach is always soon crushed by some or the other momentary saviour. Their infame and terror is also short-lived. The world cannot be 'ruled' by one man or one organization. It cannot be 'ruled' at all. Want to confirm this 'theory'. Sir Obama is the most powerful man in his country right? Well, of course, he has amazingly awesome powers (which he thankfully uses for America rather than the Gulf, contrary to some of his predecessors). But ask him one thing if you ever get to meet him while he is in his presidency. If he sanctions a bill which states that on every second Saturday of the month snowfall would happen, would nature comply? Ask our very loved honourable Prime Minister if he can order the animals of India to report at a rally of his. It's not to say that such wonders would be achieved if the world acts as one. But it's to say that if a being without conscience, acting on pure instinct, if it doesn't heed to the singular concentration of power then who are we Human Beings, who have a conscience and the self-righteousness to differ from right and wrong, to listen to the wrong of the world.

We listen to the leaders whom we perceive as one of us. The followers are mandatory for the leaders' existence, and they need something 'not so special' to follow. The unique and alien are hence segregated... and this very concept usually makes a man loyal to his religion/caste/creed/sex/organization/Etcetera respectively against the counterpart fragments. Such a dot which outstands the line holding it... the one who is special in his normality... he is The Mangoman.

*　　*　　*

Oday walked inside a room which had all the white interiors. There was white all around Oday as he turned in awe. He ran to God in a hurry.

"Tell me Oday…. Except for the two of us… what do you see in this room?" God asked.

"Ummm… That's easy… Nothing," Oday replied.

"Yes of course… it is easy… for the nothing you know… is the nothing you see," God said.

"Eh! I don't get it…," Oday said.

"Okay… Do you know Oday what was there before the Universe was created?" God asked.

"God darn it… That's too much you are asking of me… You upped the levels too soon… Can we go back to the nothing?" Oday said.

"Okay let me tell you… You must have heard of the Big Bang right?"

"Yeah… Chuck Norris' show… I know it… It is amazing… I love Howard Wolowitz…" Oday said.

"Firstly it is Chuck Lorre… and secondly… the Big Bang explosion… which created the Universe…. Ring a bell? It is one of your Human Hypotheses," God said.

"Pundit might have told me that… so what about it?" Oday said.

"Here we go… Before the big bang or the so-called Universe creation… there was nothing… not even I… I asked you what do you see in this room apart from Us… you said 'nothing' right? But as long as you can sense it or imagine it or perceive it… it isn't nothing. Even Human mind… as long as it is alive… always projects some or the other thing inside itself. There can never be 'nothing'. So before the creation of the Universe… There was NOTHING… not even a room with completely white interiors… You get me?" God said.

"Waaaiiitttt a second…… What the hellll…. I can walk and use my limbs and all… yippeeee…" Oday started jumping in excitement.

"And we are back to square zero… So Oday… you get me right?" God asked.

"Yeah Yeah… continue continue" Oday said.

"So yes… After the creation of the Universe… there were certain anomalies. I was the out-product of one of them. I was quite an appreciator of the Universal Beauty, hence I created the species on Earth using the powers granted to me by that anomaly, to explore and rejoice the beauty. There were certain refuters who tried to sway me to not 'waste' my powers. But I used them nevertheless. So the point is that you people need to Unite. And you Oday… you should work towards that goal. No matter what hindrances appear," God said.

"Okay Sir… Aye Aye to that," Oday said.

"Now you may go back to being a handicapped" God remarked sarcastically.

"Oh No! Okay I am going… Kudos" Oday took his leave.

Sameera walked inside the room.

"Sir, you didn't tell him about Mritunjay… or Him…" she said.

"Let's see what happens next…" God said.

22

A silent suburban corner of Lhasa, Tibet. The undue silence of the night was slightly broken by the heavy-bass growl of a large black tank-shaped car$_{84}$. The car door slid open. Oday stepped out of the car wearing a bat-suit with a yellow cape. He used the batclaw$_{85}$ to reach the roof of a building. From there he safely maneuvered to the inner hall.

"Pundit Come in… No signs of motion except for rats as the radar shows right now. Switching to night vision. Yeah. The infrared scan shows a few lifeforms. There are humans. Strangely though… they are cold. Maybe dead. Moving on…. Searching for the quoted stock. Nothing on the first floor… moving on to the second. So how is everyone doing at base" Oday said to Arjun across his transmitter.

Back at the Shalini Enterprise Trade-Post in Lucknow, Arjun, Shalini, Shalini's Butler and all the employees stood together in front of a massive screen which was sending video-feedback from the camera on Oday's shoulder.

"Everybody is still quite excited about you Oday… You keep doing the good work" Arjun said. Shalini was busy filing her finger nails.

"That traitor son of a bitch Jai isn't there is he?" Oday asked.

"Yeah… Though his absence is as convenient as it is suspicious," Arjun remarked.

"Wait a sec… I am getting something," Oday said, alerted by his beeping scanner.

"Whatever it is… It is huge bro," Arjun said.

"They don't seem your usual radioactive fuel or stones," A techspert prompted.

Oday opened up a huge metal container. The inside of the container showed huge missile shaped devices piled up together in a set pattern.

"What the hell is that?" Oday asked.

"Those are… missiles… Wait a second. The intel about the plutonium and uranium deal was whispered by one of the reliable aides of the old CCTV. This can't be right. What would they have missiles for?" Arjun said.

"Pundit… this is strange. The scanner picks up radioactivity from these missiles as well. And that too huge amounts," Oday said.

"What… it cannot be. A warhead cannot be that small in size. The only ones that are possibly that small are the ones virtually blueprinted under the Russian Mini-Fission-Warhead Prototype-RS646," Arjun remarked with a whimsical laugh.

"Pundit…" Oday said.

"Yo bro…" Arjun said casually.

"It reads here RMFWPRS646-EGI9 on one of them," Oday said.

"Russian Mini-Fission-Warhead Prototype RS646 coded EGI9…" Arjun screamed.

"There are about 20 or 30 of them here… I am going to the next container," Oday said.

"30 mini-warheads can destroy all the Indian capitals sir," Said one of the techsperts.

"Only if they managed to smuggle the launchers as well," Arjun said.

"Pundit… the second container seems to contain things shaped as missile launchers," Oday said.

"Holy mother of God these are RS646 launchers…" Arjun shockingly said in reaction to the picture on the big screen.

"What do you mean by mini-warheads anyway?" Shalini questioned.

"These are…" a techspert started as he was interrupted by Arjun "Let me… babe. One warhead is a nuclear bomb which can destroy thousand Eiffel Towers in one go…" Arjun said.

"That's so bad. I mean who would want to destroy the Eiffel Towers. I love all thousand of them," Shalini said as she continued to file her nails.

"There is just…" the techspert interrupted again, only to be stopped by Arjun "Never mind… Let's focus on the big picture here…"

"Okay… there are four more containers full of missiles here. Unlike GTA_{86}, we have more ammo than weapons," Oday said.

"In the peaceful land of Dalai Lama, we have an Arsenal which can destroy half of North India. Russian weapons, smuggled through Tibet and Nepal by China, to be sold to an Indian for use against the whole religious world… Now this is some globalization here… Okay… Jokes' off. Can you transport them in the bat_{87}?" Arjun said.

"I guess," Oday said.

As Oday began to think his modus operandi, the sound of clanging metal came from the lower floor. Oday stood alerted. He started scanning the lower floors. But he couldn't find anything.

"There's nothing there pundit..." Oday said.

"Yeah I know... nothing except for dead bodies. Must have been some animal," Arjun said.

"Wait a second... Dead Bodies. Where are the..." Oday's voice feedback cut off from Arjun's network.

"Oday... Odayyyy... ODAYYYY... What the hell happened? The screen went off..." Arjun screamed. Even Shalini got alarmed this time.

"It is not at our end sir... Sir Oday's comms are down," Said one of the techsperts.

"Shalini... How fast can you get clearance for flying into Tibet through Nepal?" Arjun asked.

"On to it Sir," Said Shalini's Butler.

"Just what is going on there... Hang on Oday. We are on our way..." said Arjun.

*   *   *

Oday sat naked and tied to a chair in a yellow-green haggard room. He woke up and tried to regain his full consciousness.

"Where is this place?" Oday said to himself.

He recalled being trapped by a swarm of heavily armed soldiers who had been pretending to be the 'dead bodies'.

"You are in the Kunwar's captivity" came a familiar female voice from within the shadows.

"Who is it?" Oday asked.

The woman came forward. She was Ananya.

"You... You work for the Kunwar..." Oday asked.

"I work for no one... Kunwar is my lover... I was just keeping an eye on threats against him..." Ananya said.

"You were the mole… you… and we suspected Amit… and Jai," Oday said.

"Ohhh! Amit… poor guy. He caught me talking to Kunwar over the phone. Had to kill him off for certain. And then came CCTV. He had seen me and Kunwar make-out. Had to get rid of him as well," Ananya said.

"You killed them yourself?" Oday asked.

"With these very hands," Ananya replied.

"But why did YOU disappear then, if you had such a good disguise… I mean you convinced me that there was something between us…" Oday said.

Kunwar Madhao Singh walked inside the room with a doctor.

"She disappeared because her disguise and her acting convinced even me, that there was something between you two. Not to lose my girl, I had to take certain steps," Kunwar said.

Kunwar turned Oday's seat around towards a screen. The screen showed the very building where Oday had found the mini-warheads. The Shalini Enterprise chopper hovered above the building. Arjun, Shalini and Shalini's butler stepped out of the chopper to investigate the place. Shalini's armed guards had accompanied her.

"My silly little sister… and the boyfriend… of both you and her… they wouldn't leave their dear Oday to die, would they? Little do they know that the Stock has already been exported to India. And also… there are bombs inside timed to a puny little twenty minutes," Madhao said.

"You rat… let them go… you have me. Why do you want them? She is your family…" Oday said.

"Family… Whatever the fuck you call it… It doesn't stand against my agenda… even a bit… She would be a good sacrifice. Just like you are your Father's… although he is not willing to have you dead, just crippled, but I would convince him after your demise. Sadly, Professor Nitin Trivedi is the only family member of one of the to-be-deceased who is not going to be benefited by the death," Kunwar said.

"You are gonna kill me? What are you waiting for?" Oday asked.

"I'm waiting for my father to come and corroborate. Maybe, as earlier suggested, he might wanna experiment on you for finding the reasons behind your powers. Although I would want nothing more than killing you… Meanwhile (turned Oday around again) say your goodbyes to your friends… in your heart I mean. For you would be living a bit longer than them… Okay… Sedate him…" Kunwar said as the doctor walked up to Oday and injected him with a sedative, rendering him unconscious again. Kunwar and the doctor left, closing the door behind them.

Ananya turned the screen off and walked up to Oday.

"Crippled, Tied AND Sedated… what better condition can you be in… for me to do anything I want to you…" Ananya said and bent down and kissed Oday. She soon noticed that Oday was kissing her back. She stepped back and fell in shock.

"Femme Fatale domination bondage didn't arouse me… strangely… Now this is surprising… I have finally experienced everything…" Oday said.

"How can you be awake after the sedative?" Ananya asked.

"Now Now… The thing is… I have learnt the art of keeping time. And back in Lhasa… my time wasn't over yet…" Oday broke out of the rope and stood up as clothing appeared over his body. He wore a yellow mask and cape with a uniform. The centre of the uniform displayed in big letters 'M'.

"You miss… are going to hell," Oday said rushing to Ananya to knock her out. He then disappeared.

Back at Lhasa, Shalini and Arjun, with their huge convoy, had entered the isolated building for finding traces of proofs of Oday's disappearance. Shalini caught sight of a blinking and faintly beeping red light in a corner of the building. She asked her butler to go and investigate. He went close to it. Just as he did, Oday appeared in front of him "It is a bomb… A BOMB… ONE OF MANY… RUN OUT OF HERE… FAR FROM HERE…"

"It is counting down," said Shalini's butler.

"Yes it is," Oday said.

"You are alive brother… I'm so happy… But how much time do we have… I mean for collecting evidence?" Arjun asked.

"I am not so good at keeping time here… Okay… let's run from here and then do the talking," Oday said as everybody rushed outside. They all boarded the chopper and were on their safe passage back to India, just when an RPG hit the rear rotor. The chopper hurled down in the midst of a six-lane highway, disrupting the traffic. A huge mass of cars and choppers started surrounding the crashed copter. The passengers were trying to get a hold of themselves as Kunwar Madhao Singh and Rana Teja Singh stepped down of two of the hovering choppers near the crashed one. The Kunwar held a microphone in his arm.

"Oday Singh Luhar… You and your friends have lived your days… and Shalini… you should come here right away…" Kunwar said.

Oday stepped out and ran at a lightning speed planning to attack Madhao. But his time went out in the middle of his run-up and he slowed down and fell down.

"How pitiable are you Mr. Luhar..." Kunwar said pointing a gun at Oday.

"No brother..." Shalini said.

"You come over here sister... As fast as you can..." the Kunwar said.

"You would never beat those whom the God himself has blessed with the responsibility of supporting the realm of man..." Oday said.

"And you cannot defeat a man who even the Gods cannot stop from dominating the realm of man... Well technically... one of the two men..." Kunwar said.

"Two? Oday's father is also part of this rubbish ordeal of yours isn't he? That makes three..." Arjun said. There came a sudden noise of a gunshot followed by a dark and evil laughter. There was utter silence. The Kunwar had shot. But it was not the shot which shocked them... that was inevitable seeing the current circumstances. It was the target. It was none other than his very own father Rana Teja Singh. The bullet pierced through the Rana's head and he fell down still.

"Daaaaddddd..." Shalini shouted in pain.

"Why be a prince... when the seat of the king is right there in front of you.... And as such... I hate making compromises... Unlike my father... Our new partnership would work out pretty well..." Kunwar said as Aditya Luhar stepped out of a white Rolls Royce.

"We had no use for him anymore... He served his final purpose of sympathy. As would you my son. Don't worry... I won't let you die. But as for your friends back there... Their time is up. Kill them off Madhao..." Aditya said.

Madhao raised his gun towards Shalini. Arjun ran in front of her.

"You can't shoot her..." Arjun said.

Just as Madhao loaded his pistol to take the shot, a man flew in out of nowhere and punched Kunwar in the face. He was Mritunjay. Kunwar flew more than a hundred yards across the road and got buried in a rock-rubble.

"JAI???" Oday said in a surprised tone.

"Ohhh…. That is Jai… Or if I may call you Mritunjay," Kunwar said, coming out of the rubble.

Meanwhile, Shalini was mourning beside the body of her father.

"What are you crying about Shalini? There is no need for the existence of such a paper-tiger…" Kunwar mocked with an arrogant smirk on his face.

"The end of the realms of man is inevitable… I will destroy the essence of life of whosoever stands in front of me…" Mritunjay said.

Aditya shot Mritunjay with his gun. The bullet pierced through his neck and he fell down. But only seconds later, he got up. His wounds started healing themselves at a conspicuous speed.

He turned to Arjun, who had been consoling Shalini. Arjun gazed at the jaw-dropping moment.

"What are you startled at? You think your friend there is the only one? We, who have been called demi-gods, seraphs, prophets, miracle-workers… we have been there since the beginning. I say we…though it is just I who has survived. Soon God had consumed most of his powers to grant this power of preservation and direction," Mritunjay said.

"There have been others? What happened to them?" Arjun inquired.

"They all succumbed to a plague and soon passed away," Mritunjay said.

"What plague?" Arjun asked.

Kunwar suddenly appeared in front of Arjun.

"The plague… Called Me…" Kunwar said as he turned and punched Mritunjay. Mritunjay flew the same way Kunwar had flown earlier.

"What the hell!!! How can you…" Arjun exclaimed.

"Kunwar…" Aditya murmured in a surprised and ambiguous tone.

"You go back to the car Mr. CM. This fight is going to be intense… and You sir… are our necessity. We can't lose you as collateral damage," Kunwar said.

Aditya ran back to the car without even glancing at the impaired Oday.

"Dad……" Oday mumbled in his semi-conscious condition. A tear drop ran down his numb cheeks.

"See… Me… the anomaly… the first one. I have been called Devil, Satan, Diablo, The King of Hell, The King of Demons, Shaitaan, Sathariel, Sataniel, Lucifer, and many other heart-chilling names. Mind it… I am not a reincarnation or a failed result of God using his copyright. I am the incarnation of all that is God and all that is power… I am Madhao…" Kunwar said.

"And who is he?" Arjun said pointing towards the direction where Mritunjay had fallen earlier.

Mritunjay ran and punched Madhao and flew along with him. A helicopter came close to the site and descended close to the road. Shalini's butler came to Arjun and helped him to lift Oday.

"Miss Shalini. The pick-up has arrived. Hurry," He said as the trio followed him to the chopper. Aditya Luhar came out of his car and asked his people to chase them down. Shalini asked her guards to provide cover fire for them to escape. They all safely boarded the copter and it left. The only copter to have been successful in following their chopper was soon shot down by Shalini's Butler.

"Whoa… Nice shot," Arjun said. He then sat beside Shalini to comfort her.

"Thank you Sir… Now where to?" Shalini's Butler said.

"Our trade-post… we need to collect our people and relocate," Shalini said, regathering her resolve.

"I'm sorry about your father Miss. I never liked your brother myself," Shalini's Butler said.

"Drop me on a helipad close to my home will you? I got to check on my Father. Get Oday checked up also…" Arjun said.

"Yes sir…" Shalini's Butler replied.

"And one more thing…" Arjun said.

"Yes sir?"

"What's your name anyway?" Arjun asked.

"Call me The Butler, Sir," Shalini's Butler said.

"Okay, Whatever… Just take me home… With God, Angels and Demons… It has been hell of a long day already…" Arjun said.

"Angels and Demons… hey… that's the wrong book…" Oday uttered.

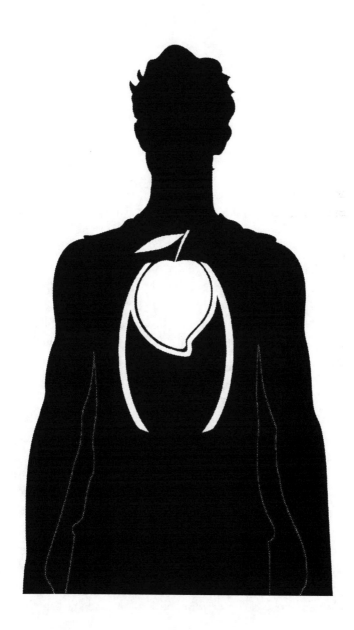

23

A secluded ravine in north-western India. The IPU president, Rajat Singhania, stood there a natural pariah. The only geographical anomaly was his car. He stood there all alone. Perhaps waiting for someone. His phone started to ring. He received the call.

"Yes Mr. Prime Minister. Oh No No I can take care of this. I have no dropout ideas. This exchange of confidantes and critical information will definitely prove beneficial for the IPU... and for the IPU alone. For that... I would ensure. As such Raj wouldn't know what to do with it in the first place. We have a General Modus Operandi. We are bureaucrats at our core.... Why would I be afraid sir? Have you forgotten already? A man who gets confused between corruption and rape, who thinks that the women of Gujrat gave Gujrat its milk, who gets nightmares from the mere idea of having to speak fractions on stage, who has solemnly stated in the media that IDU is for the young males and females to 'enjoy' and who gets up every morning at night, I am not afraid of that man. Although the confusion between the corrupt and the rapist is justified. I mean the kid gets confused amongst who's who in his party. Nevertheless, Raj Gautam is parsecs away from politics. For God sakes, politics is in his pant, not his brain. The dumbest, stupidest, dullest mind out there is Raj Gautam. Advocate Ram once said he won't hire Raj as his Office Clerk, right? I won't hire Raj as my gardener. Okay, he is here… let's talk later… Good Day" Rajat said, hanging up the phone to greet the incoming car.

Meanwhile, Rajat uttered to himself "God… Politics teaches you so much Tolerance. You have to appease your Intra-Party rival for the Prime-Ministerial Candidature. Damn you for doing good work Mr. PM. What does the diligent activist who won from Lucknow get? The consolation prize of Home Minister. Why didn't he just be like "Awwwwwwwww" while giving that portfolio to me?"

Raj stepped out of his SUV in his Yellow Bermuda-pants, White T-shirt, Black Floaters and Pink-Wayfarers. He whistled along his way to where Rajat was standing. Rajat held his laughter, contrary to the Universe which was giggling in the background at this unique specimen. Apparently, his days at the IPU had taught him diplomacy quite well. And the trained diplomat stepped forward to greet his arch-rival.

"Hello Mr. Gautam," Rajat moved to shake Raj's hand. Raj complied and greeted him back.

"Have you brought the drafts?" Raj asked.

"Yes indeed I have. Have you?" Rajat replied.

"Yep…" Raj went back to his SUV and opened its trunk. Rajat lifted the briefcase kept on his car's bonnet and awaited Raj. Raj came back with a fancy briefcase of his own.

"You can check it Rajat," Raj said.

"No," Rajat said.

"You trust is flattering," Raj said.

"Yes, I trust my actions if in case they are fake," Rajat said in a bold voice.

Raj was busy checking the suitcase he held and thus ignored the otherwise offensive and condescending remark. He suddenly got restless and turned around.

"What the hell is this?" Raj screamed.

"What do you mean? They are exactly what you asked for," Rajat replied, keeping his calm.

"How do I know they are genuine?" Raj questioned.

"You shall go and get them verified on field Mr. Gautam," Rajat replied.

"But what about preliminary varication? Where is the attestation?" Raj asked.

"What attestation?" Rajat counter-questioned.

"See my documents first," Raj said. Rajat opened up the briefcase and saw that all the pages had a stamp which read "Dr. B. Singh, Principal Secretary of Education, Uttar Pradesh" with a signature attestation at the top.

"What is this?" Rajat asked in confusion.

"I was reading the norms of verification of documents for an Indian Citizen. And it said that they are to be attested by a Gazetted Officer and only then would they be considered officially verified," Raj said. At this very statement, its structure, the words it held and the dialect of Raj, Rajat started internally pitying his position as the counterpart of Raj on the Political front. Just being in the same category as Raj was demeaning and insulting for Rajat. He was lost in his thoughts. Raj went to his car murmuring "I had prepared for such incident," while Rajat tried to construct a comprehensible sentence after the idiotic remark by Raj, the latter came with a machine gun. Rajat stood still, still confused.

"I stole it from my bodyguard. It is loaded. Now prepare to die," Raj said.

*   *   *

"Breaking News.... The IPU president, Rajat Singhania, was found lying unconscious in a card junkyard in Chandigarh. He was taken to PGI and was seen to by all the senior doctors. They have declared that Mr. Singhania has received life-threatening wounds from an unidentified weapon and is still in a temporal coma. The forensics and the CBI have also come to the aid of the IPU President and are currently investigating the reports and finding traces and proofs for nailing down a possible suspect. The car-junkyard owner has been called in for questioning. So tonight at NewsHourAndAHalf, we are going to debate on the very important question that "VVIP Racism in government hospitals and organizations." You people go through so much trouble for getting appointments in these government hospitals. But these politicians come by and encroach upon your time without any prior notification. Can this be allowed in a Sovereign, Socialist, Secular, Democratic Republic? Hash-Tag VVIPRajat. Tune into NewsHourAndAHalf tonight. Keep tweeting and Keep Watching, Times Then," Said Arlub on the television screen of Shalini's home. Oday sat in his wheelchair while Shalini and all the S.E. Techsperts stood in the big hall, gazing at the television.

"I still don't believe that Ananya killed Amit and CCTV," said one of the employees.

"What about Rajat Singhania? What do you think happened to him?" asked Shalini.

"We are still trying to figure out. We are here tracking his footsteps in reverse. We would tell you as soon as we get to know ma'am," said another worker, typing rigorously on his laptop.

Shalini started dialling Arjun's number.

"Hello. Yes, jaan where are you? I have told you so many times, bring your father here. Making tea for him huh? Okay, I would send a car whenever you feel like. Don't worry babe, I'd always listen to you," Shalini said on the phone.

She then continued to her Butler "Send two cars to Arjun's home and get him and his father here as soon as possible, Okay? Don't listen to him at all."

"Okay… But Shalini. Although Arjun is the smarter of the two of us, I still know from virtual experience that the best place to hide from Mogambo$_{88}$ is not his sister's house," Oday said. Suddenly there came a crashing sound in the balcony. They all rushed to see to it. They saw that Mritunjay had come flying down to their house. They all took a defensive stance and stood back. The guards pointed their guns at Mritunjay. Shalini interrogated.

"Why are you here?" Shalini asked.

On close observation, they all saw that Mritunjay was severely injured and more so impaled through his abdomen by a small stake.

"Help me… I promise not to hurt you," Mritunjay pleaded.

"What makes you think we would help the likes of you?" Shalini said.

Oday started moving his wheelchair slowly towards Mritunjay. He then got up from his chair, disconnected his cords and kneeled down beside Mritunjay to heal him. Mritunjay groaned as Oday took the stake out. He then hovered his hands over Mritunjay. A blue light appeared within his hand and Mritunjay's wounds started to patch up. A few seconds later, Oday stopped and came back to his chair.

"What was that about, ODAY? It seems like Arjun IS your brain… Why did you heal him?" Shalini questioned furiously.

"I only healed him half way through. Enough for him to survive his telling us all of it," Oday said.

"Telling us what?" Shalini asked.

Oday gazed at Mritunjay expecting a dramatic epilogue. The random 'Once upon a time' would have worked well for him. But Mritunjay rather asked for a drink inside the house. They all carried him to the guest room and laid him down on the bed. They surrounded him like serious investigators and he started-

"In the beginning, God tried to create the perfect being of existence. After many experiments, he could finally create the Human Being. Every being created had fragments of God's power of creation and existence. Then, whenever he saw his perfect species go astray, he created preservers as me, to help the species survive. We were the special children, with capabilities beyond human imagination, and the special right of being beside the God himself. But..." Mritunjay said.

"But... what about Kunwar... or the Devil?" Oday inquired.

"But... Just like God... there was another anomaly who looked to explore the Universe. These Universal anomalies, specific to our Galaxy, were two beings in one. The extreme Good and the extreme Bad. Together they could have had their flags in all corners of the Universe. But the other anomaly was a hasty one. Seeing this trait, God chose never to coalesce with him. Never to use him as an ally. And God used his powers in a different and slower way to explore the extremities of the Universe. That was unbearable for the Devil. The power he sought was divided amongst the beings of the world. All he sought was to integrate the beings of the world into himself," Mritunjay said.

"But why doesn't God just destroy Kunwar?" Oday asked.

"He could have. God was always the superior of the two. But he has expended most of his powers in creation. He is not that powerful anymore. The very reason the human existence is to perish right away. Damn, I am not as powerful to do that anymore," Mritunjay said.

"Why do you want to kill us all?" Oday asked again.

"You don't understand do you? If you are allowed to exist, then the Devil would use you to win. All other preservers have been destroyed. Within every man there is a God. And that God is being absorbed by Devil slowly and consistently. All that matters to you people is your puny little lifetime. Mere political motives drive humans to succumb to whatever is evil. I, the last surviving Preserver, don't see any more purpose for God to let you exist. When God would be empowered, we would use that power to destroy the Devil. But that's now just a thing my imagination. Kunwar has seized all my powers. The residue was used by me to get here. We have no resolve. This fight is over," Mritunjay said.

"What does politics have to do with this? Why choose this way when there are other more prudent ways... like destroying the earth?" Oday asked.

"The people have to actually revere Kunwar as their leader, directly or indirectly. Only then can he gain the power of their soul. Otherwise they would go directly to God. And that is what I wanted to do," Mritunjay said.

The air started getting denser and winds started blowing inside the room. Three men and two women appeared out of thin air, levitating within the room. The others within the room either fell or braced themselves out of shock.

"Mritunjay the Angel of Death. You have been charged with the murder of seven Grim Reapers including our King

Martin Messorem and General Raj," Said one of the female reapers.

"Who are they?" Shalini yelled.

"Now these are those who ensure that the souls of the dying are taken to God. The grim reapers," Mritunjay said.

"You murdered Martin? The reaper who revived my soul after I committed suicide when Arjun had left me for Shalini…" Oday said.

"That's weird… but Awwwwwwwww… you are such a good friend," Shalini remarked ignorantly.

"Yes, he murdered Martin. We are here to take him to the Eternal Gallows," said the woman.

"Aroma, you lead them now?" Mritunjay asked.

"Yes I do, and you come along with us. Your powers shall be drained and locked away," Aroma said.

"Aroma, do you know what is happening here?" Mritunjay asked.

"You cannot use another trick to escape Mritunjay. Don't stall the inevitable," Aroma said.

"Aroma. What if I told you the worst fears of the Grim Reapers have come true? What if I said, that he has been found? Alive, well and as powerful as ever?" Mritunjay asked.

"Then I would say you are again stalling by inducing fear," Aroma said.

"You think I killed Martin? I had just let him off unconscious after he came after me. And I don't even know about the other six. Believe me if you can else don't. I am rendered powerless by the one you call Kunwar Madhao Singh. Or in other words, The Devil," Mritunjay said.

Aroma closed her eyes and opened a few seconds later.

"He is right. He feels close to a human now. No more the Godly powers you had gained. And you claim that this Kunwar Madhao Singh is the Devil?" Aroma said.

"Yes, Indeed," Mritunjay said.

"We shall go and verify your claim," Aroma said and started levitating again.

"Only if you want to risk being the eighth," Mritunjay said.

"How else would we verify your plea?" Aroma asked.

"Ask him," Mritunjay pointed at Oday.

"Who is he to verify? A mere human," Aroma said.

"He is Oday Singh Luhar. The one Martin was protecting. The one God has chosen," Mritunjay claimed in a prophetical tone driving a stimulus of anxiety and importance through Oday's impaired spine.

"Oday Luhar. Yes, we heard of him. But why is he crippled?" Aroma asked.

"Ammmm… Long story. But skipping to the important part. He's right. Kunwar is the Devil. Although I don't know who killed your people, but I can say that Kunwar would definitely be my prime suspect. He evil," Oday said.

"And now we have nothing but to give in to the power of that evil. We have lost," Mritunjay followed.

"As long as we have a preserver amongst us, we haven't lost," Aroma said.

"Ahem Ahem… I just told you I have lost my powers," Mritunjay said.

"We are not talking about you," Aroma said turning towards Oday. The reapers all stared at Oday in thrilling co-ordination.

"You've got to be kidding me. At the pinnacle of our powers, none of us could beat him. And this insult for a preserver, for a prophet, you think he can stand even a minute against that Monster. He is winning… on every field. The political and the physical. We are immensely outmatched," Mritunjay said.

"What do you mean I am a prophet?" Oday asked. Everyone in that room widened their eyes peering at Oday.

"Oday Singh Luhar. As much as a weakling you might be compared to us beings of heaven, you are the last prophet, the last icicle of God's power and our last hope," Aroma said.

"He is our last hope... I have definitely lost hope," Mritunjay said.

"Last icicle of God's power. What does that mean?" Shalini asked.

"God had very little powers remaining. And the very few he had left, he entrusted in Oday. Thus he can use them only for an hour in a day. And every time he does, a fragment of God dissolves in the Universe," Aroma said.

"Another reason I wanted to destroy you first," Mritunjay said.

"Mritunjay. Although you haven't successfully advocated your stand, your case hearing has now been postponed and your absolution, if it shall be true, then is a thing for another day. For now, we are to see to Mr. Oday Luhar. He was under our former King's protection. And I, Aroma Menace, the queen of the Grim Reapers, am to see after the existence and preservation of the prophet," Aroma said.

"Good luck with that. Just do me a favour. Do kill me before dying. I don't want to see God extinguish," Mritunjay said.

"You believe the one entrusted with the ultimate responsibility is weak? He might be a weakling, but he is not weak," Aroma said.

"But it is not possible for him to defeat Kunwar. No matter what," Mritunjay said.

"The followers are the greatest power of a leader. Those who followed God are now walking in the paths of the Devil. We need to regain the support. Even sheer faith would re-strengthen God to oust the Devil from the realms of the beings," Aroma said.

"But how? The world has become very huge. No matter what, there can't be a unification. The cultures everywhere are different. China, the demographically largest, is majorly ungodly. And those in India are divided into a plethora and a paradox. Just how would you unify them? We need an immediate plan of action. Millennium of our efforts to gain unity in the immense diversity, and you think it can be done so fast and easy?" Mritunjay questioned.

"We do what they do. We play politics," Aroma said.

"Politics you say. Who amongst us bunch of nerds, fallen angel, group of Grim Reapers and two dumbasses knows politics?" Mritunjay asked.

"Arjun can help us with that. My father always praised his witty and intellectual thinking," Oday said.

"That kid. Nuh Uh," Mritunjay said.

"If the preserver persists then this Arjun can lead," Aroma said.

"But how would you unify them? What is it that you shall use? What is it that is so common and loved? What can be a possible representation of God or the Good? There is no such thing my dear. There is no hope," Mritunjay said.

Just immediately after Mritunjay's monologue, the back door slightly opened, showing Arjun's hoodied back. He came in looking down, saying "My dad's here Shalini."

He then turned around and was dumbstruck at the sight of the huge clique of visitors, including the wounded angel and the levitating Reapers. In his hand, he held a huge jute back.

"Whoa…" He gulped down his throat and took out a huge ripe yellow mango from his bag.

"Mangoes?" he asked, presenting the one he held in front of everyone.

"They are Good... Sweet (stammered)... Everyone loves them.... There is enough for everybody," he tried to regain his senses.

"Good, Sweet, Loved and Sufficient... Who might you be sir?" Aroma asked.

"I am Arjun Trivedi," Arjun answered.

"Arjun... and Mangoes... the hope is getting stronger by the minute," Aroma said, coming down.

"Oh Come on... that was just a co incidence," Mritunjay said.

"And a favourable co-incidence it was. So Mr. Arjun Trivedi. What would you say if I tell you that you are to be the next Prime Minister of India?" Aroma asked.

"Okay... I just saw you floating in the air... and now I am confused as to which one of us IS drunk," Arjun remarked sarcastically.

"He is good of speech. He shall suffice," Aroma said.

"Then you will need this," Mritunjay said, taking out a small black case from his pocket. He opened the case showing three pen drives.

"What's that?" Oday asked.

"These are all the proofs you need to bring the Ityadi down," Mritunjay said.

"Hey! You have computers in heaven too? Awesome!!!" Oday regained his senseless senses.

24

"You see what they did to Eklavya Mishra? As soon as he arranged for truce with the northern separatists, they killed him. Brutally. Shot him down with more than a dozen bullets and then burned him along with a building. They crippled my only son. Rajat Singhania, who had just allied himself with us, was attacked. Raj Gautam is missing. Our dear Rana Teja Singh has been slain at their hands. Whomsoever we bring to our cause, whomsoever we convince to unite for the front of humanity over the front of disparity, they are brought down. And by whom? Who orchestrates them? Do the real Pundits, Mullahs, Padres, Etcetera ever indulge in religious terrorism? Never. These are the self-proclaimed masters of their turf who have risen to power on the basis of domination. We, at the Ityadi, seek to bring them down. Only then can India and subsequently the whole world unite. The files are here and Kunwar Madhao would discuss them with you in the press conference later. Let's be the change, Let's be the Ityadi. Thank You," Aditya Luhar concluded his speech in his rally near the Gateway of India.

In the capital of Uttar Pradesh, Lucknow, our heroes sat in front of the big television glancing at the speech live.

"You think I can compete with that? Babe, aren't you gonna say something?" Arjun said.

"I love you. And I trust you," Shalini said as she held Arjun's hand.

"Behind every successful man there is a woman, kicking his ass to go further towards success," Arjun said in an irritated tone.

"That's what we need. The sarcastic and hysterical "quote-manipulator" Arjun Trivedi," Aroma said.

"But why do I need to become the P.M. We already have an amazingly awesome P.M. who is also pretty more experienced and specifically POWERFUL than I would ever be," Arjun said.

"Yes we have. But he doesn't know about the dangers we are facing. Although Oday Luhar is busy bringing his party president to us, we still don't know whether they would deliver and aid as asked," Aroma said.

An S.E. worker rushed inside the room.

"Sir, Madams. We have compiled all the data. As per the information Jai brought to us, we have collected CCTV footages and satellite locations and all other important tracking details of all the illicit activities going on under the Ityadi. The works range from drug deals to human-trafficking, to weapon deals, to nuclear deals. These, if and when presented before the world in a prominent way, would bring them down."

"That's Good. But what is Jai up to now?" Arjun asked.

"He is currently in para-sleep. Conversing with God regarding making Mangoes the subject of leadership," Aroma said.

"That's Good. But how does that work?" Arjun asked.

"Mangoes, as you said, are quite common. We just have to instil the idea amongst people that whoever is eating a mango supports God and his representatives and is against Kunwar and Aditya or both. They agree or don't agree, if the idea persists, our mother tree would grow. And once it flowers, it'll release the Eternal Mango. As soon as God tastes it, he would gain the support of the world and he can then bring down the Devil," Aroma said.

"But the whole world doesn't eat mangoes regularly and that dedicatedly. Mostly in the Indian sub-continent but rarely elsewhere," Arjun said.

"That's where your diplomacy comes to test," Aroma said.

"But how?" Arjun asked.

"We would start by declaring that the Mangoman supports us. Hopefully, that would gain the attention of the populous," Aroma said.

Oday appeared in the room wearing his Uniform, with Rajat on his shoulders.

"Here comes the hero. So would you reveal his identity?" Arjun asked.

"My identity? Whoa Whoa… I don't wanna risk dying," Oday said.

"Adnan is on to it. He has been creating an event over social media, inviting a gathering of people. Although against your country's laws, but that's the only immediate way," Aroma said.

"Hey… Don't say anything to me when you are water-cannoned or subject to tear gas considering the fact that the state police under the Ityadi would probably be against our cause and existence. Wait… do Reapers cry? Ok, one last question. Who's Adnan?" Arjun asked.

"It is me sir. I am the co-ordinator of the S.E. Techsperts after Amit's demise and Ananya's treachery," said a man entering the room.

"Hey… I have Union Police on my back… technically…" Oday said and laid Rajat down on the bed and started to heal him. He then sat back in his wheelchair and waited for the Home Minister to wake up. Shalini's Butler came in with a message.

"There has been a meeting scheduled between the Prime Minister and the Ityadi senior leaders. He has apparently believed the Senior Luhar's statements regarding the attack on the Home Minister. The doctors have officially declared that Mr. Rajat Singhania would not survive. The critical political situation might cause a National Emergency. Even the IDU is supporting it due to the disappearance of their prince Raj Gautam. It's all over the news. These parties might unite," the Butler said.

"But Shalini… I am worried. This is the most obvious establishment for your brother to find us at. Why hasn't he come to obliterate us off the face of earth yet?" Arjun asked.

Mritunjay came in the room.

"That is something worrying me as well. Nevertheless, the deed is done. Aroma, since I am powerless now, it is you who has to go to heaven to receive the mother seed. But there is something else which worries me more," Mritunjay said.

"I am going. You help the people here in completing their tasks. Arjun… Start the campaign. And begin it with recording his statements," Aroma pointed towards Rajat, who had now woken up, and then she disappeared.

"Good evening Sir, I am Arjun Trivedi. And this is Oday Luhar, the man who saved you," Arjun said.

Rajat started scanning himself for signs of prior injury but laid astounded at finding none.

"What is happening here? Where am I?" Rajat asked, perspiring nervously.

"Sir, let us tell you everything…" Arjun started acquainting Rajat with the happenings of the near past.

"Hey… Are any of you listening to what I have to say? I am talking about the accident which crippled Oday…" Mritunjay said.

"What about it?" Arjun asked.

"As you know, Oday didn't save you both and neither did I or any of the reapers," Mritunjay said.

"Then God must have done it," Arjun conjectured.

"No… I had a conversation with him. He didn't. And even if he wanted to he couldn't have," Mritunjay said.

"What are you suggesting?" Arjun asked.

"I believe that Kunwar saved him," Mritunjay replied.

"Now why would he do that?" Arjun asked again.

"Now that's where the 'I am worried' part begins," Mritunjay said.

*   *   *

Shalini Enterprises

The Future Is Now

(Arlub on Times Then) "A video has just gone viral on YouTube. Rajat Singhania, who is seen to have strangely recovered from his so-called "life-threatening" injuries, has given shocking revelations in that video. Let's see what Mr. Rajat has to say."

The Video Started Showing Rajat Singhania sitting on a wide sofa with Arjun and Oday standing on either of his sides. Oday wore his regular yellow Uniform.

"I am Rajat Singhania, the Union Home Minister of India. You must have seen me fighting for my life in the hospital in Chandigarh. You must be wondering as to how I survived, or if the reports of me being injured are fake? Let me tell you what really happened. I and Raj Gautam, the president of the IDU, were meeting at a specific place for possible unification of our parties against the growing Ityadi. But, we were attacked. Attacked by none other than Kunwar Madhao Singh, the son of the late Rana Teja Singh. You all must know Rana Teja Singh as the backbone of Indian Politics. Yes, he was. And that's because he held the black-money of all the major politicians and leaders of India. Thus, he had immense influence over them and their work. Whoever he supported, rose to power in the country. Aditya Luhar had recently approached the Rana for support and that was the very reason I and Raj were meeting to devise a possible counter-attack against this massive union. Now I will go a little away from the topic at hand. On my right stands the man you must have heard about in the recent past in the modern urban legends and myths. I am here to tell you that he is not mythological or a camera glitch. Whoever has heard about this hero who has been going around saving various parts of the world, they should heave a sigh of relief. Because he is as true as I am alive. As rubbish as it sounds, he was chosen by God. Yes, God; to win against the evil of the world. The only opponent he had was Kunwar Madhao Singh. The antagonist to this godly protagonist. He was against letting God's plan to be a success. He has other motives namely world domination. When I and Raj were meeting to work against their heinous motives, we were attacked. By none other than Kunwar Madhao Singh. Raj was abducted and I was left for dead. I was dumped in a junkyard, from where I was escorted to the hospital. I was declared irreparable. But then came the saviour. This man took me under his protection. He healed me using his incredible powers and gave me a new life and I am forever indebted to him. But that is not the reason that drives me towards his cause. It is the proofs that he put in front of me which made me realize what actually was going on in the country. The Home Minister didn't have an inkling of knowledge about the diabolical plans to raze the freedom of the country and then the world. On my left I have the man called Arjun Trivedi. Son of a learned professor, Arjun is deft with the modern ways. In fact, his intellect even surprised me for he has the capability to impeccably lead the people like our Father Mahatma Gandhi. Over to him. (Arjun stepped forward)

I, as Sir told you, am Arjun Trivedi. I have no idea as to how politics is done. I don't know how a country or even a state is run. Our Prime Minister would ever be much more capable of doing that compared to me. I am just a common man and I am not saying it like the 'common man activist' who is ruling Delhi. The greatest power of a common man is Faith. And his fuel is hope. When either of them is lost, people succumb to evil. And that's what is happening in the world. The fast and easy solutions are appearing more approachable to people. And that is what Kunwar Madhao Singh wants. The hastier the people, the more he would benefit. His so called idea of world unification is innately a motion for world domination. I am just asking you one small thing. Do you have faith? Not in God. Be a theist or an atheist, if there is that one thing which you can trust, the one thing which you can rely on in your worst of times and survive and you know that you can, then you have faith. Einstein once said that one day we won't believe in the existence of Mahatma Gandhi. I am sorry friend, but that day is on our doorstep. We are losing faith slowly and it is time we need to strengthen it. Hence, I will provide you with faith. I will make you believe in miracles again. How? With the help of our friend over here. He is the living proof that we have hope. Thus I ask you my friends to join us in our rally near the red fort. Don't worry, our Home Minister is accompanying us in that rally and thus there won't be any sanctions imposed. We would acquaint you with the miracles that we have witnessed in these past few months. You can help us way more than we can help you. We would give you a small token which would aid you to help us with your support. And now my friend would say a few words to you. (Oday stepped forward).

Hello Friends. I am not a superhero who is here to save the world. I am not a special someone who has been given the great power and great responsibility of saving humankind. I am just as special as you are. I am just the superhero that every being in the world is. We all are special. We all hold the power to change the world. I am just the insurance you have that it'll happen. Humanity would be saved. Don't call me a superman. Call me the Mangoman.

(Rajat then continued)
I hereby declare Arjun Trivedi as our senior ideologist. He is still too young to hold a position in the Parliament.

And I pledge that I would accompany the Mangoman in his task to save the earth from the grasps of Aditya Luhar and the treacherous Kunwar Madhao Singh. Do join the rally if you want to witness the evil revelations regarding them. Thank You. Good Day."

(Arlub) "That was more than digestible. Shocking and Jaw-Dropping revelations made by the Union Home Minister. We would soon get the statements of the honourable Prime Minister and also the subjects of the revelations that is Kunwar Madhao Singh and the Chief Minister of Uttar Pradesh Aditya Luhar. But the question of the hour is, who is this Mangoman? And also, would you be participating in this illegal rally? Tweet us back at Hash Tag Mangoman and Hash Tag RajatGoneRogue. Do join us in the debate at NewsHourAndAHalf tonight. Thank You and Keep watching Times Then."

*　　*　　*

Everybody was working in Shalini's Mansion. Just to bring God's motive to action. They were preparing their speeches and presentations for the rally. But then came an uninvited guest. Kunwar Madhao Singh himself. And unlike the way they thought he would enter the house, he rang the bell. His footage was seen wide through the CCTV surveillance. He smiled back. Everyone went to the door. They knew that if it would not be opened then the consequences could be critical. Shalini peeped through a half opened door.

"Yes brother? What do you want now after killing our father?" Shalini said.

"Oh Little Sister. Let me in already. I am tired after hours of torturing Raj Gautam. People are right. He is an idiot. Anyway, open already. Or I would destroy this stronghold of yours within a blink of an eye," Kunwar said.

Shalini opened the door wide and let the Kunwar walk in. The others gave way for him to sit on the master couch.

"Just as comfy as last time," Kunwar said.

"Why are you here Madhao?" Arjun asked in a commanding tone.

"Comes here the Union Ideologist. I am good. How are you?" Kunwar said.

Oday wheeled out from within the group.

"You dare not touch my friends," Oday said in a dramatic position in front of the group.

"I see. Professor X and his X-men[89] are here," Kunwar Madhao smirked.

"Keep a lock on your mouth, you bastard," Arjun said.

"Oh! From 'Sir' to 'Madhao' to 'Bastard'. These people are losing their manners (Got up from the sofa and walked up to Oday and bent down. The others assumed a defensive semblance.). You think this poor little hero of yours, what do you call him... YES... THE MANGOMAN... You think he can save you all? (The earth started shaking) You are underestimating me then. Ask the one you call Mritunjay when he wakes up. I guess he mustn't have told you about the scary limits of my powers... well he can't... there are no limits. Anyway (Kunwar backed away from Oday and the ground stopped shaking) I was just dropping by to see your pathetic conditions and have a laugh or two. Now I may take your leave. Good day," Kunwar said and went out of the door. The Butler closed the door behind him.

"That was scary, wasn't it?" Adnan said.

"That was more like strange. He didn't kill us. What does he want?" Arjun asked. The bell rang again.

"Who now?" Shalini said, opening the door quite causally this time. It was the Kunwar Again.

"I forgot to give you my parting gift," said Kunwar, snapping his finger. The pillars holding the mansion caught fire, invoking utter ruckus inside the house. The people started running out from all exits without thinking of anyone else. Arjun went to get the fire extinguishers.

"No spray can extinguish this fire. It is an inferno of doom… this mansion will fall down… and along with it all the 'information' you gained against me. Adios Amigos," Kunwar said, as he snapped again and disappeared. Oday had risen from his seat to fight the Kunwar. But when the latter disappeared, Oday rather engaged in fighting the fire. He used all possible techniques to stop the inferno, ranging from water, sand, ice, Etcetera but the fire did not go down instead kept rising higher and higher. Arjun and Shalini were helping to take the others out of the house. Mritunjay got up and found himself surrounded by fire in his room. He closed his eyes, trying to ward it off, but then realized that he had lost his powers. He immediately wrapped himself up in blankets and ran out of the room, cutting through the fire. He shed the inflamed blankets and came out of the house. The only ones remaining inside were Oday, Aroma and Adnan. Oday and Aroma, oblivious to Adnan's presence inside the house, on failing to extinguish the fire, came out of the house.

"Sir…" one of the techsperts called out.

"Yes," Oday said, keeping down his wheelchair.

"Adnan went inside to retrieve the documents… everything we have compiled for tomorrow's rally is there… and he went to get it," the techspert replied.

Oday began to run inside, but Arjun stopped him.

"You can't blow off the fire from inside," Arjun said.

"If he blows air on to that then the fire would strengthen. That is a foolish plan," Aroma warned.

"Air... Yes... Air... Fire needs air... Everyone except Oday take a deep breath and hold it still. Then Oday... take all the air in," Arjun said.

"Do it fast then..." Oday said.

"On the count of three.... One... Two... Three... Suck," Arjun said.

Everybody held their breaths and then Oday sucked in the air consistently to create a temporary vacuum around the mansion. The fire stopped within seconds and everybody regained their breaths. Oday rushed inside accompanied by Arjun. After they went, the building's upper dome started to fall in. Aroma, on seeing this, flew towards it and kicked it away to make it fall at a distance. She came back and awaited the heroes. A few minutes later, Arjun and Oday came out shouldering Adnan. Everybody smiled at their exit from the unholy mansion. But their smiles overturned to frowns as soon as they had a close observation of Adnan. His body had almost entirely burnt charcoal-black. They all rushed to his help. Oday and Arjun helped lay him inside one of Shalini's cars. Shalini and Arjun got in and called out for Oday. He stood with a blank expression. All he could think of was that it was his second on-field failure. The first being the small girl. The face of the girl encompassed and encircled his mind and thoughts. He wasn't in his senses. The calls of Arjun, Shalini and the rest of the lot went unheard to our hero. And he fell down and fainted.

25

G od Vs Man... a common tale told in most epics of the world. For the Good is God and the Evil is Man. But the common confusion remains... Who is mightier of the two? The creator or the created? Man's creations have always simplified his work. In a way that our dependence upon our creations is irrevocable. The more we create, the less we be. And ironically, if we judge on capability metre, the creations have certain specific perks over man. To ease the job, they have to be better than the men themselves. Take a small pen. A powerful object. Mightier than the sword, the AK-47, the fission missile and the light-saber. The one object which wrote the others out. Without a pen, no modern inventions would have been possible. Using atmospheric pressure to control the oozing out of ink in a specific pattern creating the alphanumeric system. Clever. Immensely clever. The pen can be called the mother of most inventions. And hence, these inventions can be designated as 'Indirect Evolutions of Pen'. Ranging from a Tube-light to a computer system, they are all chronological evolutions of a pen. But what when these computers would be used to create the perfect artificial intelligence? We are at a stage where we can replicate life. But what when we could create a new life. The object pen would then have not just evolved... but personified. And that creation, would be all that man isn't. A complete set of everything that man tried to create to ease his work. The perfect creation. But even if it succeeds man in capability, can it be greater than man. For the creator is the master. The created or the apprentice generally succeeds his master... but shall always remain an apprentice. Except when he is a Sith[90]. Then he would use cool one-liners and kill his master in a badass backstabbing, and become the master himself. Anyway... we can conclude that creation is a desperation of the creator to achieve his ends. And it always happens for a purpose. Who would create an intelligent organism to gain the sadistic pleasure of seeing them destroy their planet? No one in his complete senses would. And God, as has always been said, has a plan. More like had a plan. The plan went haywire when his creation went out of his hands. God is our hope... and we are his.

* * *

A humungous gathering outside the Red Fort. The gates unofficially opened to give way to the huge mass. The Netaji Subhash Metro Station was blocked. No metros stopped there that day. The cameras from all media houses encircled the podium which awaited the incoming footsteps of the Union Home Minister, closely followed by Arjun Trivedi. Arjun consistently wiped the sweat off his face. Why? Because they lacked the one thing they had promised and proclaimed. The proofs against the Kunwar and Aditya. And also Oday had not accompanied them. The only reason that he had given was that there was an emergency he had to deal with. Rajat came and greeted the people and received a warm welcome. The popularity he gained after the revelation multiplied his original fame as the president of the most appreciated political party. The start was quite motivating, but soon the audience expected the Mangoman to come forward and address them himself. There came a huge resonating call from the crowd "Man-Go-Man... Man-Go-Man." Rajat, the trained diplomat, immediately understood the consensus and stepped back for Arjun to come to the podium and greet them on behalf of Oday. Arjun nervously stepped forward. The walk from the seat to the podium was dramatically as slow as it was quick for Arjun. The first and last opportunity he had to prove his worth. He started speaking.

"Hello Friends," the mic echoed invoking immediate silence.

The cameras zoomed in on his face catching the pale expression. There were a number of huge displays and speakers streaming the young man live. The silence caught his nerves even further.

"I am here to (Microphones turned off) apologize," Arjun said, but before he could complete the statement, the mics turned off along with the cameras which displayed a static signal.

There was awkward query floating around the crowd which was rather disappointed. The situation remained constant for a while. Rajat indulged in an angry conversation with the backing technical staff. Then, all of a sudden, the displays and the speakers turned on again. The screen showed a CCTV footage of Kunwar Madhao Singh shooting his own father. Another image showed piles of nuclear warheads with subscript reading "Smuggled under the jurisdiction of Aditya Luhar and Eklavya Mishra." The crowd was startled. There were other audio recordings of the Kunwar confessing to his crimes, probably recorded through the microphone in Oday's suit. Then came the most important videos. That is, of The Mangoman. The crowd stared at respective screens with concentration. The superhero facades were all mostly covered by various CCTV recordings. The philanthropic work that Oday had indulged in, in the recent past, was almost all displayed in the video. The incredibly unbelievable powers were jaw-dropping for the gullible audience. A few sceptics stated arrogantly that it was a video editing trick and they considered it a mere 'child's play'. There were other documents with highlighted keywords indicating the cover ups for certain smuggling and other activity which went about under the Luhar Regime. Many other illicit activities were mentioned in the video with backing proofs. The twenty minutes long video came to an end. People were questioning each other, if they knew what was going on and what was the purpose of those revelations. Even Arjun was speechless as to how the video was retrieved. Then, one of the observant women in the crowd saw something strange standing. She spread the news across the crowd and people started pointing towards the top of the Red Fort. Arjun turned around. He saw that Oday stood on top of the red fort in his Uniform and held the Indian Flag in his right hand. His back faced the audience and co incidentally showed his yellow cape curling to the wind in the shape of a huge mango. There was again pin drop silence; Silence to an extent that it almost gave way for the sound of some wavering. The Indian Flag, the Cape or both. Oday turned around to greet his fans. But he accidentally stepped on his cape and lost balance and started to fall urging an immediate wooing. The sceptics assumed a snobbish persona, only to be immediately silenced by the hero's floatation in the air. Yes, Oday started floating upside down in the air. There was instantly a loud cheer in the audience. Even Rajat and Arjun clapped at the wondrous spectacle. Oday slowly descended down and approached the microphone. "I am sorry friends, I had to take the mic away from my dearest partner Arjun Trivedi. But I am just here to say that I am just the one with the gift of superpowers. They are meaningless without the right direction. He gives me the direction. He gives me the motivation and hope. He is the one with the gift of leadership," Oday said in a dramatically slow dialogue. The crowd positively hooted in amazement. Arjun came to the microphone and before speaking asked Oday about the source of the video.

"Adnan... he didn't go to retrieve it. He went to safeguard it online. On investigation by our members, they found proper first-hand backups online. He sacrificed himself. He didn't go back in to come back out. He went to safeguard the data and martyred himself in the act," Oday said as a tear ran down his eyes across his mask. Arjun came to the podium with teary eyes and started with a re-established confidence.

"Here beside me stands the Mangoman. Why Mango you might ask? Super being too clichéd, we thought what can be both new and funny, common and questionable, strange and weird. Something easy to remember and celebrate. Something not hated anywhere. Unless you are allergic to them Of course. The Mangoman is not a superhero. Either of those words doesn't play any role here. The Mangoman is a concept. A concept that declares that everybody is equal. Everybody, from our dearest Prime Minister to Sir Rajat Singhania standing beside me, everybody is equal and has equal say in the world. Everybody is just as better than the other as the other is than him. Nobody is special. But everybody has a speciality, which we call their duty. If everybody performs their duties honestly and earnestly, without trying to presume powers over others, then we shall unite. Unite into the Mankind that God had foreseen. The man beside me is just like you and me. He is no different. His abilities are his duties bestowed on him by God himself. But he is just like you, me or the Prime Minister of India. For each one of us is a Mangoman," Arjun said. His words started inspiring the crowd and they started admiring him just as much as they did the home minister.

He continued "Thus, I would like you all to help us. Yes... help us. We would like you to declare your support to the philanthropic work we have taken upon ourselves. Whenever we think of one world, the second thought which strikes our mind is that WHO WOULD RULE THE ONE WORLD? AMERICA, RUSSIA OR CHINA? Let me tell you... the one who shall rule the unified world is the seven billion people of the world and not one man or one parliament or country. That's our ambition. To see unity in diversity. And I request all of you to help us achieve that. It won't take much effort. You just have to go to any local vendor and buy a mango and preserve it in your homes. As foolish as it sounds, this is the way you can donate to our cause. If you do not have the means to buy one, then we will send you one. Just write to us. We will do as asked. We just need support. We are not making or bringing a government here. We are just propagating an idea. The idea of The Mangoman."

The crowd became ecstatic after a few seconds' pause of deep thinking. The idiosyncratic idea pitched by the heroes strangely had an unexpected positive and wide reception. This boosted their morale. Then Oday came to the mic.

"Many have sacrificed themselves for our cause. And that is sad, because it is misanthropy at its highest. Not their sacrifice... but their murder. Yes... murder. One Amit, One

Chatur Verma and One Adnan... all three have martyred themselves to help us reach this platform. Let us not let their sacrifices go in vain... let us commemorate them by moving a step further towards their ambition... the ambition of acceptance... the ambition of unity," Oday said.

A helicopter hovered over the crowd. They cleared a circle on the road for the copter to land. It landed safely and from within came out Shalini and her Butler. As per instructions by the Home Minister, everybody made way for the guests to come up to the stage. People, at first, were confused after identifying the sister of the antagonist of this rally's agenda. They started jeering against her uncontrollably. She came up and Arjun said "She is the daughter of the late Rana Teja Singh and the sister of Kunwar Madhao Singh. She has recently witnessed her father being slain at the hands of her brother. She is also the partial owner of the assets of the Rana. Unlike her brother, she is not being a hindrance to our cause but is supporting us outright. She is our sole sponsor. In her tough times she has decided to completely deliver towards her cause. Please give a wide round of motivating applause for the one and only Shalini Teja Singh," Arjun's words aroused the crowd to shed trepidation for Shalini. Shalini and her Butler escorted the Home Minister and Arjun to the helicopter for their cinematic exit. Oday floated over the crowd to give them the last show for the day. But in a horrible natural Déjà vu, as soon as the chopper took off, an RPG came in from nowhere and hit its rear rotor. The crowd panicked and immediately it sparked a stampede crushing many of those who were just moments ago enjoying the show. Oday went below the chopper and held it up and safely placed it down extinguishing the fire. He tried to calm the alarmed crowd but his attempts were unsuccessful. There were multiple cries for help. Oday first tried to help the injured, heal as many as possible and escort certain others to safety. But then he was informed by Arjun regarding the identity of the attacker. Arjun told him that he had seen the origin of the RPG at a distant building's rooftop. He testified that the attacker was none other than the infamous Aryaman Mirza. Oday jumped high to get a positive ID of the attacker. He used hawk-vision to confirm that it was indeed Aryaman and thus he was going to engage, but the cries of the people reverberated loud in his ears. He could only resort to helping the ailing crowd. Before he came down, he saw that Aryaman confidently grinned back at Oday, almost to intimidate him. But Oday gave in to the much more needed of his two emotions and started helping the people. The feeling of guilt of not being able to sufficiently help the needful engulfed Oday. The service, which had just started off as a tedious job to 'help' five, as a time-consuming and monotonous 'job' which Oday wanted to have done with as soon as possible, was now something Oday couldn't get enough of. From feeling the work as a drab, to feeling Good after working to feeling bad after not being able to work to his content, Oday had seen all the phases. Arjun and the others also helped normalize the situation. But soon, it was observed that most of the audience had dispersed away. When Oday was almost done with handling it, Aryaman had already escaped. "All this... and just by a mere weapon of fear, they won..." Arjun said.

*   *   *

"Come out you Coward and fight me. Come out right now," Oday called out for Kunwar Madhao Singh outside his palace in Dubai. His mobile phone rang consistently in his pocket. He took it out and saw that it was Arjun and rejected the call. He repeatedly rejected successive calls due to his colossal anger. His mind was clouded and he couldn't think straight. All he could think was to achieve his vengeance on Kunwar for the water had reached its high-boil.

"Hello Mr. Mangoman," echoed a rough whisper around Oday.

"Appear now if you dare… and face me man to man," Oday yelled at the top of his voice.

A dense fog engulfed the whole place within seconds, impairing Oday's vision.

"You will die today," Kunwar said and moved to grapple Oday. But Oday intercepted his approach and tackled him using his select audio-visual expertise.

"You forget… I can be anyone…" Oday said, blowing the fog away. He was holding Kunwar's hands tight in his grip and was getting ready to beat the villainous leader.

"Why are you so angry? It wasn't your father I killed," Kunwar said.

"Angry… yes you get it right… I am angry… and let me use that," Oday said as he began expanding, with his skin turning dull green. He transformed into the hulk, still gripping Kunwar's arms. Then Oday let his right arm go and took a stance to punch Kunwar. He groaned loud in preparation for his big blow and then punched. A huge mass of dusty air flew off the scene. And when it cleared away, it showed them in almost a similar posture. The only thing different was that Oday's right huge green arm held still attached to Kunwar's left cheek. The Kunwar had completely blocked the massive punch with his bare face without even trying to defend. Kunwar started rising up in the air. And in the same posture, started pushing Oday down into the Earth. Minor cracks in the air soon converged into a big crater and by the end of Kunwar's counterattack, Oday lay senseless below his feet.

"Quite presumptuous of you to come and fight me like that... when the most powerful of you preservers were slain within just seconds of me starting to fight. And now when I have usurped Mritunjay's powers, even God, in his prime, cannot outmatch me," Kunwar said.

*   *   *

"He didn't pick up even now... Track him down... and Fast... He must have run out of powers already," Arjun declared his primary worry.

"What then? He has gone after Brother. Even if we track him, none of us can fight him back. And those who possibly stood a minor chance, are either powerless or are busy enchanting some enigmatic poems," Shalini said.

"They are still on to it, aren't they?" Arjun asked.

"Yes... six hours since they began," Shalini's Butler said.

Arjun and the others were all currently temporarily stationed at the Home Minister's Gomtinagar Residence in Lucknow. He went to the back kitchen garden to have a look at Aroma and the other reapers chant away in their polygonal formation. They all sat in a meditative state, humming strange chants. At the centroid of the polygon was a small and wet mango seed. Mritunjay stood beside the group, leaning against a pillar.

"Is it any good?" Arjun asked.

"We'd see... not yet..." Mritunjay replied.

"Sir… we got Oday sir's location… he is in Dubai," said one of the incoming techsperts.

"Dubai!!! What in heavens is he doing in Dubai?" Arjun said surprisingly.

"Dubai… There is our palace in Dubai," Shalini said, following the techspert.

"Palace… Why is that more intriguing than supernatural angels?" Arjun remarked, turning towards Shalini.

"Yes… Kunwar's personal hideout. That place has ALWAYS been heavily guarded. Even I have never been there. I just know of its existence," Shalini said.

"Let's inform Rajat sir. He might help," Arjun said.

"He is busy talking to the Defence Minister, arranging for permanent counter-attack teams against the Kunwar. But I do know someone who can help… should I call him inside? He is waiting in the guest room," Shalini's Butler said.

"Oh… Let's Go there ourselves," Arjun said. Everyone except the celestial beings started to leave the garden, only to stop when they heard a sudden beaming sound. Arjun turned around. It was the mango seed which was glowing yellow and sounding regularly, all like the fictitious dragon balls[91].

"What next?" Arjun asked.

"Look closely," Mritunjay prompted.

Arjun went up to the seed to find that a small sapling was growing out of the glowing seed.

"This is something… isn't it?" Mritunjay passed his rhetoric.

"Our little start-up is getting investors already… awesome," Arjun said.

"Now go bring your hero back. We need him here to defend the reapers," Mritunjay said.

26

Oday lied conscious yet paralyzed on the floor. He held the very crooked posture, resting on the floor against his right side waist, in which the Kunwar had thrown him inside that hall. A dramatic theatre hall that is. Lying within the massive gap between two successive VIP rows, Oday's calls for help in the solitary hall went unheard. Moreover, the deafening intensity of the theatre mics, set to some irritating and monotonous default tone, harassed the powerless Oday. Powerless, since he had expired his daily share. The images of the little eight-year-old girl, of Adnan, of Amit and of Chatur inundated his thoughts and his conscience. To his understanding, his successive whole-hearted trials for living up to the expectations of God had all been successive failures. Tears dropped down his eyes. Maybe because of guilt, maybe because of being unable to safeguard his ears against the incoming noise. But it was not all. His agony magnified when the screen turned on, displaying the regular High-Definition SMPTE colour bars, with the speakers tuning to the 'humming' test. Oday moaned in pain. But then the torture came to a halt.

The screen now showed the back of a small girl with long hair. The girl started murmuring while sobbing.

"I was alone. He did horrible things to me... I trusted you, but you helped him instead. I trusted you... and you killed me. YOU KILLED ME... YOU..." the girl screamed and then burst into tears. Oday started crying as well. Then all of a sudden, the girl's cries turned into periodic and devilish laughter. She then looked up. Her face was eviler than the most horrifying of sightings. Perhaps the basic fundamentals of horror movie directors, that is using the innocence of children as a terrifying weapon, aided the girl's motive of giving chills down Oday's spine. She then continued in a strange and manly voice "You don't know, do you? You can't possibly beat me. I reside inside everyone... I am everyone and everything." The girl said and transformed into Kunwar Madhao Singh. The scene then switched over to a small warehouse. Three masked men, tied to three chairs, sat in the middle of the room. Kunwar went across from left to right, removing their masks, revealing Amit, CCTV and Adnan respectively. He then went beside the right most, saying "Your saviours shall not see the next dawn", and then took out his pistol to shoot all three at once in a row. He then walked away. The three bled out completely creating a huge puddle of blood. Oday was now shivering with anger. Then the three got up and sat back in their chairs. Their blood-clad faces slowly transformed into three separate Kunwar's faces. All three then spoke at once "I am everyone."

Then, came the ultimate surprise. The screen turned off and the speakers switched over and came a familiar yet confounding voice "Earth to Everyone... Come in Everyone... Wait... Everyone IS earth, right? My bad..."

"Who is it?" Oday shouted.

"Oday... It is me... Wait a second you can't see me. And not like John Cena you can't see me, the real you can't see me. My bad again," came the voice again.

The screen turned on again showing the face of CCTV.

"Tadaaa... hello Oday. In the words of the great Arnold Schwarzenegger, I'm Back," CCTV said.

Oday immediately thought that it was Kunwar who was again messing with Oday's mind.

"Stop it already you fucking asshole. In a few hours I would gain my powers back. I am kicking your ass then," Oday said.

"Hey... No kicking asses bro. I am here to help you. I said... I am CCTV. That idiot Ananya thought she had me. Nobody gets Chatur Champakdas Tilakchand Verma unless Chatur Champakdas Tilakchand Verma wants them to get him. The person who died was a small fake token, one of Kunwar's allies, whom I had left for the bitch to devour. Now enough of storytelling, let's get out. Brace yourself. Wait a second, you already are naturally braced. Okay then, this will begin the normal CCTV way," CCTV said.

"And that is?" Oday asked.

"Kabooooommm," CCTV said, the screen turned off and exploded up in flames. A Hummer came in through the fire. CCTV stepped out and escorted Oday to the car and reversed out of the hall into some yellow garden.

"How do we plan to escape the fort?" Oday questioned CCTV.

"Plan? CCTV never has a PLAN to escape. He just... escapes... and if you are asking me what I have... then I have that," CCTV said, pointing towards something in the sky. He helped Oday look up to glance at the huge number of fighter-helicopters surrounding the palace.

"Oday come in, are you Ok?" came Arjun's voice over the car radio.

"Pundit... How the hell did you arrange this kind of an arsenal?" Oday asked.

"Well… let's say I had help from the Government of India. The Prime Minister's recent visit to UAE helped our latest allies arrange for a quick fly-by and rescue operation," Arjun said.

A chopper used a huge electromagnet to lift up the Hummer. Right after they were in the air, the other choppers loaded up their weapons surrounding the central building. Arjun then gave the final verdict "Let's Mango the shit out of them."

"What the hell do you mean by that?" Oday asked.

"Well, now that your so called stupid alter-ego is so famous, why not make dialogues out of it," Arjun said.

"That's lame… even for me," Oday said.

"Attack Already you morons," Arjun commanded his air legion and it unfolded its devastating wrath on to the fort. Rocket after rocket, Missile after missile, bullet after bullet, the whole complex was rubbled within minutes. Then the attackers waited for the conflagration to come down, to confirm a positive hit. From within the burning buildings came out many of Kunwar's faithful minions, all burning up in flames. Then came out the one who alerted Oday. It was Ananya. Her back was on fire and she had almost fumed out in flames. She used the last of her energy to point at Oday and then fell down just outside the door. The gory scene was too much for Oday and Arjun to bear with. But Rajat asserted that 'sometimes war is a dire necessity'. Though the sole purpose of that war wasn't served yet. The target, that was Kunwar Madhao Singh, his death had not been confirmed yet. Then all of the radio frequencies of the attacking force were hacked by an unknown source. The next thing they heard was Kunwar Madhao's voice.

"Oh! I see… You have an army AND a hulk. But… lemme tell you Mr. Oday Singh Luhar… Not even your

God can kill me anymore. I… am invincible," Kunwar said through the radio. The choppers were then ordered to leave the site, for they had quenched their fly-by duration. All of them flew away. The last being the one carrying the Hummer. Oday and CCTV were the only ones to witness the Kunwar walk out of the burning building. He stepped over the deceased Ananya's face and smiled again. Oday was furious. All he wanted was to jump out and kick the satanic prince. But he had to wait more. He wondered whether God had a plan. And if he did, then what role was Oday to play in that plan. Was it the same role that he was playing? If yes, then he felt sheer under-confident about a glorious victory. If no, he felt all the same. Oday's fate was now in close relation to the fate of the planet and its races.

*   *   *

"They say I am a killer. Working for the remnants… working for the Etcetera, all I have ever learnt is peace. Showing morphed videos of my newest ally, the Kunwar, the son of my late friend Rana Teja Singh, they expect to persuade the people who have shed sweat and blood to unite the sections under one name… The Ityadi. Arjun Trivedi… his father Nitin Trivedi was recently caught in the Central University Paper Leak scam. Having mercy on the man and his family, we just had him removed from the University. We didn't file a case on him. I know that the Supreme Court and the laws are the ultimate judges… and I apologize for taking decisions in my hands out of the humanity and pity in my heart. But he and his son have been consistently looking for an anchor to take the Ityadi down. And that fallacious anchor was provided by one Shalini Teja Singh. The sister of the Kunwar was first held in high praises in mine eyes. But soon, we found that she held biggest grudges against her brother for being the preferred child due to his naturally adept leadership. The late Rana never differentiated between his children and gave everything in his capability to either of his beloved children. But Shalini needed the crown, needed the chair. And for that chair, she gave herself away to Arjun, luring him to her cause. Arjun and Shalini, together, conspired and got the Rana killed. And they set out a concrete plan to take down the Kunwar. Having common ends, both of them co-ordinated to take us down. But, their concrete was nothing compared to the scratchproof steel of the Ityadi. We are here standing. They tried their best, but when they couldn't kill us, they retired to using the very party as their ally that they had earlier attacked. Yes… Mr. Rajat was attacked by this creature who calls himself The Mangoman. And he used these diabolical abilities of his, achieved through some ungodly and illegal technology, to hypnotize our possible ally. We want to take everyone along. But he stopped us. These people now claim to be the ambassadors of the righteous. But I would just say… fake as much as you want… use any façade or camouflage… Ityadi is not coming down," Aditya concluded his speech and the huge crowd cheered in appreciation.

*　　*　　*

Aroma and the other reapers continued their harmonic and consistent chant surrounding the now emergent sapling of the mango tree. The seed continued glowing. Oday sat in his wheelchair, expressionlessly gazing at the wondrous scene. For the past three hours Oday had been there, he had seen the magnificence of creation at its prime. He saw leaves bud out of the sapling's branches and the stem broaden out, the roots clutch the ground and the seed glowing bright and still. Aroma stopped the chant, and after hours of sitting, stood up and walked out of the group towards Oday.

"It is beauty isn't it?" Aroma said.

"Yes indeed. It's growing so fast," Oday said.

"But not fast enough," Aroma said.

"What do you mean not fast enough?" Oday asked.

"We don't have sufficient followers yet. We need more. MANY MANY more," Aroma replied.

"So what should we do?" Oday asked.

"You and your friends… you should get more followers," Aroma said and went back and sat again in her meditative state.

"That was… not… the answer…" Oday said.

Arjun came in from behind.

"Whatch'ya doing Suckhead? What are the fairies up to?" Arjun asked.

"They are… singing again. Pundit… I think we should have another rally," Oday said.

"Exactly my thoughts. That belligerent statement by your dad… it has like destroyed our reputation," Arjun said.

"How can you be so calm? He defiled your father's reputation as well. And as I can recall, you take insults to your dad really seriously. The one time you have ever seriously beaten me up was when I said that your father looked like a monkey," Oday said.

"I look like a what?" came Arjun's father walking inside that room.

"No Sir… Nothing. So Arjun… why so calm?" Oday asked.

"We needed a bigger campaigner… a bigger ambassador than Rajat," Nitin said.

"Who can be a bigger campaigner than the Home Minister of India? Wait a second… what do you mean needed?" Oday said.

* * *

"Brothers and Sisters… The 'good days' our party had brought to your doorstep… an evil power has been trying to take those days away from you… Would we allow someone to encroach upon our peace?" the Prime Minister spoke in front of an immensely huge mass of audience. The audience gave its cheerful consent.

"Would we allow some madmen to take over our country?" he continued as the crowd applauded more in approval.

"Would we allow our hopes and our heroes to fall to their knees?"

The crowd cried out loud in appraisal for the Prime Minister. Arjun appeared on the stage along with Shalini.

"They say that I prostituted myself for him to kill my father. I… loved my father. His life was taken right in front of my eyes. And this is the man, Arjun, I love most after him," Shalini said to the crowd.

"They blamed me and my dad for certain strange crimes. I… don't even want to say anything about that. I just want to say to you people… my fight… our fight… is not against Kunwar Madhao Singh and Aditya Luhar. I don't even care what wrongs they do and what paths they choose to cover them up. I don't even care they call me names. In fact, our fight is not AGAINST anyone… Our fight… our struggle… is FOR peace and unity. Fight to Unite… let's raise a mango," Arjun said.

Then Oday came flying in his yellow suit and descended in front of a microphone. He stayed there for a few seconds.

"Our saviour... the Mangoman is forever dedicated in our service," Arjun said.

The crowd was silenced. It strangely made way for a group of four men carrying a woman's body up to the stage. The Prime Minister's guards stopped them. Then came a loud cry from amongst the crowd "Hear me out."

The PM asked his guards to stand down. The cry was from an old woman. She came close to the stage and screamed at the top of her voice "Six months ago... my husband passed away in a train accident. We were rendered poor and helpless. My young daughter was the one entrusted with the job of supporting this small yet broken nuclear family. Yesterday... robbers entered our house. My daughter begged them that all the money we had was being saved up for setting up the shop which might earn us our livelihood. She rebelled... and was shot on the spot. I don't care about money... I don't care about food. I can starve till the next century... but they took my only happiness from me... they took away everything. I ask you... you emissaries of peace. Where were you? Where was this saviour you call Mangoman...? Where was he when she was killed in cold blood? I spit on you all," the woman said, picking up her slippers and throwing them at the Prime Minister. The guards immediately took a hold of her. She wept loudly and angrily. The PM and the others were asked to leave the stage, to evade a possible stampede of the now not so accommodating crowd. Oday, against the instructions by the senior diplomats, came up to the microphone.

"I'm really sorry about your daughter," Oday said.

The crowd threw insults at his face. They were also questioning the same thing to him that is "Where were you?"

"Leave her... I beg of you," Oday asked the guards. The PM and the others were waiting for Oday to come along with them. But he waited. He conjured the right combination of words to be put against the angry lot.

"I...." Oday uttered, but his voice was predominated by the screams of the crowd.

"Hey... come here. Let's try this later. We might start a riot over here... The PM has been hit... do you understand the significance of that?" Arjun whispered from behind.

Oday left the mic and turned back for a second. He walked for a while and then stopped. He then gazed at Arjun for a while, at the gestures that Arjun was making to him to 'Hurry Up'.

For him, his responsibility was now evident. And there were no evasive measures to be undertaken within the walls of that responsibility. He knew it. It was his moment. He took a grasp of his mask and tore it off, shocking his friendly spectators on the back stage. He gave a blissful smile and turned around. The crowd was shunted in silence. Oday walked up to the mic and said "My name is Oday Luhar... and I am... The Mangoman...."

27

The practically isolated Kashmir Valley of Northern India. And not just inclusive of the various no-man land stretches. On either front of POK and COK, the Indian Armed Forces seemed to have resigned away. Not because of some incapability of the Indian side against the hostile neighbours. But because of some informal trilateral conference held between the three countries. Unfortunately, the Indian was represented by none other than Aditya Luhar. The sides were polarized against each other and the prospects of conflict seemed inevitable. India, for a change, was a mere witness and a third party to this emerging and prudent friction. It wasn't just a war between Pakistan and China... It was a war of the religious and the ones without religion. The presumed bound class of 'lower' race humans was to be razed away from the earth, as suggested and directed by Aditya Luhar. China and Russia were in his complete support. For the first time, the annexation of a territory of the Indian subcontinent was just a secondary objective of a war in that region. The so-called philanthropic ideal of world unity was to be achieved, for the good of the masses, as claimed by these fake leaders. But the procedural hush and rush would have only benefitted one and only one person. Kunwar Madhao Singh. And how? To fight off rebellion, people committed horrid crimes at instances succumbing to their inner devil. Divergence from the path of God would make them fragments inclined to go to the Kunwar Instead. And the rebels, those he had directly or indirectly aroused against the ones with faiths, they would be the easiest and most prominent in numbers of his targets. Overall, a majority of the created would ascend and dissolve in Kunwar, making him the prime being. But this diabolical (literally and hysterically) plan of the Kunwar was not known to his followers as well as protestors. At least most of the protestors. None of them could have digested so much supernatural at once. All he had was 'I am good'. And all they had was 'We are good'. They… as in our very own heroes.

Yes, so where were we? Yes… in the beautiful pseudo-heaven of Kashmir. The soothing silence was broken by sounds of heavy military vehicles appearing from either side and somewhat converging close to the border. The army commanders from both sides stepped out and held their microphones up to announce their decisions to each other. The Chinese General spoke in his broken English, declaring that the Federation of Pakistan was now to accede to the People's Republic of China. If they said yes then they would be spared. If they said no, then they would be forcefully annexed. And if they didn't reply within twenty-four hours, then their nation would be nucleated away from being available for habitation.

The Pakistani Soldiers became furious. They held up their rifles aiming at the Chinese. The Chinese did the same. Just like when during the classical ages of war, the enemy archers used to load their bows right in front of each other with the spear-equipped soldiers ready for jousting their spears while getting impaled themselves, the two armies faced each other. It was a foolish practice overshadowed by arrogance. Then came some wise-ass and devised the rule of everything being fair in war. Even hide and seek, setting traps, attacking from the rear, Etcetera, all of which was sheer cowardice for the arrogant and usually devastatingly losing rulers. But that practice seemed to have been revived. Maybe clouded by their hastiness, but they held guns at each other, completely aware that there'd be no one left to tell the martyrs.

The Chinese commander smiled in mockery and asked his soldiers to step back. He then turned around. The Pakistani commander didn't quite appreciate the gesture. He said to his Lieutenant that he was now going to send his reply much before the time of delivery. He aimed at his counterpart and took a clean head-shot. The Chinese Commander fell down and died at the instant. There was all out shooting between the sides and now they were all running around, zig-zag, searching for proper hiding platforms. Sanity had finally arrived in their idiotic brains. The war had kick-started. Soldiers continued dying one after another. But all of a sudden, all the bullets stopped mid-air. The guns of the shooters started floating away in the air. They were all terrified of the unholy sight. Ironically, most of them recalled God in this time of worry. Theist or Atheist, when the going goes bad, then the hope becomes God. Their guns floated in the air for a few minutes and then disintegrated and fell on the floor. A few seconds later, believing that it was a doing of their enemy, both sides ran towards the no man's land. There was a huge wave in the stretch which then rose up in flames. They all stopped again, wondering as to which demon was doing this. Few hundred metres away, Oday stood in his yellow uniform, flying in the air as the silver surfer[92], assuming the stance to extinguish the fire now when the war had presumably ended. He spoke out loud "Listen you Soldiers. You have dropped the weapons which inflict damage on others… Now shed those which inflict damage on thyself."

The people were alerted at the strange voice. Oday then swept away the fire. The enemy in line of sight again, the people grabbed stones, pebbles and weapon fragments and started hurling them towards each other. Oday felt ignored. He understood that they needed a deterrent.

"They never understand unless you are large… and destructive," Oday said, transforming into the Hulk. He jumped and then punched down the earth, creating a crack in between the engaging armies. The crack held them back. He then appeared in front of them in his normal form. He walked up and removed his mask.

"I ask of you to stop this stupid battle for Unity. If you wish to Unite… then Fucking Unite… Killing and enslaving is no unity," he said to the Chinese.

"And you… you people just need reasons to use that overloaded arsenal of yours, don't you? I understand you are insecure about your illiteracy, lack of communication and convincing skillset, it doesn't mean that the only means of diplomacy and negotiations you enforce is force. That cannot be an ideology of a state of a humanitarian religion," he said to Pakistan.

"Who the hell are you to tell us? You Indian… How dare you mock away on our face like that? It is your turn after China," the Pakistani commander said.

"Unlike our Paki friends here… we have beaten you people already. So you don't want another taste of that medicine, do you? If you interfere then you shall be personally killed. Although we are officially allying with the next Government of India…" the Chinese second-in-command said.

"Government… What do you mean by next government? To be headed by my father, you mean? Is Aditya Luhar, your Ally, to be the next Prime Minister of India? Who decides that?" Oday said.

A man stepped forward from amongst the Chinese lot and said to Oday "Kunwar Madhao Singh decides that. And yes… he sends his regards…" He then threw a big knife towards Oday which stabbed through Oday's chest. A few others stepped forward and threw their sharp weapons aiming at Oday. The collective knives caused Oday to fall down on the ground. The mottos and slogans began yet again on both sides as they prepared for an all-out brawl. They now entered the no man's land, where Oday lied, and exchanged ruthless punches and merciless kicks. Oday ignorantly got up and found it quite intriguing to be in the middle of that fight. He slowly walked out of the area and side-lined himself. The soldiers fought intensely, but then the one, who had first thrown a knife at Oday, caught sight of the hero witnessing the fight from the side. He alerted his comrades. The fighters from both sides soon became aware of this miraculous sight, that is Oday standing holding out all the knives, that had stabbed him earlier, gripped tightly in both of his hands.

"Hasn't the Kunwar told you? To be able to even stand, I need powers. I need to transform. Thus I always keep myself mutated into one or the other superheroes. This time, luckily, Wolverine," Oday said, dropping down the knives.

"You…" the soldier said, running towards Oday.

"You guys don't ever get moved by small fries… Let's see how you handle the wrath of Shirohige₉₃," Oday said and started to transform again. This time, his skin didn't go green and neither did he stop transforming at nine feet of height. He grew and grew, turning whiter and paler. He retained his facial structure, although his whole body multiplied in size. He grew huger than ever and then punched the air$_{94}$, cracking it. The ground started cracking very fast and the quake raced along the no man's stretch towards the peak behind him. The peak got rubbled in an instant. It was now that the warring sides stopped and surrendered to this heavenly power of Oday. After catching their attention, he transformed back to his original state and started the monologue which Arjun had made him learn by heart.

"What preposterous war is one which is waged on life… yes… life… that is the one classification we have. Our species, faiths, genders or any other classification is not our identity. God or Not… we are all the same. Disparities are there in our minds. No war can remove them. For the irreligious, you people have evolved over the ethics provided by religion, right? Then why behave so naïve? Why stoop so low? If you have achieved the knowledge that was to be originally imparted by religion, then why succumb to killing? Is that the ideal that you self-taught yourselves? I am sorry… but you all need the path of God. To the religious… if by joining hands, touching your head on the floor or by lighting candles you could have reached God… then Ravan, Osama and Hitler would have been Prophets. To reach God you need the one thing that people overlook in these enigmatic times. Bhagwan, Allah and God… all have ever propounded the path of Self-Righteousness. Don't wrong others… and God won't wrong you. Do right others and God would ever shower his blessings on you. Read the Gita, Quran or Bible carefully… you would find that there is some strange similarity in the principles. Religion was not created by God. It was a path created by salient and holy prophets in their specific time zones to propound the path of God. All they wanted was that the humanity that they knew should not be party to evil. I am no prophet... but that is all I want too. And in these modern times of global connectivity... the humanity I know involves the whole world. So to either of you... what is the knowledge I am talking about? It is to know that you can have a much more beautiful and successful life if you ward off animosity and intolerance for the existence of alternate faiths and beliefs and live symbiotically with universal acceptance. I don't know what will you achieve by warring foolishly. You will just lose your lives and be lost in history when you could have enjoyed the beautiful gift of life you have. Now it all depends on you... I am not a supreme being who can control the human beings and their actions. I could have merely made you aware of the truths... and I have done that... I would now take your leave," Oday said. He then witnessed the men taking a few steps back and returning back to their stations in their respective territories. He waited for fifteen minutes till they had all dispersed. He then sighed in relief and disappeared.

*   *   *

Inside Rajat's Mansion in Lucknow, the revolutionaries conferenced on the plan of action against the Kunwar, now that the world was officially aware of Oday's identity. Oday appeared in the drawing room.

"Hey Suckhead! Me and Sir Rajat were right now discussing the way we can enhance our rallies with technology, just like during Prime Minister's Lok Sabha rallies. So yes... how did it go in Kashmir?" Arjun said.

"Your words are like magic Pundit. I mean some people convinced me that I am too gullible. But now I realize that it is you who is over-convincing. So not my bad. My powers were like nothing compared to your philosophies. Thank God I had enough alone time in front of the mirror, chanting and memorizing the paragraph. That war has been avoided. Other than that, how is the tree going? It had grown four or five branches the last time I was here," Oday said.

"Let's go and see it," Rajat said.

They all walked to the garden to see the tree. The sapling had now grown to be a huge tree with hundreds and hundreds of leaves.

"It has grown further… a lot more in just forty minutes," Oday said.

"Yes… the seed is glowing faster than ever. You have many followers now…" Mritunjay said.

"Oh… just how many exactly?" Oday asked.

"Six Hundred and eighty-six million, seven hundred and twenty-one thousand and two hundred and fifteen followers… and now nineteen… and now twenty-six… These many have raised mangoes in your support," Aroma said with her eyes closed. She then continued her chanting.

"Whoa… that is… flab… flab," Oday said gazing at Arjun, expecting a cover-up for his fumble.

"Flabbergasting," Arjun gave the pointer.

"Yes yes… that… So many followers of the Mangoman," Oday said.

Then Shalini's Butler came in with a message.

"SIRS… AND MADAMS… The technicians have caught an unofficial displacement of nuclear warheads across the world. It seems like the whole world is now getting ready to retaliate against the threat that they see in every other country," Shalini's Butler said.

"What… It is time we take care of that as well. Oday… how much time do you have left?" Arjun asked.

"I guess just above ten minutes," Oday said.

"Okay… you Butler… go and get the stats of geo-location of the alleged movement. And Oday… Go Dr. Manhattan$_{95}$. You need to transmute these nuclear missiles far into space and then disintegrate them. And also come back… Ok?" Arjun said.

"Affirmative…" Oday said and started transforming into a glowing blue creature.

"You'd have him destroy so many warheads at once?" Rajat asked.

"I'd have him destroy all… even the ones we have…" Arjun said.

28

"In a strange course of events… the world's nuclear arsenal has disappeared from the face of Earth. Stranger is the fact that where the launchers and missiles were supposed to be, there are mangoes. One for each. This has all occurred in the last twenty-four hours. The countries are all blaming each other… there are unilateral sanctions all around from anywhere to anywhere. The country leaders are now revealing their dichotomous stands on the subject. The very nations which preached disarmament in the past are now mourning over lacking the power to destroy the world. On the NewsHourAndAHalf tonight, watch as we debate this subject of two-faced powers… Keep tweeting on Hashtag Atom Bombs Become Atoms. Keep tweeting and keep watching Times…." Arlub's voice stopped midway as the television network seemed to have been hacked. All across the world, all networks were hacked. Television screens, computer screens (of those streamed to internet), Radio frequencies, smartphone screens, Etcetera… every media was hacked and started streaming a voice and/or video. The video jumped off with a symbol of the Mangoman. Then it showed Oday on his wheelchair and Arjun standing beside him.

"Recently, you must have noticed that the nuclear missiles of the world have been disintegrated in space by the man beside me, Oday Luhar. It was an initiative to strike off the fear latent within all our hearts. We are taking all drastic steps to avoid war. Now the countries which have lost most of their power are looking about to blame certain nation or organization. And we're sure, after watching this video, they would want to deal with us personally and on the battlefield. I would just want to urge the citizens of all those furious nations, be truthful… have we done anything wrong? We have destroyed the nuclear power from the world… from all countries. This drastic step was necessary to remove mutual fear from minds… since only acting against your personal fear and enemy would make one the enemy of all. And we don't seek to be the enemy of anyone. We hereby declare that the world is atomic-free. Oday left the symbol of peace and integrity back at the places where the missiles were supposed to be… You know what they are… so let's work for peace and unity… Let's fight the common evil that is hatred. Let's raise a mango… Kudos… Take Care…" Arjun spoke and the hack was released.

At the Indian Prime Minister's residence, everybody celebrated the massive hacking operation. World's best hackers and technicians sat in that room, laughing cheerfully along with Arjun, Oday and the others. They switched on the TV to see the Global News and response of the nations. Some praised the move… others criticized it for removing the only deterrent against war and thus increasing the chances of war. They called back at Rajat's residence to inquire about the tree. And evidently, its growth reflected a common consensus in support of the heroes. There were more than a billion supporters now. The movement had officially gone global. The social media was clustered with selfies and comments declaring support for the Mango Movement. People raised mangoes all around the world. Success was not far in the eyes of Rajat, Arjun and Oday. As they celebrated in a huge hall inside the PM residence, an uninvited guest showed up as a visitor. It was Aditya Luhar. He had come as the Chief Minister of Uttar Pradesh, on account of presenting the woes and cries of his state to the Prime Minister's Office. The Home Minister and the other officials went to the guest room to passive-aggressively greet the visiting CM. Arjun and Oday were asked to accompany the Home Minister, but Oday denied having to meet the father that he was so ashamed of.

Arjun asked the Home Minister to allow for Oday to be absent for that meeting. He himself went in. It had been just a few minutes that the meeting had started, when Oday, who was switching through TV Channels, found a shocking news. The News showed that Aditya Luhar, the CM of Uttar Pradesh, was found dead inside his Lucknow private residence. The news sources claimed that Aditya had committed suicide for being ashamed of his wrong doings. There was even a letter that he had written, in which he had apologized to Oday for siding with the evil Kunwar Madhao Singh. Oday was startled. But then the channel frequencies were hacked again. Oday inquired and was told that it was not one of their hackers doing it. The screens turned black and showed a man sitting in a shadow of another man. He came forward to reveal his identity. He was Aryaman.

"A huge trend is going on against my master. 'Raise a Mango' they say. We urge you to do the same… if you want to get in the Kunwar's bad side. We won't see if you are good, bad, child, adult, mother of ten, Etcetera. If you are against us… if you are with those fake saviours… then we won't lure you through diplomacy or give you deterring warnings.

Kunwar Madhao is a pragmatic man. So rest assured… if you are against us, without any second thoughts, we would obliterate your existence off the face of Earth, History and Time. So if your friends or family are stupid enough to give into these maniacs, then I recommend you console them. Use force if you can; in the end only life matters, doesn't it? (Came up to the camera) Doesn't it Oday? Don't you think your friends would be safer if they are on the more powerful and risk-free side? Otherwise, wherever they hide, the Shalini Mansion, The PM residence, we shall get to them," Aryaman spoke in the screen and then the channels were restored.

Oday wheeled down the corridor as fast as he could have to reach the visiting room. He opened the door to see that the meeting was going peacefully. Aditya Luhar seemed perfectly okay.

"Dad, the news said you committed…" Oday said, invoking silence in the room.

"Son… Hello… Yes… I did…" Aditya said.

"What do you mean?" Oday asked.

"I meant… he did…" Aditya said. His eyes contracted and turned red and he gave a wide and evil smile.

"It is him… the Kunwar," Oday screamed. Aditya transformed into the Kunwar and threw his chair towards Rajat. Oday intervened and stopped the chair midway.

"Run out from here…" Oday screamed. Arjun escorted everyone out of that room.

"All of you are going to die today…" Kunwar said as his hands caught fire. He threw a fireball towards Oday. Oday stopped it. He then flew and grabbed Oday, nailing him across the walls and pillars of the PM's residence. Oday tried to intercept Kunwar's powerful attack, but he seemed powerless in doing so. As such, only a fragment of his daily power-share was left. He tried transforming into Goku, Superman, Whitebeard, The Sage of the Six Paths[96], Saitama[97], Dr. Manhattan, Hulk, Thor[98], Jean Grey[99], Etcetera; But nothing could stand the seemingly eternal strength of the Devil. Kunwar mercilessly punched Oday, who had transformed back to his original state.

Kunwar said "I'd kill everyone except for you... Let's see how you take that."

"Oday... Odayyyy..." came a loud call from Arjun, who stood in the messed up portico. The Indian Army and National Security Guard had appeared at the scene. They had surrounded the area and were devising quick interception plans against the Kunwar. The shelling had started. Kunwar laughingly went in front of the bullet shower and took them head on. Meanwhile, Arjun briefed Oday regarding his own personal action plan.

"You need the One Above All[100]..." Arjun said and then took cover behind the broken fountain. Kunwar was planning to burn the combat team alive. He noticed that the ground below him was shaking and harsh gushes of wind were flowing all around him. He turned around and saw that Oday was not at the sight that he had left him at. He took a moment to sense out Oday's location. But he was nowhere to be found. A tap on his shoulder and he turned again. Oday stood with bright white eyes. Kunwar punched him. Oday took the punch on his face without even an inch of vibration.

"You... are.... Not... God..." Oday said and punched Kunwar in his abdomen. For the first time did Kunwar bleed through his mouth. Then Oday grabbed him and flew up. He broke through what was left of the roof and flew way high up to the sky. Then he started his fall. Below, Arjun was taking the guards' help and also convincing them to leave the area since it was out of their control. The area was quickly evacuated. Arjun braced himself behind a parked heavy truck and awaited the return of his friend. Then he saw an incoming ball of fire from the sky. Yes… Oday's extreme velocity had made him catch fire. He screamed loud, pushing the Kunwar down into the ground. The ground cracked open as Oday tunnelled inside. Strangely, Arjun realized, that there was no crater. He went near the crack and hoped for his friend to return. After a five-minute wait, Oday climbed out. He was completely out of breath and fell weakly on Arjun's shoulders. Arjun worriedly and hurriedly laid Oday down on a secured floor. He scrutinized Oday's body to find any serious injuries.

"Where is he?" Arjun then asked.

"I dropped him near the earth's core… He can't possibly come alive…" Oday said in a faint voice.

"Sucker's finally seen the end of days… Fucking Kentucky Fried Satan…" Arjun exclaimed to cheer Oday up. Oday gave a small laugh and then coughed out blood.

"What gave you the One Above All idea?" Oday asked.

"Well… I figured… if nothing else can beat him then the classic tale of God Vs Devil might come in handy," Arjun said.

"What if it hadn't worked sucker?" Oday said.

"Well… Honestly… I had my bets on the Kunwar all along… But I am also glad it worked…" Arjun said and they both broke into laughter.

"You think that worked…" came a voice from behind Arjun. Arjun turned around to see that it was Kunwar drenched in blood. His eyes were black and his veins all flexed. Oday tried to get up but he had expired his share for that day. Arjun grabbed a broken pole lying beside him and took a defensive stance. Kunwar slowly walked towards him.

"Pundit… Run… Go away from here…" Oday said.

"You can take your best shot…" Kunwar said arrogantly. Arjun hurled the pole and hit directly at Kunwar's forehead. The latter didn't even fret. Arjun repeatedly tried, only to cause more dents on the pole. Then Kunwar grabbed the pole and burned it to fumes within seconds. Arjun stepped back and tried to protect Oday. All Oday saw was a bloody hand, piercing through Arjun's lower back. Kunwar had punctured through Arjun's abdomen. Arjun only groaned in agonizing pain. Oday screamed out for help. He asked the Kunwar to leave his friend but he did not listen.

"I said… I would kill all your friends. See you later… as an upgraded Evil…" Kunwar said and disappeared. Oday was about to lose his senses. His vision was fading. The last thing he saw was Shalini who had come to their help with backup. And then he passed out.

*   *   *

Oday opened his eyes and found himself crippled in a part of AIIMS Emergency Ward. Seeing him wake up, the nurse called in the visitor. In came Mritunjay with a bouquet of red roses.

"How's Arjun?" Oday said, sitting up using his powers.

"Hey Hey… save your powers. Although you don't need them now," Mritunjay said, pushing Oday back down.

"What do you mean?" Oday asked.

"A lot has happened since the fight yesterday," Mritunjay said.

"Yesterday? I have been out for a day?" Oday asked again.

"Sadly… Yes… And also… your friend survived… miraculously…" Mritunjay said.

"What happened? How is he doing?" Oday asked.

"I'd be getting to that… But lemme finish off first. After the fight yesterday, the whole world became aware of the dualism between the Kunwar's words and actions. The live feeds and official reports declared him an assassin who intentionally attacked the Prime Minister of India and his office. Your dad's letter also helped the case. In his letter he had declared Kunwar's plans against the world and everything and also apologized for his wrongdoings. Thus… now… more and more people are supporting the only group challenging and confronting the Kunwar directly… that is our little gang of men, women and monsters… The tree is growing. We have above three billion followers. Within a day we have had the official support of many republic nations… We will soon reach four billion and have a clear upper hand against the Kunwar. If more than half the humanity clearly supports God, only then would he regain his Prime self. It is a time for joy… but yes… your friend. He is struggling for his life. Although I am not that worried about that," Mritunjay said.

"What do you mean you don't care?" Oday got startled.

"Calm down young man. You can anytime heal him. Although…" Mritunjay paused midway his speech.

"What… Although What?" Oday asked.

"As I have told you already… God has been weakened, and every time you use your power, you further cause the weakening. And the power of healing is channelled by the chalice of creation. You have used it quite a few times already. And after recent events, God has been weakened a lot. I suggest you don't use it right now. You should wait for the budding of the Mango and let God eat it first. Then you can heal as many as you want. Or else you might risk losing your powers altogether," Mritunjay said.

"You yourself said that I don't need them. Take me to Pundit… I shall heal him right away. I don't care if I have to die to save him…" Oday said.

"Keep the emotions inside your pockets… we have a duty as preservers… Arjun would be kept alive for sufficient amount of time… You would have ample time for healing him. The doctors are working him well and good… We need to focus on securing the area around the tree," Mritunjay said.

"I want to help him…. Let me go…" Oday got up and started to fidget as Mritunjay held him down. Mritunjay's phone started to ring.

"Okay… just a second my friend… Don't go anywhere… hearty request…" Mritunjay said, walking out of the room. He then received the call. It was Shalini's Butler.

"Mritunjay- Hello… Yes…

Butler- Sir… Come right away… we are being attacked by the Red Army being led by Aryaman. Bring Oday Sir along. We need his help. Security forces would take a lot of time to be here.

Mritunjay- What the hell is happening there?

Butler- We just reached four billion… and as soon as we did… there was gunfire all around the house. Sir Rajat Singhania has been evacuated from the back door and taken to another safe house.

Mritunjay- What? What are Aroma and the others doing?

Butler- They are still in front of the tree. I guess they are doing some final rituals for the bud is now growing. The tree shall flower soon. Shalini Ma'am and the technicians are back at our place. I have ensured they don't come out of there. It is very risky.

Mritunjay- Is the Kunwar there as well?

Butler- No Sir… Fortunately no.

Mritunjay- Why attack now? When the tree is complete? Wait a second… That Kunwar is a bastard.

Butler- Why? What happened now Sir?

Mritunjay- He caused all this. He intentionally antagonized himself in front of the masses so that we can rise to popularity as quickly as possible. He wanted the souls, didn't he? He had a quicker and more effective plan to gain the humans all along. And we were the minions executing it for him. He wants to have the fruit for himself.

Butler- But… that can just be eaten by God… isn't it?

Mritunjay- To attract the theists AND the atheists we used the object as the power and not the subject. The mango holds the power… it can be used by anyone. But a normal being most probably can't handle all of it. Only supreme creatures like God can… and in this case… I am sorry to say that the one in the same category as God is the Devil. We have to stop him Butler… otherwise it is the end for us. Armageddon, Doomsday, Two Thousand Twelve… whatever you want to call it… it is on our heads. I am going to wake up Oday now. He along with the reapers might be able to hold off Kunwar till the time the fruit is delivered to God. Got to Go. Take Care. And good job showing remarkable bravery and intellect during war times… Bye…" Mritunjay hung up the phone. He went inside the room calling for Oday and removed the curtains from around the bed. The bed was empty. He ran to the washroom to check for him but it was empty too. Mritunjay threw his newly gifted phone which hit the wall and broke apart. "Why the fuck did I let that idiot out of my sight? If I just had powers…. God… Help…" Mritunjay screamed out loud and the voice resonated throughout the hospital premises. A band of nurses came in and warned him to keep silent or leave the hospital.

29

The Mango Tree had grown through the roof of Rajat Singhania's house. It stood tall at over a hundred metres. The tree was flowering. Unlike the typical mango tree, this one grew just the one flower. The flower slowly but visibly transformed into an unripe mango. The ripening had started. The reapers' decibels had reached a new high for they were about to sum up their ritual. The guards were busy apprehending the red army militants surrounding the block. Indian Army, stationed at the Central Army Command Post in Lucknow Cantonment, was also notified regarding this civil war. People had started evacuating areas across the Gomtinagar locality of Lucknow. Then came the trump card of Kunwar's plan, that is he himself. A bright red shining-shoe was seen slowly and classily approaching the paramount complex. The Kunwar mockingly wore fluorescent luminescent horns, signifying his natural identity.

"Years and Years I guised as this blunt business-tycoon… I have followed infinite cycles of birth to reach this convenient point in the chronology of man. And finally… I see victory… over this and all the other realms. After gaining this fruit of eternity… the Universe would be mine," Kunwar said and took flight. He moved ahead towards the Tree. The ground started shaking and cracking, opening up the house in two halves. The tree trunk and base were in his complete vision. But the reapers were now not stationed there.

"You are still trying to win this so called 'war' of yours… Let me tell you… It is war for you… just mere slaughter for me…" Kunwar said. Then out of thin air appeared the reapers, surrounding the Kunwar in the air. A blue wave emerged from all of them, visibly penetrating through the Kunwar. The attack continued for a while but when the smoke cleared, the Kunwar was seen standing still, whimsically laughing off the considerably puny attempt compared to his powers. He then turned to Aroma.

"The queen bee…" Kunwar said and warped to grab Aroma through her neck. She tried to punch herself out of this grapple. A heavy bassed gush of wind started flowing. The reapers turned to see the cause behind this event.

"You Bastard…. Where is Arjun?" came Oday's woe through the air.

"Oh! The hero has finally arrived to die…" Kunwar said, leaving Aroma and raising his hand to his sides as a sarcastic welcome gesture for Oday. Within seconds, Oday flew along with Kunwar and the fight had begun. Aroma ordered her reapers to aid Oday as she attempted to extract the fruit and escort it to God for ingestion. A sounding of various tanks and army trucks came from the nearby highway. The 1/11 Gurkha Rifles, the finest of the Indian Army, had appeared to intercept the troublesome elements led by Aryaman. They were followed by fighter helicopters and also various Mikoyan Supersonic Aircraft as air support. They would have arrived earlier, but they were ordered to safeguard the VVIPs to secure locations first. The arrival was delayed since in the eyes of a soldier, every living soul was a VVIP. Now, a huge radius around the tree was only populated with the heavenly creatures, the militants, the Armed Forces Personnel and also Shalini's Butler. Kunwar struggled to fight off the others so he could take the fruit for himself, and that too before Aroma could pluck it out. The Armed Forces Command Intelligence, administering the operation, then received an alien feed phishing through its systems and hence interrupting their interception network and radar. The experts could just witness their systems being hacked cause apparently the master stroke was sourced from some extremely skilful ethical hacker(s). Then, on their backup frequency, they received on-field news that two unidentified helicopters had been seen trying to invade through to the red zone. But the patrolling copters couldn't deter their movement since their automated weapons were also jammed by the hacking party. It was Shalini accompanied by a few select techsperts. She had come to the aid of the Good warring side. She stepped down with her helpers at a small safe distance from the premises. They had brought certain Search and Eliminate equipment which would identify nearby targets as allies and enemies and electrocute them if they fell under the latter category. They all dispersed to plant the equipment at diverse spots to cover up the area. Shalini went further inside to see how Oday was keeping against the massive strength of the Kunwar. And just as she thought, he wasn't keeping well. He came flying and fell beside Shalini.

"Oday…" she said.

"Shalini… Pundit… You know where he is? I searched everywhere. He is not there… he cannot be found…" Oday said.

"What… I thought he was at the hospital with you. I told Jai to ask you to heal him…" Shalini said worriedly.

"That's what the issue is… I can't… I have expended that power of mine. Only when God powers up after eating that mango then I can use it further," Oday said.

"What! Then we should get on to it…" Shalini said.

"Get on to what?" Oday asked.

"Getting that Mango…" Shalini said.

"But how did you reach here anyway? There was a huge Army blockade in air and land…" Oday said.

"The technicians hacked through their radar and other geo-locators while CCTV jammed their communication frequencies and weapons. It was a necessary evil…" Shalini said.

Then, there came electrocution noises all across the block. Militants were being knocked down everywhere. The efficiency of the system seemed perfect. But Oday did not realize that while he was indulged in this conversation with Shalini, most of his supernatural allies had been taken down. He turned around to see that more than half of the reapers had been ripped apart by Kunwar. And the ones remaining, including Aroma, were having a hard time even breathing as Kunwar manhandled them.

"I should really take off. They need my help. I have certain duties to live up to you know. As the Mangoman…" Oday said and prepared to take off but was stopped by Shalini.

"We have a plan to retrieve the Mango through our covert intrusion from the ground itself," Shalini said.

"I cannot let you fight here… Pundit would kill me…" Oday said.

"I have MY duties to live up to… as a human. And you cannot stop me from it. If you want to help, you can," Shalini said.

"Okay then… what's the plan?" Oday asked.

Kunwar had dealt with the reapers. Aroma was the last one standing, or should we call levitating. Being the most powerful of the reapers, she was obviously supposed to be the last one. Or the Kunwar might have felt dramatic pleasure in killing her last. As such, he was much more powerful than all of them. He asked Aroma to give her final speech when Oday flew up and floated beside Aroma.

"Oh Nice... The Mangoman is still alive... I almost forgot about You. My bad... I was never too good at remembering wannabe weaklings. Or what you call as Preservers. Hence I always kill them. Although... you are a special one Oday. You are many folds less powerful than any of the others, but you are still different. You are one of the few who have been chosen and not created. So... why don't you just go God like last time? Oh Wait! I know Why not. Your God has lost his voodoo. And turning God is like a power too heavy for him to channel. The finale, like the preliminaries, has been lost to you Sir. And this is the moment where the cinematic villain says that 'Back Away and I might spare your life'. But sadly, I never had the taste for Cinema. So... Just to say... You ARE going to die no matter what you try," Kunwar said.

"Wait a second... Wait a second... Peace... I call Parley... I call truce..." Oday stopped Kunwar from delivering his final blow.

"What now?" Kunwar asked.

"Well... since you are usurping the God seat... wouldn't it be a necessity to have a right hand. I mean every king has a general.... Every superhero has a sidekick. And when God retires... I can work for you. I am just a freelancer. I can work for anyone. I mean you need support. You cannot take the burden of the Universe on to yourself," Oday said.

"You traitor. Seven Hells… why did God choose this creature as a preserver. He is a mutineer. I would kill you right away," Aroma said and started towards Oday to punch him. Kunwar appeared between the two.

"Stop there… This is interesting… Let him talk," Kunwar said, throwing Aroma across the block. She vanished away inside a building.

"So… what were you saying?" Kunwar asked.

"I was saying…" Oday constructed a convincing statement, something which Arjun had always aided him with. He then noticed behind Kunwar that near the tree, the militants were being taken down one by one and Shalini's Butler was climbing up and was almost half way up. Kunwar saw the direction of his eyes and almost turned around to see for himself only to stop at Oday's request "Let's go down and discuss it in a civilised way." They both descended down slowly and reached the ground. But, unfortunately, their presence near one of the electrocution devices triggered an identity check.

The machine rose up and spoke "Kunwar Madhao Singh… Hostile…" and released an electrocuting trap on to Kunwar Madhao. It did not cause even the smallest of damage but alerted the Kunwar.

"What the hell is this?" Kunwar said and turned around and focussed his eyes, and saw that everybody was attempting to reach the top of the tree. He turned back.

"Here goes nothing…" Oday said and grappled Kunwar through his waist and disappeared along with him.

Meanwhile, Shalini and the others were safeguarding the radius around the tree to aid Butler's attempts to reach the top. But a few distant metres from the tree, Aryaman was trying to get a clear shot at the Butler with his sniper rifle. But before he could pull the trigger, CCTV arrived at the scene "Hello Sir… How is it Going?"

"Well, if it isn't my rogue-ex-assistant. I believe you are here to attempt to stop me, aren't you?" Aryaman said.

"Stop You… Naah. I am here to give you the return gift I wanted to give Ananya," CCTV said, taking a grenade shaped metallic cylinder out his pocket and then throwing it midway between the two.

"Just the failure you are, you forgot to unpin it. And even if you had done that, at this vicinity, you would die in the explosion. You have never been the smart one have you?" Aryaman said and returned to sniping.

"Who said anything about a grenade or an explosion?" CCTV said invoking curiosity in Aryaman's head. Aryaman turned to see the grenade, and on a close observation, he realized that, in fact, it wasn't one. The cylinder transformed into a huge stand with 360-vision senses and spoke out "Aryaman Mirza, Hostile Confirmed…" and gave out a huge visible wave of current rendering Aryaman unconscious.

"These kids and their technology these days…" CCTV said and went beside Aryaman and took a selfie.

"Has Tag War, Hash Tag Mangoman, Hash Tag Beat The Hell Out of Ex-Boss…" CCTV said.

In a wasteland on the opposite side of the Earth, the two main battling individuals reappeared and started another round of their brawl, which mostly involved Oday devising innovative methods to dodge Kunwar's deadly attacks. Oday was completely relying on defence.

"By now… the Mango must have been taken by them and delivered to God…" Oday said.

"Don't be that hopeful. If that were the case, then you would have given me some competition at the least. But your source, your God, is just as weak as you are," Kunwar said.

"You might be right... but it very well would be safely segregated from your reach... The Mango," Oday said.

"Sir... if I cannot get the Mango myself... then you shall bring it for me..." Kunwar said.

"And why would I do something that stupid?" Oday asked rhetorically.

Kunwar then disappeared and reappeared a second later with Arjun in his hand. He had clutched Arjun's skull in his palm and held him out forward to make Oday identify him clearly.

"Pundit..." Oday said.

"No No... I would crush his skull if I witness you drifting even an inch from your spot... even if it is because of some wind..." Kunwar said.

"Is he dead?" Oday inquired in a shivering voice.

"No... not yet. But he would be if I don't receive the Mango... and don't overthink and believe that your God, after gaining his powers, can revive him like he revived you. This man has already been branded by me. If he dies, I would get him. So there is no way you can revive him... Only I can heal him back to his healthy state or kill him right at this instant. So... the job's on your shoulder... What do you choose? I am waiting right here... Go bring me that Mango..." Kunwar said.

Oday wiped the tears off his face and took some time to think it out. He then warped back to Lucknow. He walked through the army blockade. They let him through after identifying him as the Mangoman. His absent-mindedness didn't even let him realize that he had reached the Home Minister's residence. Shalini came running and embraced him.

"We got it... We got it... Yeiiiiii..." the overjoyed Shalini said to Oday. "Where is it?" Oday asked.

"It is with my Butler. He is taking it to Aroma… she crashed in a nearby building. We have won Oday… we have won…" Shalini said.

"Okay… I'll be back within minutes…" Oday said and jumped high. He landed right in front of the Butler who was climbing the staircase of the building Aroma was in.

"So… we finally have it… show it to me…" Oday said. The Butler took out a big, bright-yellow and juicy mango from within his blazer. Oday was astounded at its sight. Aroma came in from behind. She was limping due to excessive injuries. "Oh! Aroma… sorry for troubling you with the false statements before. I was just stalling for these guys to be able to steal the mangoes…" Oday said.

"Yes… I realized… None of God's preservers have ever deviated from their paths. I trust God before I trust anyone and he cannot be wrong. I was just playing along with you…" Aroma said.

"That is… impressive…" Oday said.

"Give it… I shall take it to him…" Aroma said… coughing through her statements.

"You are injured… and I still have time… I shall be the one to take it… you rest for now…" Oday said. They then saw a black Land Cruiser stop outside the building. The left front door opened and Mritunjay walked out. He called for Oday.

"He is here… let's take the Mango and the good news to him first then. He'd be glad that we have succeeded our heavenly objectives," Aroma said. Oday took a moment's pause and then agreed. They came down and met with him.

"There it is… the Eternal Fruit… Can I see it for a minute?" Mritunjay requested. Aroma gave it to him for inspection.

"I can feel the faith in this object... Take it to God As soon as possible Aroma..." he suggested.

"Give it to me... I would take it... She has done so much already. Let me do my service as well..." Oday said.

"Very well... You go then..." Mritunjay said and handed the Mango to Oday. Oday immediately disappeared.

"So How did you reach this place?" Aroma asked.

"This young and kind lady gave me a lift from the airport," Mritunjay said.

"She was waiting for you there? Or is she a taxi driver?" Aroma asked.

"Wait... now you make me wonder as well... She had a baby with her. Why would she divert her course unless she wanted to be here? Anyway, secondary subject that is..." Mritunjay said. The car in which Mritunjay had come, it had left the spot and had halted beside the Home Minister's Residence. From inside the car, came out Ria Mishra. She held a pistol in her hands. She sat down and took cover in a corner and carefully peeped out to aim for Shalini. But suddenly came a beep.

"Ria Mishra... daughter of Late Hostile Eklavya Mishra... armed... probable hostile..." the machine said, electrocuting Ria who fell down unconscious. Back at the other side of Earth, Oday stood in front of the Kunwar. They both held objects of utmost importance to each other, respectively in the other's hands. Kunwar held Arjun and Oday held the Mango.

"Oh... You brought it... amazing... now let's commence the honourable exchange..." Kunwar said. Oday was lost in his own void. His eyes were open but he couldn't see. His body stood there, holding the mango... but he was somewhere else. Across dimensions, he was walking in a park beside God.

"Why am I here? Arjun would be killed… Let me go… I am really sorry but you have been mistaken… I am not your chosen one," Oday said.

"Oday… I won't ask much of you. It is not my survival that I care about. It is Mritunjay's department. I care about being survived by my beloved children… just like any other creature. The step you are going to take won't save your friend. It would end up you all being destroyed altogether," God said.

"But I have no choice… I'd rather die than have to live with Arjun being dead because of me…" Oday said.

"Oday… from the start I have told you son… I trust you… you are the one who shall cause the change. Directly or Indirectly… but it is you… it is you who shall decide. Think for a while," God said.

"But thinking was Arjun's department…" Oday said.

"Then think like him… I did not choose you to follow Mritunjay and Aroma… take your outstanding decisions yourself… Listen to your heart… Just like Vijay did… you don't need approval… just go out there and be the Mangoman…" God's concluding speech echoed through his head as Oday regained his senses.

"Hey moron… did you die or something… or are you just deaf?" Kunwar said.

"Yes… I am alive… and can hear it all quite clear…" Oday said.

"Then hand it over…" Kunwar said, pointing at the Mango.

Oday held the mango forward and with his thumb picked its top. He then tightened his grip and placed it against his mouth. Within seconds, he sucked the Mango dry. The Kunwar was infuriated. Before Oday could decide his next move, Kunwar snapped Arjun's neck, throwing

281

him down towards the ground. Oday flew in to catch Arjun. Kunwar then caught the sucked out mango and then disappeared.

"Pundit... PUNDIT... NOOOO" Oday cried out loud. The ground started shaking intensely, changing the topography of the whole place. There was a thunderstorm. A white aura formed around Oday. His eyes also turned white. He was filled with vengeance to his core. But then he recalled that he had others to protect. Seven billion others. He lifted Arjun's body and came back to Lucknow. He walked towards Shalini and the others, with Arjun's body in his hands. Shalini broke into tears. He laid Arjun down and started mourning. The skies slowly turned black and heavy rainfall started.

"What happened to the Mango? You delivered it right?" Aroma asked. "No... I couldn't..." Oday replied.

"What..." Mritunjay was devastated.

"What would we do now? Kunwar would destroy the earth..." Aroma said.

"I would stop him..." Oday said.

"After having that much power... I mean he was already so much stronger than any of us. You can't possibly beat him in this state..." Aroma said.

Oday got up and closed his eyes, feeling the raindrops on his face. They somewhat merged with his teardrops.

"Who said that Kunwar ate the Mango?" Oday said and started walking ahead.

"What do you mean?" Mritunjay asked.

The ground started shaking again and the white aura appeared around Oday, stunning everybody at the scene. They made way for Oday. Oday jumped and took off. He flew and flew farther towards space and on reaching the vertical limit, found Kunwar flying there as well. He opened his eyes again.

"The brave hero is back again... to save the earth... How many more defeats would you need to understand I am a supreme being. So what if you have the power of faith with you now? I am still stronger than you..." Kunwar said.

"You don't understand do you? But I understand now... my purpose... it is way beyond your puny comprehension. It was always I who was to defeat you... Not God..." Oday said.

"No Superhero from ANY book can defeat the power I possess..." Kunwar said arrogantly and then laughed away in his snobbery.

"Are you sure? Or are you forgetting certain books entailing the defeat of the evil at the hands of the good... that is the devil at the hands of the God?" Oday said.

"You are going to be God now again, aren't you? Be anyone you want to... I am ready this time..." Kunwar said.

"I apologize but this time.... I am not anyone... I am... EVERYONE..." Oday said and disappeared. His periodic whispers were heard around Kunwar. A huge scabbard appeared near Kunwar's waist and he drew a white sword from within it. He swung the sword in a particular direction where Oday appeared to swing his own black sword against the former white one. The sky below them seemed to have been divided in black and white. The heavenly duel had begun. They were both fighting on equal terms.

"No one other than the God can challenge me to this level... How is it possible for you?" Kunwar said, dripping in sweat.

"Never forget... amongst every creature lies a fragment of God... when that fragment unites... physically OR mentally... then it channels the power of Good... the power of God…" Oday said and continued his duel. The Kunwar's sword broke. "How is it possible?" Kunwar said.

"I, now, am not only using the swordsmanship of every fictional or non-fictional character ever recorded in history… but also that of every swordsman on earth right now… and that too all at once… My weapon is just as strong…" Oday said. Similarly, they tried fighting using all combat weapons, but Oday stood victorious. In all matters of speed, strength and technique, Oday stood out as the superior one. After a heavy round of fist fight, both of them stood facing each other with Kunwar ever more tired and injured than Oday.

"Why… How can this happen?" Kunwar said restlessly.

"What would you do now?" Oday asked.

Kunwar recovered and started laughing.

"What are you protecting… there wouldn't be any earth left when I am done with it…" Kunwar said, turning towards the earth. He then created a black ball of fire with his hands and threw it towards the earth.

"Noooo…." Oday screamed and rushed below the ball and tried to stop it. But he couldn't push it back. To stop it, he ingested it. The Kunwar then came down at where Oday was. He started laughing again and then said "I knew you would do that… I knew it… and now… when You have taken in that much dark energy of destruction, there is nothing which can ever save you," Kunwar said and started rejoicing his moment of apparent victory. Oday's body had already started turning red due to internal damage and poisoning. His veins flexed, Oday seemed helpless in avoiding his slow death. But just as Kunwar laughed away his intellectual domination, his body felt a little strange. He then turned to Oday and saw that Oday's body was mutating. And a few seconds later, his own body started mutating as well. The clothes remained intact, but either of their faces and structures switched. Now, strangely, Kunwar seemed to experience the same pain that Oday was experiencing seconds ago. "What is happening?" Kunwar asked.

"The perks of having a thing for Cinema… I bet you never saw The Matrix, did you?" Oday said. Kunwar's flying ability started to dissipate and he started falling down, catching himself mid-air at regular intervals. His eyes were pitch black and slowly his face and the rest of the body was drying up and turning black as well. There was an explosion inside of him and he started descending in a free fall. Oday flew in close to ensure that he did not escape this one. Back on the ground, everybody was mourning Arjun's demise. Aroma and Mritunjay were both criticizing Oday and also revering him as their last ray of hope. Then came a loud bang close to them. A car alarm started off and then died down. They all rushed towards the crash site and saw that a blackened and thin Kunwar Madhao Singh had fallen over a black Land Cruiser. Aroma carefully went close to check on him and found that he had been defeated. "The Devil… after Centuries… has finally been slain at the hands of the Preserver… By God' Grace, we have WON…" Aroma said and the other reapers joined in her chants of celebration. Mritunjay walked to them and laughed in relief. Oday came in flying from above. The people below him awaited him. They called out in co-ordination 'Man-Go-Man… Man-Go-Man…'.

Without even waiting for a second to listen to their praises, Oday straightaway went to where Arjun lied dead.

"Pundit… Get up… Come on… Who'd tell me what to do next? Who'd be my guide and my best friend? Whom would I listen to rock songs with? Come on…" Oday said in grave remorse.

"He has no chance of waking up... his soul has been destroyed when you destroyed Kunwar over there..." Mritunjay said.

"Hey! Be easy on him... you didn't destroy anything. Kunwar did. And you just did away with the evil that was Kunwar Madhao Singh..." Aroma prompted.

"There must be a way..." Oday said.

"The power of creation is the only way to reinstate life in an organism... it lies only with God... but he needs the soul which has been destroyed..." Aroma said.

"There is one way... power of succession," Mritunjay said.

"Stop it... Don't tell him that..." Aroma said.

"Hey Hey... I am just keeping him informed... not that he would use it... I know for a fact he wouldn't..." Mritunjay said.

"Tell me... Whatever it is... tell me..." Oday pleaded.

"Okay... if you will to then listen... the power of succession is entrusted in celestial beings or preservers as a last resort. In cases where an important human or any other organism or celestial being suffered death, another celestial being CAN revive him. But the consequences are not very good. He has to give up his life and create a fresh soul for the other to revive him. And you know... when you don't have a soul... you die..." Aroma said.

Oday grabbed hold of Arjun's hand and closed his eyes.

"You are not thinking of doing it, are you?" Aroma asked.

"Even you don't understand. My true purpose is this only. I have now realized. My powers... what are they? What can they do? Unbelievable wonders... I know. But that's not what the people need. People need direction and leadership. I cannot ever provide that. I can maybe personally guard them to the best of my abilities... but I can never lead them. Whereas he can. I now understand why he(God) said that I have to lead directly or indirectly. I am not a leader. I may have more strength and speed than any other being on earth, but that doesn't mean I can lead them or rule over them, does it? Has it ever meant that? Being powerful is not a luxury... it is a duty. And here I am performing my duty. Now that there is no Kunwar Madhao... I don't think the world needs my powers as much as it needs a leader like Pundit... If you don't agree with me, still, don't stop me. I have decided...." Oday said and looked upwards with his eyes closed. He stayed that way for a few seconds and then opened his eyes wide. There was a flash of bright light emerging from his eyes impairing everybody's vision temporarily. When they regained the sense of sight, Oday was nowhere to be seen.

"What happened?" Shalini asked, wiping her tears.

"Where'd he go?" she continued.

Arjun's abdomen started healing itself. His face regained colour from its pale state and he started coughing. He opened his eyes and woke up.

"Whoa... Where am I? What'd I miss?" Arjun said.

"Arjun..." Shalini said, rushing in to hug Arjun.

"Whoa... why are you crying? And where is Suckhead?" Arjun asked.

"Oday.... Oday..." Shalini broke down.

*   *   *

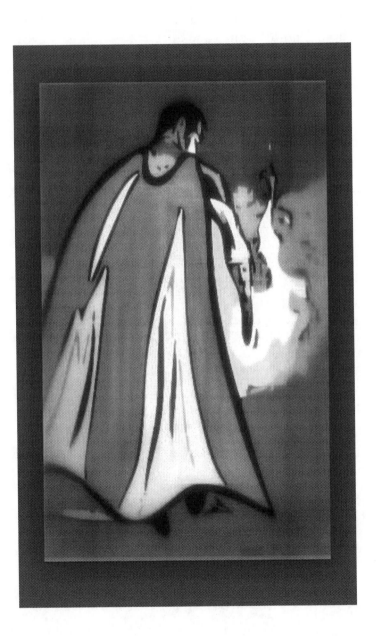

It was evening time around the Home Minister's residence. The place showed only a few signs of the living. Ria woke up after hours of being electrocuted. She walked back to where she had parked her car. The sight pissed her off a lot. Her car was completely nailed inside the ground and over the broken bonnet lied a blackened unconscious man. She went close to inquire about the happenings which led to that. She moved to tap the man on the shoulder to wake him up, but as soon as she did, the man sublimed into black smoke and disappeared. From behind the smoke, appeared a breathless Aryaman banging on the bonnet.

"You are Eklavya's daughter," Aryaman said, regaining his breath.

"Yes... Who are you?" the alerted Ria investigated.

"I am Aryaman... I worked with your father... somewhat... I'd be back in a second," Aryaman said.

Ria was terrified. Seeing the direction of the diffusion of the smoke to inside the car, she suddenly realized that her young infant was also accompanying her in that car. She thought to herself that even though the car was equipped with the best safety machinery and the baby was strapped in his car seat, it was impossible for any living organism inside to survive the disastrous crash. She started crying and screaming and opened the back door using a closely lying rod as a lever. Her hopes were restored miraculously and the baby was lying completely fine and that too without a scratch. She went in close to embrace the infant out of exhilaration. But, she then saw something stranger in the kid's hand. A sucked up yellow mango. On observing closely, she saw that the small hole on the top was glowing with a faint humming. She gave in to her curiosity and grabbed it from the kid's hand and peeled the cover off revealing a brightly and loudly glowing mango seed. A car started honking behind her. It was Aryaman again.

"Bring your infant. We are to leave this place immediately..." Aryaman said.

Ria took her girl out as the infant continued to grip the mango. She took a seat and inquired "Where to?"

"To Nainital..." Aryaman said.

"What's there in Nainital?" she followed.

"One Raj Gautam..." Aryaman concluded.

30

The Best way to find yourself is to lose yourself in the service of Others.

-Mahatma Gandhi

There is no passion to be found playing small – in settling for a life less than the one you are capable of living.

-Nelson Mandela.

Do not wait for leaders; do it alone, person to person.

-Mother Teresa.

A man is made by his beliefs. As he believes, so he becomes.

-Lord Krishna, Gita.

The mind is everything. What you think you become.

-Gautam Buddha.

*   *   *

A month had gone by since the war. The city of Lucknow was being cleaned up. The UNO had evolved into a much stronger and globally significant organization for the countries had now allied in thoughts. The political ego clashes had been minimized and righteous governing had become the fashion of the day. The martyrs of both heaven and earth were commemorated at their respective realms. For the first time in the history of Pakistan's existence had it agreed to a truce over the Kashmir issue. The peace talks reached a new high and subsequently both the countries signed official pacts acceding equal territories of the disputed zones. The population, Hindu, Muslim, Sikh, Christian, Etcetera, was given the democratic choice of going to either side. It was all led out in an organized and secure fashion. Similarly, many a settlement of bilateral issues viz. Russia and Ukraine, Iraq and Iran, China and Japan, Argentina and England, Etcetera were initiated. The Ityadi party and its propaganda had dissolved with Uttar Pradesh coming under the Presidential rule. Mritunjay was learning the ethics of being a human and on Rajat's recommendation, he had become an integral part of the IPU. Raj Gautam was still missing, making it the backup NewsHourAndAHalf Debate for Arlub. Arjun had shifted to Shalini's place with his father. They were both planning to get engaged. Realizing the significance of the responsibility entrusted to him by Oday's sacrifice, Arjun had become a full-time National and Social Activist and was himself planning to enter politics. But not 'politics'. For that, he should have been acquainted with Aditya's laws of politics. A month had gone by since Oday passed away yet just like the first day, Arjun found silent solitary hours in the day sitting in front of the big television screen, scrolling through the media images of the two of them. Shalini could comfort him to an extent but he always kept his pain to himself. His father decided for his son to tie the knot with his partner and hence they were getting engaged soon. The Prime Minister adorned the City of Lucknow regularly for his meetings with none other than the hero of the world peace, Arjun Trivedi. He desperately missed the idiotic and baseless comments of Oday. Every once in a while, he used to grab the Uniform Box that he had assembled along with Oday, now containing only Oday's yellow mask (after he had stopped wearing it, he used to keep it in that box itself). He used to take it out, wear it over his face and try to mimic Oday's speech and actions in front of the mirror. He used to stand in front of the mirror and chant away in a heroic dialect "Here comes the Mangoman... I am the Mangoman...". One fine day, while he was indulged in this performance of his, Shalini's Butler came in with a delivery package. To avoid awkwardness, Arjun began with his small talk while opening the package "You never told me your name man..."

"Sir... You can call me The Butler..." the butler said.

Arjun opened the package to find the remaining uniform of Oday. There lied a note within "Washed, Steamed and Ironed... just as you like it..."

Arjun got the worst of Goosebumps... his heartbeats rose and kept rising till he lifted the uniform to see what lied below. His heart then paused. For below, lied a big and juicy mango. The Butler had resigned from the room. Arjun kept the box down and went back to the mirror. He took the mask off his face, held it beside himself and gazed at it through the mirror. He smiled and said "Here Comes.... The Mangoman..."

... To be Continued ...
(Dawn of Alfonso)

REFERENCES

1. **Merman-** An intelligent amphibious organism with superhuman strength in the Anime called One Piece.
2. **Murphy's Law-** An epigram stating 'Anything that can go wrong, will go wrong'.
3. **Richie Rich-** A *Harvey Comics'* fictional character who is famous for his family's extravagant lifestyle.
4. **Richmore-** A para-clone of the famous Mount Rushmore in the Richie Rich Universe, with the Presidents' faces being replaced by the faces of the Rich Family. It is the treasure-hold for the family heirloom.
5. **Arjun Pundit-** A Bollywood Hindi Action Flick starring Sunny Deol as the Social Revolutionary 'Arjun Pundit'.
6. **Karan-** The name of Salman Khan's character in the movie Karan-Arjun.
7. **One Piece-** A Japanese Manga and Anime written by Eiichiro Oda.
8. **Straw Hats-** The name of the leading Pirate Crew in the One Piece Universe.
9. **Goku-** The protagonist of the Japanese Anime called 'Dragon Ball' by Akira Toriyama.

10. **Chichi-** Goku's Wife in Dragon Ball Universe.

11. **Vegeta-** A leading character in the Dragon Ball Z Universe.

12. **Bulma-** Another leading character and Vegeta's wife in the Dragon Ball Z Universe.

13. **Naruto-** The protagonist of the Japanese manga and Anime called 'Naruto' written by Masashi Kishimoto.

14. **Hinata-** A leading character and the wife of Naruto in the Naruto Universe.

15. **Nami-** A leading character in the One Piece Universe.

16. **Sanji-** A leading character in the One Piece Universe.

17. **Luffy-** The central protagonist of the One Piece Universe.

18. **Hancock-** A character in the One Piece Universe who had fallen in love with Luffy.

19. **Oda-** Eiichiro Oda, the writer of One Piece.

20. **Gwen Stacy-** Spiderman/Peter Parker's love in the 'Amazing' Spiderman Universe. Considered by Oday and Arjun as fake love.

21. **Merry Jane-** Spiderman/Peter Parker's love in the Original Spiderman Universe. Considered true love by Oday and Arjun.

22. **PS4 black Fifa 15 Ultimate Version-** The Fifa Football Special Edition of the Sony Gaming Console called PlayStation 4.

23. **Zoro-** A leading character in the One Piece Universe.

24. **Chimpanzee Glass-** A mistaken reference to the Gorilla Glass technology.

25. **ALS Ice Bucket Challenge-** A challenge whereby a person dumped a bucket of ICE over his head to spread awareness about Lou Gehrig's disease.

26. **Jerome Carpenter-** The infamous case of the young lecherous kid who died of a heart attack due to successive forced emissions.

27. **Game of Thrones-** An HBO original T.V. series written by George R.R. Martin, famous for all its central characters dying by the end of every season.

28. **Darth Vaderish-** Darth Vader is the hero/anti-hero/villain from the Star Wars movies who is most famous for having the strangest of a heavy baritone and the regular 'Sigh' in his dialogues.

29. **Manga-** Japanese Comics are called 'Manga'.

30. **DC-** The English Comics which published Superman, Batman and all characters of the Justice League Universe and beyond.

31. **Marvel-** The English Comics which published Iron Man, Spiderman, Hulk and all characters of The Avengers and beyond.

32. **Raj-** The Indian Comic Universe which published Superheroes such as Doga, Nagaraj, Etcetera.

33. **Iron Man-** The famous superhero of the Marvel Universe.

34. **Andy-** The fugitive protagonist from the famous flick called 'The Shawshank Redemption'.

35. **Shawshank-** The name of the prison where Andy was held.

36. **Son Goku-** Again a reference to Goku, the protagonist of the Japanese Anime Dragon Ball.

37. **Instant Transmission-** Goku's ability to teleport instantly between any two points in the Universe that he could locate through his senses.

38. **SSJ3-** Super Saiyajin Three is the third Super transformation of the alien race of Saiyajins in Dragon Ball Z.

39. **SSJ God-** Super Saiyajin God is the fourth chronological transformation of Saiyajins in Dragon Ball Z.

40. **Hulk-** Reference to the Marvel Universe Green Monster 'The Incredible Hulk'.

41. **Shadow-Clone-** One of the many abilities of the protagonist Naruto of the anime 'Naruto', whereby he can make clones of himself using hand signs.

42. **Rasengan-** Another ability of Naruto where he can create a ball of body energy which creates an intense push on impact.

43. **RasenShuriken-** Naruto's ability to add the elemental energy of Wind/Fire/Etc. to his Rasengan.

44. **The Big Bang Theory-** The famous geeky SITCOM by Chuck Lorre.

45. **He-Man-** The most powerful of the *Masters of the Universe* by Mattel.

46. **Spidey sense-** The instinctive power of prediction of the Marvel Comics famous superhero Spiderman.

47. **Flash-** The DC Comics superhero with the power of superhuman hypersonic speed.

48. **James Bond-** The Fictional Super-Spy in a suit created by Ian Fleming.

49. **Quicksilver-** The Marvel Universe Superhero with the power of superhuman speed.

50. **Metal Claws-** Reference to the self-healing superhero from Marvel Universe called Wolverine. He has metal claws which he can voluntarily release and retract from between either of his hand's knuckles.

51. **Magneto-** The Marvel Universe Superhero with the power to control metal.

52. **Dende-** The Alien Character from Dragon Ball Universe who has the special power of healing both major and minor injuries.

53. **DBZ-** A reference to Dragon Ball Z.

54. **Otaku-** The Japanese word which means 'Geek'. Here it symbolizes an Anime and Manga geek.

55. **Electro-** The supervillain from the Spiderman series having the power to absorb and emit electrical energy.

56. **Conqueror's Haki-** One of the three types of Hakis (or Willpowers) in the One Piece Universe which gives one the ability to predominate over someone else's conscious, rendering him powerless.

57. **Green Lantern-** The DC comics Superhero with the ring providing him the power of creating and voluntarily controlling a green physical aura.

58. **Three Swords-** Reference to the fighting style of the swordsman from One Piece Universe who generally uses three swords (Two in hands and one in the mouth) in his unique three-sword-style.

59. **Spiderman-** The Marvel Universe Superhero having superhuman strength, senses and agility and also the power to create and manipulate spider-webs.

60. **Byakugan-** One of the three visual powers in the Naruto Universe, which provides the User extreme observation, scanning and analysis capabilities which those without visual powers don't have.

61. **Diglet-** Reference to the Anime Pokémon and its super-animal Diglet which has the power of digging.

62. **Wand-** Reference to the wands used by the Wizards in the fantasy world of Harry Potter Flicks.

63. **Lumos Maxima-** The magic spell used by Wizards in Harry Potter Universe to illuminate a dark area.

64. **Neo-** The name of Keanu Reaves' character from The Matrix.
65. **Smith-** The antagonist of the 'Matrix' trilogy.
66. **Magellan-** One of the many antagonists of the One Piece Universe with the power to produce liquid poisons of all varieties from his body.
67. **Poseidon-** The Olympian God of the Sea holding complete mastery over the element of water.
68. **Golden Trident-** Reference to Poseidon's weapon.
69. **Invisibility Cloak-** One of the three *Deathly Hallows* in the Harry Potter Universe. It is a cloak which makes the one wearing it invisible to the sharpest of eyes.
70. **Daredevil-** A Marvel Universe blind superhero who compensates his vision impairment with his enhanced auditory senses simulating the echo phenomenon used by a bat.
71. **Professor X-** The Marvel Universe Psychic-Superhero having the power to control and take over other's brains.
72. **First Class-** Reference to the era in the Marvel Universe when Professor X and his aides were young. In his old age, he is shown to be crippled and hence the young impersonation could walk.
73. **Expeliomus-** The most common magic spell in the Harry Potter Universe usually used to disarm someone.
74. **Stupefy-** As the name suggests, this Harry Potter Universe magic spell is used to paralyze someone just as they are.
75. **Obliviate-** A Harry Potter Universe magic spell used to erase someone's specific memories.
76. **Raised his hand-** Reference to the way Darth Vader telekinetically controls objects.

77. **Floating in the air-** Reference to one of the powers of the Matrix Trilogy Protagonist 'Neo' using which he can decelerate and halt projectiles.

78. **V-** The masked protagonist of Alan Moore's novel and also the inspired flick of the same name, 'V for Vendetta'.

79. **T-800-** The model of the robotic character portrayed by Arnold Schwarzenegger in the Terminator Series.

80. **Billy the Puppet-** The toy avatar of the sadistic antagonist from the 'Saw' movie series.

81. **Anti-venom-** The Marvel Character whose one of many superpowers is to scout for diseased/ailing people/animals and another is to detect nuclear radiation.

82. **Supernatural-** Reference to the 'Angels' from the TV Series called Supernatural by Eric Kripke, who hold the power of healing people instantly.

83. **Gyojin Karate-** Reference to the specific fighting style of Mermen/Fishmen in the One Piece Universe.

84. **Tank-Shaped Car-** Reference to Batman's supercar in the DC Universe.

85. **Batclaw-** A Mini-Carabiner used by the DC Universe super-detective to maneuver around the city.

86. **GTA-** Acronym for the famous virtual reality game series created by Rockstar Games called 'Grand Theft Auto'.

87. **Bat-** The aero-mobile used by Batman to traverse faster.

88. **Mogambo-** The Famous Antagonist from the classic Indian flick 'Mr. India'.

89. **X-Men-** Reference to the Mutant Superheroes from the Marvel Universe Comic/Movie series of the same name.

90. **Sith-** Reference to the Misanthropic Superhuman Cult in the Star Wars Universe.

91. **Dragon Balls-** Reference to the seven magical spherical and numerically marked objects in the Dragon Ball Universe, which when brought together held the power to grant the collector any wish he had.

92. **Silver Surfer-** The Marvel Universe Extraterrestrial Superhero whose power resided in his surfer.

93. **Shirohige-** Reference to the One Piece character 'Whitebeard' also known as the 'Strongest Man in the world'. 'Shirohige' means 'Whitebeard' in Japanese.

94. **Punched the Air-** One of the primary abilities of Whitebeard.

95. **Dr. Manhattan-** The Superhero from the 'Watchmen' who accidentally transformed into a living and infinite mass of nuclear energy.

96. **Sage of the Six Paths-** The father of the Ninja race in the Naruto Universe.

97. **Saitama-** The Superhuman protagonist of the Anime 'One Punch Man'.

98. **Thor-** The Norse God of Thunder who also found a place in the superhero Universe of Marvel.

99. **Jean Grey-** The extremely powerful mutant from the X-Men Universe.

100. **One Above All-** The Marvel Universe adaptation of the general conception of the omniscient, omnipotent and omnipresent, or God.

ABOUT THE AUTHOR

Rishabh Dubey is a young author from Lucknow, India. Appreciation for the imaginary made him a fantasy aficionado, building his passion for writing. He embraced the ideal of 'imagination becomes innovation' and took to giving shape to all his imaginations. He plans to continue writing with growing knowledge and experiences.

Author's Weblog: http://keatzz.com
Author's Email ID: keatzz.dubey@gmail.com
Facebook Page: www.facebook.com/raiseamango
Webpage: www.raiseamango.com
Goodreads Page: www.goodreads.com/author/show/15122559.Rishabh_Dubey
Instagram Page: www.instagram.com/letsraiseamango
Twitter Page: www.twitter.com/raiseamango

Printed in the United States
By Bookmasters